MORE CHEERS FOR JESS LOUREY'S
MURDER-BY-MONTH MSYTERY SERIES

November Hunt

"Clever, quirky, and completely original! This taut and compelling mystery—with a twist on every page—is edgy, entertaining, and irresistible."—Hank Phillippi Ryan, Anthony, Agatha, and Macavity Award-winning author

"Jess Lourey skillfully navigates her way along the razor's edge of the traditional mystery. A masterful mix of mayhem and mirth . . . [and] a fun read all the way through."—Reed Farrel Coleman, three-time Shamus Award-winning author of *Hurt Machine*

October Fest

"Snappy jokes and edgy dialog . . . More spunky than sweet; get started on this Lefty-nominated series if you've previously missed it."—*Library Journal* (starred review)

"Lourey has cleverly created an entertaining murder mystery . . . Her latest is loaded with humor, and many of the descriptions are downright poetic."—*Booklist* (starred review)

"Funny, ribald, and brimming with small-town eccentrics."—*Kirkus Reviews*

September Fair

"The very funny Lourey serves up a delicious dish of murder, mayhem, and merriment."—*Booklist* (starred review)

"Lively."—*Publishers Weekly*

"An entirely engaging novel with pathos, plot twists, and quirky characters galore . . . Beautifully written and wickedly funny."—Harley Jane Kozak, Agatha, Anthony, and Macavity-Award winning author of *A Date You Can't Refuse*

August Moon

"Hilarious, fast paced, and madcap."—*Booklist* (starred review)

"Another amusing tale set in the town full of over-the-top zanies who've endeared themselves to the engaging Mira."—*Kirkus Reviews*

"[A] hilarious, wonderfully funny cozy."—*Crimespree Magazine*

Knee High by the Fourth of July

Shortlisted for a Lefty Award from Left Coast Crime and chosen as a Killer Book by the Independent Mystery Booksellers Association

"Mira . . . is an amusing heroine in a town full of quirky characters."—*Kirkus Reviews*

"Lourey's rollicking good cozy planted me in the heat of a Minnesota summer for a laugh-out-loud mystery ride."—Leann Sweeney, author of the Yellow Rose Mystery series

June Bug

"The funny, earthy heroine is sure to stumble her way into the hearts of readers everywhere. Don't miss this one—it's a hoot!"—William Kent Krueger, Anthony Award-winning author of the Cork O'Connor series

"A funny, well-written, engaging story . . . readers will thoroughly enjoy the well-paced ride."—Carl Brookins, author of *The Case of the Greedy Lawyer*s

"Jess Lourey is a talented, witty, and clever writer."—Monica Ferris, author of the bestselling Needlecraft Mysteries

May Day

"All the ingredients for a successful small town cozy series are here."—*Publishers Weekly*

"A likeable heroine and a surfeit of sass."—*Kirkus Reviews*

"*May Day* is fresh, the characters quirky. Minnesota has many fine crime writers, and Jess Lourey has just entered their ranks!"—Ellen Hart, author of the Sophie Greenway and Jane Lawless Mystery series

NOVEMBER
HUNT

OTHER BOOKS BY JESS LOUREY

May Day (2006)

June Bug (2007)

Knee High by the Fourth of July (2007)

August Moon (2008)

September Fair (2009)

October Fest (2011)

FORTHCOMING FROM JESS LOUREY

December Dread (2012)

NOVEMBER
HUNT

A Murder-By-Month Mystery

jess lourey

MIDNIGHT INK
WOODBURY, MINNESOTA

First Edition
First Printing, 2012

Book design and format by Donna Burch
Cover design by Ellen Lawson
Cover illustration © 2011 Carl Mazer
Editing by Connie Hill

Midnight Ink, an imprint of Llewellyn Worldwide Ltd.

Library of Congress Cataloging-in-Publication Data
Lourey, Jess, 1970–
  November hunt : a murder-by-month mystery / Jess Lourey. — 1st ed.
      p.   cm. — (The murder-by-month mysteries ; #7)
   ISBN 978-0-7387-3136-0
1. Minnesota—Fiction. 2. Murder—Investigation—Fiction. I. Title.
  PS3612.O833N68   2011
  813'.6—dc23
                                                                    2011038549

Midnight Ink
Llewellyn Worldwide Ltd.
2143 Wooddale Drive
Woodbury, MN 55125-2989
www.midnightinkbooks.com

Printed in the United States of America

©Jane Bailey Photography, Inc.

ABOUT THE AUTHOR

Jess Lourey spent her formative years in Paynesville, Minnesota, a small town not unlike the Murder-by-Month series' Battle Lake. She teaches English and sociology full time at a two-year college. When not raising her wonderful kids, teaching, or writing, you can find her gardening and navigating the niceties and meanities of small-town life. She is a member of Mystery Writers of America, Sisters in Crime, the Loft, and Lake Superior Writers.

ONE

TOM STAMPED HIS FEET on the hard-packed snow. "It's cold enough to freeze a shadow."

His partner nodded. "It's so cold, it'd freeze the balls off a pool table."

Tom chuckled. It came out in white cumulous puffs. "It's so cold I think the rock rattling around in my boot is my big toe."

"Amen to that." Clive knew it was his turn, but damn, if it wasn't 20 below in the sunshine. It wasn't funny any more. "Pass the coffee?"

"Sure, if you can remind me why we agreed it'd be a good idea to muzzleloader hunt the last week in November." He tossed the silver thermos. It caught a dazzling ray of clean winter sunlight before landing neatly in Clive's gloved palm.

He didn't even consider removing the gloves to twist off the cap. The zip of a vacuum opening was followed by the rich aroma of dark roast. "It's the only time it's allowed."

"Not what I meant." Tom dropped his weight onto the hay bale with a labored huff and began to pack his rifle. It was tricky work in this frigid temperature. If he hadn't just popped off his last round at a white-tailed buck well out of his Thompson Omega Z5's range, he'd be as happy as a clam in butter sauce.

"I don't know if you heard the news," he continued, "but it turns out we can buy meat at a grocery store. We don't need to freeze our hair off in a hay bale fort drenched with deer whiz." Drawing in a breath for courage, he stripped his hands down to thin polar gloves and dropped a hundred grains of powder into the barrel from a pouch at his side. Next came the .50 caliber round. He grunted when he packed both with his ramrod. His hands felt like two wooden planks with chopsticks where the fingers should be. "Toss me the primer. And I wouldn't yell at you for moving the sun heater closer."

Clive obliged on both counts. "We shouldn't have brought it at all, you know. Animals catch wind of it, we might as well be on a beach in Mexico for all the deer we'll see."

Tom rubbed his hands together briskly in front of the glowing orange circle before yanking the breech on his rifle. He shoved in the primer with cold-clumsy hands, tapped the breech closed, and thrust his hands back into fur-lined gloves with a sigh. Jabbing his mitts toward the heater, he rubbed them together until sensation returned in the form of intense, tingling pain. "I mentioned we can buy meat at the grocery store?"

"You did." Clive kept his eyes nailed to the lunar-white landscape. "But a ten-point rack looks a helluva lot better than a t-bone mounted over your fireplace."

Tom grinned, and it cracked the icicles on his mustache. "That *was* a ten-pointer, wasn't it?"

"Yup, and if you had let it get close instead of shooting wild, we'd be on our way home right now. Might be days before we get another chance like that."

Tom moved in next to Clive, still smiling. "I dunno. That might have been the only deer dumb enough to stick around for the winter."

Despite his complaints, there was no place in the world he'd rather be the last week of November, and he knew Clive felt the same. They'd been hunting buddies for over forty years—turkey, duck, deer, even elk the year one of them was lucky enough to get a license—and the colder, the better. It was especially peaceful during muzzleloader season, when all of the hobby hunters returned to the city, packing up expensive gear that was smarter than they were and leaving only the locals, those with enough pioneer blood still bubbling in their veins that they'd roll out of bed before the sun had seriously considered rising, pull on six layers of clothing, and trudge to their pickups, which would start as often as not.

Clive nodded. "Looks that way. You check the salt lick before we set up shop? Maybe the deer finished it off and that's why we've only seen the one."

"I checked it two weeks ago when we came out bowhunting."

"But not since?"

"Not since," Tom said, taking the hint. He stretched his arms skyward until his back made a satisfying pop. "Anyone ever tell you that you're lazier than furniture? You're lucky I have to water the trees anyhow. Watch for that big buck while I'm out there."

"I'll be doing nothing but."

Tom left the relative shelter of their hunting blind, a cube of hay four bales high and four across to keep them out of sight and scent of the animals. He crunched over the surface of the snow. Fourteen inches of the white stuff buried the ground, but at this temperature it turned hard as rock, squeaking underfoot. The air was dry, and the sun refracted off a billion ice crystals on the ground and the trees. It was blinding. He couldn't be happier. All this time hunting together had fine-tuned their relationship into a comfortable marriage of shared interests, a tolerance for quiet spells, and a mutual admiration for one another's skills. Clive watched his old friend footslog across the landscape. This was dedicated hunting land, over 400 acres of woods, water, hills, and prairie just across the Otter Tail County line. A mutual friend owned it, and though he charged the city folks to use it, his comrades hunted on it for free. The blinds and hunting stands were already in place, but this late in the year, they were responsible for checking the salt licks and, if they could get away with it, corn piles.

A cracking sound toward Clive's left yanked his attention. Something rustled in the copse of trees two hundred yards up. Tom must have heard it too because across the snow tundra he froze, staring in the direction of the same grove.

No birds sang. No wind blew. There were only two men on the frost-scorched landscape of a Minnesota November, the clean blue scent of cold cracking their nostrils. The silence lasted until the magnificent buck stepped out of the woods and into the open. He sniffed the air and barked, low in his throat, a warning sound. His rack reached toward the sun, all fourteen points glistening like polished wood. The proud beast glanced across the unbroken

4

prairie toward Tom, who stood as motionless as stone. He was 100 yards from the massive beast and an equal distance from his gun.

Clive already had his rifle at the ready, perched over the top of the blind. His breath tore out short and shallow. In one slow but fluid movement, he brought his hand to the trigger. He squinted and focused down the sight. His target was in range, a clean shot. He couldn't feel the press of the metal lever through his thickly gloved finger, but he knew he was pulling it toward him, every tiny movement tumbling the powder closer to the spark. His heart was racing, pounding, forcing hot blood to his hands and feet. The bass snap of his trigger, when it finally came, was drowned in the momentary explosion of black and red flame out the end of his rifle. The pungent tang of fired gunpowder filled his nostrils.

Tom fell to the ground instantly, his blood a violent raspberry red staining the snow. One hundred yards away, the buck sprinted back into the woods, unharmed.

TWO

THE THERMOSTAT ON MY car was out, or so I figured as I used the tender meat of my hand to scrape a peephole on the inside of my windshield. Thirty years in Minnesota teaches you these handy bits: mosquitoes are attracted to white clothing and pretty much anything else you'd like to wear, a three-party government with a former professional wrestler at the helm isn't the laugh riot you'd think it'd be, and if your car runs great except for the heater, it's probably your thermostat.

It was the "probably" in that last piece of wisdom that hung me up. As long as I pretended my car was just a four-door snowmobile with a radio, I could remain in the dark. Once I brought it to a mechanic, though, I risked hearing that my flux capacitator, or some other ridiculously expensive and hard-to-reach part, was shot. And then I'd need to choose one of three options: retire my beloved teenaged Toyota Corolla and take out a loan to buy another car, dip into my meager savings to repair her, or pretend that I misunderstood the mechanic and return to blissful ignorance.

*I'm sure your car is at peace with Schmidt, too, Mechanic. Thanks
and have a nice day!*

Just thinking about it made my shoulders tighten. At least my
Toyota blocked the wind. That would suffice for now, record-cold
November be damned. I wiggled my toes inside their good-to-72-
below Sorels and rescraped the windshield spy-hole. Being no
dummy, I was driving slowly to compensate for my lack of vision.
I didn't need to drive far, a three-mile hop skip from my place to
visit a friend I hadn't seen since October. He'd called last week
with surprise good news, and today was the first day that worked
out for both of us to celebrate.

We'd met this past summer, right around when I was acquiring
my Battle Lake sea legs. This west central Minnesota town had a
downside, no question—not a single ethnic restaurant, no movie theater within 20 miles, and at least one mysteriously dead body floated
to the surface every month, give or take—but you couldn't beat the
people. Every last one of 'em would charge into a burning house to
pull out a stranger. Of course, immediately afterward, they'd head to
the Turtle Stew to whisper about how it was almost certainly poor
housekeeping that had caused the fire in the first place. It was the
timeless small town dance of solidarity versus privacy.

I'd found myself cutting in last spring when my friend Sunny
coerced me into leaving Minneapolis to housesit her doublewide
resting on the most beautiful 200 acres this side of the Mississippi.
I'd agreed, leaving behind six graduate credits in English, a waitressing job, and a boyfriend who tackled lovemaking with as much
patience and skill as a monkey trying to figure out how to change
the TV channel (*one … of … these … must … be … it …*). Made Battle Lake look pretty good.

7

The town had treated me well in many ways. For example, for the first time in my life, I had enough friends to form a basketball team, were I so inclined. No one treated me like a pariah for my father's crimes, as they had in Paynesville, the tiny town I'd grown up in. And shortly after arriving, I'd landed a full-time job running the library after a homicide opened up the director position, proving that murder has its perks if you're not the dead body. I also wrote a recipe column for the local paper as well as freelance articles, and three weeks ago I'd bowed to the Fates and begun pursuing my private investigator's license. Mrs. Berns had planted the idea in my head. "This many dead bodies in your vicinity, you either got to be a mortician, a cop, or a PI, or people start to talk," is how I believe she'd put it. We both agreed that the first option was gross and the second unlikely, which left only the third. That required undergoing certification training and tracking down a lawyer or licensed investigator who'd let me work under them for 6,000 hours. It was a daunting number, to be sure, but I'd gotten nibbles.

Oh, and did I mention I was in a relationship with kind, smart, sexy Johnny Leeson? I'd been spanked by the cosmos enough to recognize it's bad luck to brag, but here's the truth: Johnny is so hot that women cross their legs to keep from involuntarily whistling when he walks by. I know you're wondering how I scored a hottie with a body like his, and to be honest, I'm as baffled as the next person. All I can tell you is that it happened, and I'm glad every day for it.

That's not to say I'd become magically stable. In fact, certain that it was only a matter of time before I messed it up, I'd put clear parameters on our fledgling relationship: we'd keep separate lives, no "L" word until I gave permission, and no going beyond third base for the first six months. This was a seismic shift for me. I had a history of starting relationships with a trip to the bedroom, and it had never worked out particularly well for me. I wanted something better this time, and every after-school special I'd ever watched had convinced me I'd have to keep the relationship vertical to get it.

The point I'm trying to make is that I was in a good place in my life and as nervous as a funeral giggle because of it. This fine world would come crashing down around my ears soon. That's just how the dice had always rolled for me. Until disaster struck, though, I was determined to make the best of it, starting with this afternoon's celebration with Jed.

As long as me and my fridge on wheels could survive all the way to his place, that was. Man it was cold out. That's one more thing you learn from thirty years in Minnesota, by the way. Once the temperature drops to the double digits below zero, there's no point in applying adjectives. Cold is cold. I tugged my Swedish ski cap lower to protect the numb tips of my ears and breathed into my gloved hand to warm my nose. The heated air made my fingers ache in contrast.

In our conversation last week Jed hadn't mentioned what we would be celebrating, probably because it hadn't occurred to him that I might want to know. I smiled, sending white puffs of frozen breath through my teeth. Sometimes Jed acted like he hadn't paid his brain bill, but that was his charm. He was one of the last innocents, a Shaggy minus Scooby Doo. His parents owned the popular Last Resort, and he still lived with them, serving as their man

Friday as well as the oddjobber fix-it guy for many Battle Lake residents.

I slapped my hands on my thighs to circulate the blood and visualized a steaming cup of cocoa. Jed's mom had concocted the most amazing hot chocolate when we'd last gotten together in October, laced with a hint of mint and topped with homemade whipped cream. I salivated at the memory, then remembered that Jed's parents always flew to Florida for the winter, leaving just before Thanksgiving. That meant they'd hit the skies around the same time Jed had called me.

Maybe I could talk him into going to the Shoreline for veggie chili and fresh cornbread, I thought, as I hung a left on Lakeshore Drive. I caught sight of the Last Resort sign a half a mile ahead. The deep snow buried its bottom quarter, so anyone not from around here wouldn't know to "Turn Right to Claim Your Slice of Summer Heaven!" Maybe it was intentional, with that line serving as a paint-based barometer.

In the winter, this touristed side of the lake became a sparsely populated stretch. I caught only glimpses of the landscape through my tiny sighthole, and the lack of peripheral vision was beginning to make me claustrophobic. Maybe Jed could help me rig up an electric space heater in the car. Spurred by that hope, I flipped my turn signal and eased up on the gas in case the driveway was icy.

Too late, I realized that there was no driveway. I plowed into a monster drift of thick white snow broken by the occasional gray-limbed shrub. My foot attacked the brakes, but not before my front tires buried themselves in a snowbank. I swore like a one-legged sailor, my hot words freezing the second they left my mouth and dropping to the ground like ice cubes. Probably they'd roll under my seat and be forgotten until they thawed next spring, popping like soggy, four-letter firecrackers.

I gunned the car forward and back, forward and back, but it was no use. My vehicle was stuck as a pig in the slaughter trough. I flicked off the ignition and shouldered my way out. The frigid air pierced my cheeks like needles. I yanked my scarf over my nose and breathed shallowly to avoid the crackling pain of mucus membranes freezing from the outside in.

Except for my ragged breaths, it was utterly silent outside my vehicle. Glancing around, two other facts struck me: the Resort's driveway hadn't been plowed since last week's heavy snowfall—hence my stuckness—and the mailbox was so past full that the carrier had left a bag of letters tied to its front.

Shielding my eyes against the setting sun, I stared down the 200-yard drive to the main house and eleven cabins that comprised the Last Resort. Not a single light shone in any of the buildings, and I couldn't make out footprints or shoveled paths. I replayed last week's conversation with Jed. Had he sounded down? Mentioned leaving town? I ignored the warning thud of my heart.

Tightening my wool scarf, I slogged to the mailbox, which was placed conveniently on the shoulder of Lakeshore Drive. It was too cold to take off my mittens, so I used my hands like crude tongs to paw through the letters. The oldest was an electric bill, postmarked the day after I'd spoken with Jed. A glance in the bag showed me that the carrier had dropped the most recent mail off today. But nobody was picking it up. A chill icier and more personal than the winter wind licked my spine.

What had happened to my friend?

THREE

"Need a lift?"

I refrained from asking him whether it was the thick white crust that had formed on the surface of my scarf or my frozen-open eyeballs that had tipped him off. "Please."

"Not a great day for a jaunt," he said lightly, leaning over to roll up his window and open his passenger-side door.

I stepped up into his truck, awash in the smell of cigarettes, fast food, and sweet heat. These basic human comforts tamed my smart-ass tongue. "I'm afraid to look whether or not my legs are still attached."

He chuckled. His laugh was deep and out of place in his wiry body. I guessed he was in his early sixties and, judging by the rainbow pompom on his blue cap and smile lines creasing the corner of his eyes and mouth, not an immediate threat. I would have gotten into Satan's corduroys, though, if it'd rescued me from the deep freeze. "They're still attached, though I'm not sure they'd have taken you much farther. WCCO says it's supposed to drop to 40 below with windchill tonight."

"Hmm. Sounds cold." See? That's how we roll in Minnesota.

"That your empty car I passed at the Last Resort?" He aimed a thumb toward his rear window. My Toyota was a mile back. Not possessing a cell phone and having established that there was no sense in staying in a heatless vehicle as dark fell, I had to choose from which direction to seek help. I was equidistant from the intersection of the better-traveled county road on the left or an occupied-looking house on the right. Given the light traffic I'd witnessed tonight, I chose the right. Unfortunately, once I reached the driveway, I saw it was as drifted over as the resort's. It was too late to turn back and too cold to cry, so I'd put my head down and pushed on toward the next house. The only sound had been the chuffing of my boots on the snow and my ragged, cold-seared breath pushing through my iced-up scarf. The frozen moisture on my exhalations had turned the front of my scarf into a ragged, chafing patch of sodden, icy wool that scratched my face raw. I focused on that pain to take my mind off the humming numbness licking at my toes and fingertips. I'd constructed a mantra as I walked, a word for each step: *one, two, Jed I'll get to you, three, four, we'll be cold no more.*

I nodded. "It's my car." The warmth was awakening painfully frozen nerves in my outer perimeters. "It's stuck. You don't happen to have a tow rope, do you?"

"I do." He executed a neat three-point turn with his old Ford.

"Then you're my winter angel."

He smiled mighty cryptically for a man wearing a pompom hat. "Lucky timing and a tow cable don't make a man an angel." His solid truck ate up the icy road in seconds. Just past the Last Resort driveway, he coaxed it into reverse and backed in behind my car, requesting my keys and hopping out before I had an opportunity to ask if he needed help. That's okay. I wouldn't have. The ache of sensation returning to my fingers and toes was agonizing.

I swiveled in my seat and watched him yank a thick nylon rope with an evil-looking hook on each end out of the bed of the truck. He disappeared for a moment into the space between our vehicles. I heard the scrape of metal on metal before he popped back into view. He walked around the side of my Toyota, slid in quickly, and started her up. Doubtless he was putting it in neutral and warming her for me. I could have saved him the trouble, but it would have only stolen the shine off his kindness. He returned to the cab of the truck, bringing a wall of cold with him. Tiny icicles decorated his beard and mustache like tinsel. "You're lucky you weren't out here any longer. It's cold enough to freeze the smile off a clown."

He accelerated the truck and freed my girl without any fanfare beyond the solid thump of iced wheels releasing. I thanked him sincerely and left the heated glow of his cab for the rock-cold seat of my Toyota. I grimaced. My thawing tips were immediately refreezing. I slid her into first gear and sped away like a fox from a trap.

I was closer to town than home and chose the former. The Fortune Café on the north side of Battle Lake not only had the nearest phone but was owned by my good friends Sid and Nancy. I didn't want to be alone if Jed didn't answer. I parked the car and limped through the ice-crystalled door of the Café.

It was late for the Fortune, a retrofitted 1920s house turned bakery that now specialized in coffees and teas, and homemade bagels, pastries, and soups. The air smelled of roasting coffee beans and cinnamon. Except for the owners and a smattering of customers playing Scrabble at a round table, the restaurant was empty. "Mira! Is that you?"

I unwrapped my frozen scarf. "Parts of me. I might have lost my nose and a toe or two, but I'm hopeful I've still got the big ones."

"Oh my God! It's freezing out there! Come over here and sit by the fire. Sid, get her some hot tea."

The fireplace tempted me obscenely, but I held out my hand. "First I need to find out where Jed is. I was supposed to meet him tonight, and no one's at the resort. It doesn't look like anyone's been there for a week." I kept my voice even.

Nancy took in my pink cheeks, glossy eyes, and tight mouth. She shook her head and clucked. "Didn't Jed tell you? He's moved next to Kathy's Klassy Kwilts. You know, where Herb's Wienery used to be?"

I melted, relief warming me faster than any fire. Jed's body wasn't rotting within inches of the phone he'd tried to crawl to after slipping and breaking both legs and one arm. I took a deep breath and redirected my brain. It liked to spend a questionable amount of time picking over gruesome possibilities when left to its own devices. Instead, I pictured the building Nancy was referring to. Herb's had lasted all of three months. I think it was the owner's unfortunate resemblance to a cow, from his big brown eyes and his droopy jowls to his tassly brown hair. It made you feel bad to eat a hot dog in front of him. Whatever the reason, Herb had packed up his saddlebags and moved the wienery to greener pastures last spring, the third restaurant in as many years to go under in that location.

"Jed's drained all the water from the resort's pipes and moved out for the winter. Too expensive to heat." She pushed me onto the couch and pulled off my boots to bring my toes closer to the fire. "He didn't tell you, did he? And you went out there and saw the driveway was unplowed, most likely, and figured he'd died in his sleep or maybe been eaten by bears and no one else had noticed?"

It's weird how your worries sound stupid when someone else says them out loud. Weird and annoying as hell. "He told me to meet him at his place," I said, a little defensively. "You'd think he'd have mentioned he'd moved."

Nancy nodded agreeably. "You'd sure think he would have. You going to leave your snowpants on? You'll warm up quicker if you get your skin closer to the fire."

Her kindness worked, and my peevishness began to melt incrementally. Tiny increments. I'm no quitter. "I thought he might be hurt out at the resort, maybe dead."

She clucked again and took the tea Sid had brought over. "I'm sorry."

Sid perched herself on the edge of the couch. "What's this? Jed forgot to tell someone something important? Next you'll be trying to tell me that a skunk stinks."

She was right. It was completely in character for him to invite me over but forget to tell me where he was living. It wasn't his fault I'd driven into a snowbank or that my thawing extremities felt like they were simultaneously on fire and frozen. I sighed and made a conscious choice to let go of stress at the exact moment that the door chime jingled. We all swiveled our heads to see who had entered, and I cursed under my breath. It appeared that stress wasn't ready to let go of me.

FOUR

Mrs. Berns was my best friend. She was also in her eighties and a beautiful package of white curls, deep wrinkles, and saucy wit. When her husband passed a decade earlier, she'd thrown off her housewife shackles and become a skilled cougar, chasing men half her age and catching her fair share. I loved her to death and back, but the expression on her face revealed that something was seriously wrong. I shot to my feet, disregarding the bone-deep pain of frozen toe tips. "What is it?"

"I need a seat."

I led her over to the couch with Nancy's help. Mrs. Berns was still sporting a light scar on her face and a limp, markers of the life-threatening car accident she'd been in five weeks earlier. This close, she felt frail.

"Can we get you some tea?" Nancy asked. Sid was already on her way to the kitchen.

"Not unless that's lesbian for 'brandy,'" Mrs. Berns said, settling into the sofa.

Nancy smiled. "'Fraid not. We've got a chocolate croissant with your name on it, however."

"Now you're talking some sense." Mrs. Berns stretched her feet toward the fire and took stock of me, her eyes squinting as she looked me up and down. "Went for a walk in this beautiful weather, by the looks of you."

"Forget about me. I haven't seen you this stressed since, well … ever."

She harrumphed, her face dropping back into the peaks and valleys of strain. "You know that funeral I attended this afternoon?"

"Tom Kicker's?" Nancy asked. "Sad situation."

I nodded in agreement. Everyone in the county knew Tom, or at least knew of him. He'd founded Battle Sacks thirty years earlier. The business had started, legend had it, when he couldn't find a knapsack sturdy enough and with enough pockets to hold all his hunting gear. Swearing he could do better, he'd cut up an old canvas tarp and created the first Battle Sack. Since that time, the name had become synonymous with quality outdoor gear, and he'd expanded the line to include sleeping bags, hiking and camping equipment, and even a line of high-quality bows. The company had quickly outgrown the shed he'd originally started it in, and he'd constructed a factory on the outskirts of Battle Lake two decades earlier. Battle Sacks was the largest employer in the five-county area. All had been golden until last Saturday, when its founder had been shot and killed in a tragic hunting accident. The story had even made the *St. Paul Pioneer Press*. "I bet there were a lot of people at the funeral."

"The church was full to the top. Really good food, too. You know those First Lutheran ladies make the best bars. I've got some extra here, if you're interested."

I tried to stop her from digging in her purse. "I'm good. So you're stressed about the funeral?"

She almost had her head fully tucked inside her grocery-bag-sized purse. Her voice was muffled. "Not that so much. Funerals can be a good time, depending on who you sit by. It's the meeting with his daughter that's set me off kilter."

"Hallie?" Nancy asked.

Mrs. Berns pulled her head out of her purse. "That's her. She's my goddaughter, you might know. And she's as convinced as the nose on her face that it wasn't an accident that killed her father."

FIVE

THIS BROUGHT SID BACK from behind the counter. "What? But he was out hunting with Clive. Those two have been friends since high school."

Mrs. Berns made a dismissive sound. "I know that, you know that, the whole county knows that."

"So why does she think he was murdered?" I asked. Clive actually my neighbor, in a country-mile sort of way, and a recluse as far as I could tell. There was a rumor among the high school crowd that he'd murdered his wife and children and fed them to the pigs years ago. I'd never put much stock in it. Every small town in Minnesota has an aging bachelor who's been designated as either the fed-his-wife-to-the-pigs man or the trap-and-eat-children-for-fun guy. It's just one more way we punish the single in society. Clive was gainfully employed, and on the rare occasions when our paths crossed, his hunched body language and smell labeled him a loner with a borderline drinking problem, not a murderer. As far as I knew, Tom was his only friend, and I think Clive liked it that way. In fact, I'd wondered if he'd started the pig-feeding rumor himself to keep people away.

"That's for you to find out," she said.

I coughed involuntarily. "What?"

"I told her you'd talk to her. Said you'd come over tonight, as a matter of fact."

"What?"

"You already said that."

Feeling had finally returned to all the previously frozen parts of my body. Problem was, it was that high-pitched nerve pain that your body doles out as it decides whether or not you have frostbite. I tried to ignore it. "It was relevant both times. Why on earth would you tell Hallie that I'd talk to her?"

"You're a private dick, aren't you?" She smiled innocently. She'd been tickled when I'd agreed to seek out my investigator's license because it gave her countless legitimate opportunities to say "dick" in mixed company.

"We've talked about this. I don't have my license yet, it'll be years before I do, and you don't get to call me a dick. Besides, what is there to detect? A man was shot by his friend while they were hunting. He died, and the friend claimed it was an accident. If that's good enough for the police, it's gonna have to be good enough for Hallie."

"How many murders have you solved in the last six months? Seven? Eight?"

"And not a one of them on purpose."

"Well, now you've got some purpose."

I shook my head. "I want to be a small-town investigator. You know, the boring stuff. Online research, credit checks, maybe a cheating scandal or two. Nice and safe."

She changed tack. "You won't talk to a grieving woman on the night of her father's funeral?"

I groaned. Guilt was my kryptonite. "Why do you do this to me?"

"You love it, and you know it."

"It won't do any good, me talking to her." I was already caving.

"We'll see."

"Tonight?"

"Yes."

"I'll only consider it if you'll come with me." I wasn't very good at dealing with emotions, mine or others. I guessed there would be a lot of the latter.

"Wouldn't miss it for the world."

"Fine. I'll do it. It shouldn't take long to convince her that a librarian isn't her best bet if she wants to prove a murder."

"Right. Or for her to convince you that she might be on to something." She indicated my hands, which I'd begun flexing to burn off the last of the frost-stiffening. "Now that I've spilled, why don't you explain why you looked like you'd been shat out a snowman when I came in."

I updated her on my afternoon—no Jed, got stuck, walked across the tundra, rescued by a stranger, found out Jed moved.

She nodded as if it all made perfect sense and then zeroed in on the part that affected her. "You better get that heat in your car fixed soon. I need you to drive me to Minneapolis on Wednesday."

"What for?"

She returned to her purse and came out with a pair of sunglasses as big as dinner plates. "Gonna visit my daughter in Sedona." She enunciated every syllable: *C-doe-nuh.*

I'd met her daughter, Elizabeth, at the hospital after the car accident. She was good people. "What time's your plane leave?"

"Nine p.m. I scheduled the flight so you'd have just enough time to close up the library before driving me down."

"Very thoughtful," I said. "When're we leaving for Hallie's?"

She looked over her shoulder, her expression annoyed. "As soon as I get that chocolate croissant I was promised."

———

I knew who Tom Kicker was, of course, and had seen him around town. The same was true of Hallie. I could have picked them both out of a crowd, though I'd never exchanged more than a few words with either of them. "How do you know the Kicker family?"

Mrs. Berns sat next to me, furiously scraping the inside of the windshield as I drove. Dancing ice shavings turned the inside of the Toyota into a roving snowglobe. "That's a potentially interesting question, but how's this for a better one? What sort of goat-roping idiot drives a car without heat in Minnesota at the end of November? I'm just curious, mind you. Making conversation, if you will." She was shivering so violently that her teeth clattered like castanets.

"I'll get it fixed. I just haven't had time." I shot her a sideways glance to see if she was buying it. Not only was she not in for a penny, she looked ready to whack me with the scraper.

"You wet-pantsed chicken. You're afraid of what the mechanic is going to tell you, aren't you?"

"Unh unh. Just busy." I steered the conversation back to the Kickers. "You must be 20 years older than Tom, and I never heard you talk about him. How'd you get to be Hallie's godmother?"

She returned to her scraping. "I didn't know Tom that well, tell you the truth. Hallie joined my church while she was still in high school. She was having some problems at home but was never too specific about them. Her family wasn't religious, so Sundays were her excuse to get away. She and I hit it off, and when she decided forever ago to get baptized, I agreed to be her spiritual guide."

I snorted. Talk about letting the wolf guard the sheep.

"I'm multi-faceted," she huffed. "Now step on it before my niblets freeze off."

Hallie lived in the rich part of town, which, given the size of Battle Lake, was right next to every other part of town. Her house was an old Victorian, the kind with a four-season porch, gingerbreading on the outside, and lots of turrets and crannies. *I bet a person could get a lot of thinking done in a house like that,* I thought, following Mrs. Berns up the well-traveled front walk. A soft snow had crept in and the streetlights were lit, imparting a faded, Norman Rockwell feel to the block of grand old houses.

The stampede of footprints leading to Hallie's front door suggested she'd entertained a traveling army recently, which made sense given her father's death and funeral. They must have all gone home because only one light shone in the window. The door was answered before Mrs. Berns finished knocking.

"You came. I wasn't sure if you would." Hallie was in her late forties, and because she was a little short and a lot round, I'd

24

always assumed she'd be nice to hug and smell like fresh-baked cookies up close. Right now, though, the pinched look around her eyes and mouth suggested the only thing she wanted to hug was her pillow and a bottle of Valium.

"I said I would. Now let me in. I'm so cold I can't feel my liver." Mrs. Berns pushed her way inside.

"Hi," I said, holding out my hand. The growl of a car coming to life rumbled from the end of the block, followed by the sound of a windshield being scraped. "I'm Mira. I don't know if we've ever been formally introduced. I'm sorry about your loss."

She smiled, but it didn't quite reach her eyes. "Thank you for coming. You probably think I'm ridiculous, asking you here to talk about my dad's shooting. The police are certain it's an accident."

The car at the end of the block took off, its tires making a crunching cornflakes sound on the newly fallen snow. I tried to keep my shivering within the myoclonic range. "But you're not?"

"Where are my manners? Come in and have a seat. Can I get you something to drink?" She closed the door behind me and led us into a grand den stuffed with soporific-looking sofas and velvet-backed chairs. My second fire of the evening crackled in the fire-place, and through the heat-tempered glass shielding the front and the back of the fire, I could see into the room on the other side.

"Brandy," said Mrs. Berns. "And Mira gave up drinking a month or two ago, but I predict she'll be back in the bottle soon. Want to start tonight, dear?"

I shot her the stink eye. Her social filter, flimsy under the best of circumstances, must have frozen entirely on the way over. "I'd take some hot chocolate, if you have it."

"Of course. I'll be right back."

She turned a corner and a light illuminated the glass on the other side of the fireplace. I realized it was the kitchen I was seeing through there. Suddenly, I was dying to explore this majestic house. "How much do you think a place like this costs?" I whispered to Mrs. Berns.

"Less than it would in Minneapolis. You're going to snoop, aren't you?"

Bugger that she knew me so well. I'd always struggled to pass a closed door without at least jiggling the knob. If it was unlocked, a peek couldn't hurt anyone, could it? It was an affliction, but there were worse ones. "No. I need to use the bathroom."

"Okay. It's the third door on your left down that hallway. Let me know if you find anything interesting."

I stuck my tongue out at her and left the warm firelight. The hallway was graced with what I assumed were the original tin ceilings and elaborate crown molding. I stretched my hands as high as they would go, and the ceiling was still seven feet away. The walls were decorated with dark wood chair rails and dozens of family photos. Most of them were of Hallie when she was younger, standing alone or with a dark-haired version of her father and the woman I guessed was her mother. I couldn't remember if Tom Kicker had been divorced or widowed. I'd ask Mrs. Berns later.

Whenever the three of them were posed together, they looked happy, all sunburned noses and wide smiles. I recognized Minnesota landmarks in many of their photos—the Paul Bunyan statue in Brainerd, Split Rock lighthouse in Two Harbors—looming behind a grinning Hallie who in the earliest photos was missing teeth. As the photographic timeline progressed, she grew taller and then rounder, and by the end of the line-up, she'd graduated to curled hair, bell bottoms, and the large eyeglasses favored by shop teachers and fans of the Bay City Rollers.

Tom must have snapped most of the photos because he appeared only in a handful, though at the end of the wall, he was front and center in a fishing shot. I recognized Clive. The other two men were strangers to me. The photo appeared about five years old, judging by their clothes and the gray peppering their hair. The four of them stood on a dock, holding a muskie so huge they each had two hands on it. Tom was laughing, mouth open, and the much-older man immediately to his right seemed to be sharing the joke. Clive and the other fellow looked stiff, but it might have been the way the late afternoon light fell on their faces.

I heard Hallie return to Mrs. Berns and pulled myself away from the photos. I really did need to use the bathroom. I hurried to the end of the hall. All the doors on my way were open, so I could see right into an office and a neatly kept spare bedroom on my right and a fabulously oaky and well-stocked private library on my left. I steered into the bathroom and did my business, forgoing opening any of the cabinets. I actually do have a curiosity line that I won't cross.

My hot cocoa was waiting for me when I returned. "Thank you," I said, accepting the steaming mug. I dipped my pinkie in the liquid, felt it was exactly the right temperature, and took a big swallow.

I opened my eyes and saw Hallie smiling at me, this time from her eyes. "Good stuff?"

"You have no idea. This is the first time I've been completely warm in hours."

"I'm glad." She sat in the love seat at an angle from the sofa. We could all converse with one another comfortably, but she seemed not to know where to start.

Mrs. Berns, however, didn't suffer from that affliction. "So you think Tom was murdered."

I choked on my hot chocolate, but Hallie took it in stride. "I do. I know it sounds crazy, which is why I haven't told anyone but you, and now Mira. It's just a feeling I can't shake. Well, that and the fight."

"Fight?" I asked, against my better judgment.

Hallie nodded and took a deep slug of her drink. It was also in a mug, but I'd wager twenty dollars it wasn't hot chocolate. "I don't think they wanted anyone to hear it. I'd stopped in late at the plant last Friday to pick up some work—I've been the bookkeeper for twenty years, my first and only job, really—and saw my dad's truck out front. I was surprised because he was supposed to be hunting with Clive for the weekend. I walked to the main office and was going to go in when I heard the voices. It was Clive and my dad, arguing."

I placed my empty mug on the end table, wondering if maybe I should have paced myself. I was starting to feel sleepy, like a well-fed kitten. "How do you know it was Clive?"

She shot me a glance I couldn't read. "Clive has been in my life forever. I'd recognize his voice anywhere."

"What were they arguing about?" Mrs. Berns asked.

"That's just it." Hallie sat forward in her chair, her face haggard. "I don't know. Clive yelled something about nobody finding out, and my dad said something back, too quiet for me to hear. He wasn't a yeller, never had been," she added, almost as a plea. "Then

Clive yelled at him to wait just a week. Well, as soon as I realized it was those two, I didn't want to be a busybody. I left."

Mrs. Berns arched her eyebrow at me. *See, some people choose not to be nosy*, it said. I aimed my own eyebrow back. *Women who lie in glass cougar dens shouldn't throw stones*, it said.

Hallie sniffled, and we both returned our attention to her. "If I'd known it was the last time I'd have seen my dad, I'd have gone in there. I'd have hugged him and asked what they were fighting about."

Her words stacked a heavy load on my back. In that moment, I recognized what Hallie was doing and why we were here. She wanted to change the outcome of this story. I'd attempted the same thing when I'd lost my own dad. When someone who is sewn tightly into the fabric of your life dies unexpectedly, you become desperate to rewrite history, to "what if" every moment in the space-time continuum until you're crazy with misery and guilt. My father had been a sloppy drunk who'd killed himself and two people in another car in a head-on collision. My high school had somehow acquired his crushed Chevy Impala and displayed it on the campus as a cautionary tale. I was forced to walk past it every day of my senior year, and still, given all that he'd put me through, I'd tried to paint him as a misunderstood hero that I could have saved. I imagined it was a hundred times worse if your dad had been a decent person. Best to reset her compass quick and clean.

"Look," I said gently. "I know it can be hard to lose someone you care about, but Clive and your dad were good friends. People who know each other well fight, and then they make up. I'm sure that's what you heard—friends having a meaningless argument. It couldn't have been that bad if they went hunting together after-ward, right?"

She gripped her mug like it held her spare heart, and rose to her feet, her voice trembling. "But that's it, don't you see? My dad and Clive have been hunting together for decades. They were pros. Clive knew his way around a gun better than his own hand. There's no way he'd accidentally shoot my dad. No way. It had to be on purpose."

"But why?"

She fell back into the chair like a popped balloon. "That's what I need you to find out."

Mrs. Berns downed her brandy in a swallow and strode over to Hallie. She put her arm around her. "You'll have to accept that it may have been an accident, dear. But if it was murder, our Mira here will figure it out."

"What?"

She glared at me over her shoulder. "You might want to get either your hearing or your vocabulary checked. You seem to not be processing things too well."

"But—"

"But nothing. I already told Hallie you'd look into it. I'd do it myself if I wasn't on my way to Sedona." *C-doe-na*. She returned to her place next to me on the couch and twisted the vulnerable skin underneath my arm.

"Ouch!" I swatted at her hand. "I'm not a real detective. I'm not even a real librarian."

"Now, now. You're a real dick deep down, even if you don't yet have your license." Mrs. Berns' eyes glistened. "Take your future by the reins. Just last week you were telling me you need to get a

30

million hours of apprentice work in before you can be licensed. Hallie already spoke with her lawyer, and he said he'd hire you to investigate this. You get paid, Hallie gets help, and you get closer to being licensed."

Hallie nodded vigorously.

I sighed. This whole plan would all make perfect sense in a loony bin. I looked at Hallie square. "Hallie, I'm an English grad school drop-out who was promoted to head librarian when her boss disappeared. Everything I know about investigating murders has come from trying to save my skin or reading a book. You sure you wouldn't rather hire a professional?"

Hallie sat forward, speaking earnestly. "The closest private investigator is in Fargo. He would stand out like a sore thumb around here. I need someone who can ask questions without people being suspicious. I'm now the owner of Battle Sacks, and I have too many employees I'm responsible for. I can't afford any more negative publicity. Think how it already looks, the owner of an outdoor supply company dying in a hunting accident."

She had a point, and the more sense she and Mrs. Berns made, the less I liked it. "I need to think about it."

They let me off at that. We left a sad-eyed Hallie, and Mrs. Berns nagged me for not having heat the whole fourteen blocks to the nursing home. I made sure she made it to her room safely even though the stress of the day caught up with me and hung off my body like a hundred sand bags. I dragged myself back to my car and navigated the icy roads all the way to my mailbox, where I pulled out a stack of bills. I drove down the interminable driveway, plugged in my car, let out my dog, and called Jed to make certain he was safe. He was, and so apologetic that it was difficult to muster up anger. We made plans to get together later in the week.

I possessed barely enough energy to brush my teeth, but a letter on the top of the pile caught my attention. It was from an unfamiliar bank, and it looked official. It could be good news, right? Maybe I'd inherited. Or maybe I owed. I cranked the house's thermostat to 72 degrees and listened to the click and then hum of it kicking in. The letter stared at me. I brushed my teeth, let the dog back in, ran fresh water for both animals, peeled off my clothes, and hopped into bed.

Who was I kidding? I heaved myself up and went to the letter.

Dear Ms. Miranda James:

This letter is to inform you that your school loan deferment period ended on May 1st. We have had difficulty tracking down your most recent address; as a result, your account is in arrears. This is your last notification before a collection agency is…

I balled up the letter and tossed it toward the basket. It looked like I would be taking on Hallie's case after all.

SIX

TWO DAYS LATER, AFTER I'd dropped Mrs. Berns off at the airport, I called Hallie to say I'd take the case. It was a funny, TV detective thing to say. I assured her that it was unlikely I'd uncover anything, that I might be wasting her time, and that there were easier ways to let go. She listened to it all without changing her mind, and set up a lunch appointment with me and her attorney.

We met over Tator Tot hotdish—special order vegetarian version for me—and dinner rolls at the Turtle Stew, Hallie still appearing shattered by the loss of her father. Her skin had a gray hue, and her hair and eyes were dull. It must have been shock that kept her buoyed the night of the funeral, because she appeared to have aged ten years since that evening. It broke my heart. She continued in her conviction that I take the case, and she didn't blink when her attorney from the Litchfield Law Firm offered me a $500 retainer. I almost choked on my own spit when I saw the check, but I tried to play it cool. Possibly my wide eyes and muttered, "No way! That's a lot of cheddar!" gave me away, but then again, we're always harder on ourselves than the rest of the world is, right? The $500 wouldn't solve my money jam, but it'd put a nice dent in my back payments.

Hallie's lawyer informed me that I had complete freedom to handle the case any way I wanted, which made me realize, sadly, that I had no idea how to handle a case. Fortunately, I'd had the foresight to order *Private Investigating for Morons* for the library at the same time I'd contacted the Minnesota Private Detective and Protective Agent Services Board to look into the state licensure requirements. I vowed internally to rifle through that puppy after lunch. Surely there would be a numbered list outlining the steps to follow when cornering a killer. Even better would be a guide that explained how to convince a woman that her father had died in an accident rather than been murdered, while simultaneously unearthing $500 worth of information for her. I'd keep my fingers crossed. Amid the Turtle Stew's bustling noontime crowd, we finished our food and small talk before all three going back to work.

The library had been slow this time of year, especially these weeks between Thanksgiving and Christmas, even though I'd tried to make it an inviting place to visit. Right before she'd left for Sedona, Mrs. Berns had helped me to decorate the library's ceiling with snowflakes strung on paperclips and lavish twinkle lights around the doors, windows, and shelves. I loved Christmas lights, and it showed. There were now corners of the library where you could read by the tiny glittering bulbs alone. It made the whole space warm and cozy.

I reviewed my to-do list. I had the Saturday night Love-Your-Library fundraiser to prepare for, an annual after-hours event where the city paid for food and drink to thank our donors. Other than that, my schedule was clear beyond personning the front desk, shelving returned books, and helping the occasional patron stalwart enough to brave the screaming cold that had gripped the town like a thousand icy fishhooks. We were setting record lows, and most people didn't venture out unless they were forced, myself included. That left plenty of time to get caught up on my newspaper duties and flesh out a strategy for investigating Tom's death.

I figured I'd start with the easy stuff—the newspaper job. I plunked myself down at the front desk computer and halfheartedly searched for recipes for my "Battle Lake Bites" column featured weekly in the *Battle Lake Recall*. When Ron, owner and editor of the *Recall*, had first directed me to discover food representative of Battle Lake back in May, I'd passive aggressively sought out the strangest, Norwegianest recipes I could find, from deer pie to tur-ducken. And readers couldn't get enough of it. Ron had requested that my recipe theme between Thanksgiving and Christmas be holiday-related, and if possible, centered on entertaining. He was hoping for dips and toothpick-in-a-weenie-type magic, I knew this, but I had to give the people what they wanted

My first hit on "weird holiday food" was scrapple, because what can go wrong when you start out cooking with a whole pig's head? Next was beaver tails, which I liked the sound of until I found out they were the Canadian version of elephant ears and included no actual beaver parts. A half an hour later and still nothing weird enough had jumped out at me.

Disheartened, I spent the rest of the afternoon tending to the rare library patron, reading my *Moron's Guide* and taking notes on surveillance and interrogation, and confirming that all was a go for Saturday's donor-appreciation event. By the end of the day, I had yet to come up with a plan for tackling Hallie's case. I wished Mrs. Berns was still around so I could bounce ideas off her, but I didn't want to interrupt her vacation.

Jed would work as a Mrs. Berns stand-in, I thought, as I locked up the library and scurried to my car. I flicked on the portable propane fish house heater in my back seat and cracked the windows so I wouldn't suffocate. Mrs. Berns had a friend toss it in so she wouldn't be cold when I drove her to the Cities, and I'd buckled it in the back seat like a fat gray Buddha with a glowing red circle for a head, the whole unit roughly the size of a two-drawer filing cabinet. The heater was designed for a larger space, and even on its lowest setting, gave off enough heat to leave a tan. In fact, we'd had to roll the windows halfway down. By the time we'd pulled into the airport exit, Mrs. Berns was down to a puckered fire-engine red bra, her elastic-waisted slacks, and bare feet. I'd settled for rolling up my sleeves and gathering my hair in a ponytail. The heat was better than frosted windows and freezing fingers, though, and I'd talked Mrs. Berns' friend into letting me keep it until my car was fixed. Whenever that might be.

Once my windows were defrosted, I drove a few short blocks to Jed's new place. Battle Lake looked like a ghost town, with snow drifting across the road in place of tumbleweeds and not a sane person to be seen. The dusk-lit street lamps glowed oddly, the cold warping their light and giving it an underwater quality. It was eerie. I parked my car in front of the empty storefront Jed was now occupying and shot out. The subzero air smelled like steel, and the only sounds were the shriek of the wind and the repetitive echo of a loose binding whipping against the post office flagpole.

I ran to the front door of the shop, not bothering to knock. Fortunately, it was unlocked. It was a relief to put a door between myself and the keening weather. I unwrapped my scarf and breathed in the warm air. I'd managed to let go of any lingering peevishness toward Jed from the day I'd gotten stuck in his drive-way. The thing about him is that he is as sweet as he is absent-minded, and it's impossible to stay mad at him for long. I hadn't spoken to him since that day, so this would be a nice opportunity to clear the air.

"Jed?" Immediately inside the door was a large, wood-floored room, empty except for a few tables off in a corner. Clanking and hammering emanated from the back room. When he didn't answer, I pounded the snow off my boots and headed off the welcome mat and toward the rear of the building. There I entered a room that looked like it had been an industrial kitchen at one time, but was now dominated by an enormous black, shed-shaped furnace. My first thought was that the witch in *Hansel and Gretel* would have loved it. My second thought was that I bet it'd keep a house mighty toasty. Jed was pounding on the back of the massive furnace, and another body was stuck inside, his legs sticking out like Santa's from a chimney.

"Mira!" Jed looked up from his work, grinning dopily. He was seven or so years younger than me, with the bearing and demeanor of a black Lab puppy, all skinny and full of barely suppressed wig-gles. He was wearing a sleeveless t-shirt and long nylon shorts. His curly dark hair was pulled back into a ponytail, the loose strands held off his face by a patterned handkerchief. "You made it!" He loped over to hug me as if we hadn't seen each other in years instead of weeks.

I couldn't resist smiling back. "Hey, Jed. Who're you cooking?" I pointed at the man in the oven.

"Ha! That's Monty. Monty, come on out and meet Mira." He turned back to the furnace and tugged on the legs.

The man inside grunted and then crawled backward like a crab out of its shell. When he emerged, I recognized him immediately.

"My savior!"

"Hunh?" Jed said.

I held my hand out to Monty. He was sweaty but his clothes appeared clean. I'd expected whoever was in there to be covered in soot, so the furnace must be brand new. I noticed for the first time that he was a small man, lithe and only slightly taller than my 5'6". "This is the guy who picked me off the side of the road when I got stuck in your driveway. Thank you again."

"Well, it is a small world," he said, adjusting the same rainbow pompom cap he'd been wearing the other day. I saw close-cropped hair, brown shot with gray, before he yanked it back tight to his ears. "You must be Jed's friend Mira, then. Your car running okay?"

"Except for the heater."

"Probably your thermostat," they both said in unison.

I rolled my eyes and changed the subject. "What're you two up to?" I indicated the furnace and the exotic-looking equipment on two large tables in the middle of the room. Jed had a reputation for undertaking creative and financially irresponsible projects, like the canoe fleet he'd tried to carve from whole logs before giving up and constructing a Huckleberry Finn raft. He was a gifted handyman despite his goofiness. In fact, I'd heard he was a genius with machines, though a village idiot with money. I was pretty sure Mrs. Berns had offered that evaluation.

"Glassblowing!"

I walked around the stove. "Really?" I liked blown glass almost as much as I liked Christmas lights. "Here in Battle Lake?"

"Yup," Jed said. "Monty is the expert. I'm renting the space, and the equipment is his. He's going to teach me!"

"Wow." I glanced over at Monty, who was smiling proudly. "Where'd you learn to blow glass?"

"All over the world, but mostly Turkey."

I stopped to study him. "How'd you end up in Battle Lake all the way from Turkey?"

"*Back* in Battle Lake," he corrected me. "I'm from here originally. Left a long time ago. Guess you can't shake the home dirt off your feet for good, though, 'cuz here I am." He scratched his head underneath the hat, making the pompom shake. "Came back for my father's funeral a few months back and never left. I figure I finally know what I want to do. If you'll excuse me." He crawled back into the maw of the furnace, leaving me with a beaming Jed.

"This is the surprise you called about?"

"Yup. Monty is a master. He's teaching me everything he knows. We just got the furnace a couple days ago, and the rest of the supplies should be here before the end of the week. Battle Lake glass is going to be famous! Pretty cool, hunh?"

"Pretty cool," I agreed. "But this is going to take a while to get off the ground. You still working odd jobs?"

He reached for a rag and wiped his fingers. "I s'pose I'll have to. I had a winter job lined up at Battle Sacks. Was going to be their line mechanic, but I lost it before I started. Got a call a few days ago saying it was no longer available."

My heartbeat ratcheted up at the mention of Battle Sacks. "You heard Tom died, right?"

"Yeah, the hunting accident. My parents are going to be so bummed. Tom was a stand-up guy."

"Did you get hired before or after he died?"

"Right before. And unhired right after. Nobody could tell me exactly why."

"I'm sorry." In my head, I was scrambling to see if the weirdness of that fit with Tom's death. Deep down, I didn't believe that Tom had been murdered, but I'd taken money from Hallie to look into it. I didn't want to admit that the cash had been a main motivator, but I knew I would not have taken the case otherwise. On the drive to the airport. I'd come straight out and asked Mrs. Berns if she'd really thought Tom had been murdered.

"It's hard to say. Hallie was right that Clive knows his way around a gun, but he also drank like a horse. The best hunter can make a mistake when he's got whiskey finger. Then again, it's hard enough to hit an animal when you're aiming at it, let alone a man by accident. I can't quite swallow that 'a hunting accident' is the whole story here. Even if I'm wrong, if you take the case, you'll give Hallie the time and attention she needs to ease her into the idea of her dad being asleep with Jesus."

"So you don't think this is a snipe hunt?"

"I think there's only one way to find out."

He was right, unfortunately. Odds were better than good that Tom's death was accidental, but I'd been hired by Hallie to investigate, and I had to take her concerns seriously. And as luck would have it, here was Jed helping me out. "Say, if a person wanted to get a job at Battle Sacks, how would they go about it?"

"Maybe the newspaper?"

"Is that what you did?"

"No," he said, sounding surprised. "I was just in the Fortune one day, fixing the espresso maker for Nancy. The HR lady from Battle Sacks was there eating lunch. She mentioned they'd need a new line mechanic soon and I should apply. It would have been the perfect job."

"I'm sorry," I repeated.

"No biggie. One door opens and another door closes."

I was going to correct him but thought better of it. Now that I had serendipitously gotten an entrance into investigating the Tom Kicker case, I was itching to leave. "I should probably get home and feed Luna and Tiger Pop. They've been alone all day."

Jed reached over to an ashtray and lit up a sweet-smelling hand-rolled cigarette. "You want any of this first?"

I shook my head. I'd never seen the appeal in smoking something that made me hungrier and more paranoid than I was by nature. "No thanks." I looked around the remodeled work area. "This looks like a really good deal, Jed. I'm excited for you."

He nodded like a Muppet, his mouth full of smoke, and walked over to the furnace. He reached inside to pass the joint to Monty, who seemed fully prepared to accept it. I believed I was witnessing how these two had met. Pot smokers in a small town always seem to find one another. "Yah, it's an awesome deal. I'll make you something as soon as we're up and running." His voice was deep with the sound of trapped smoke. "What would you like?"

"Thanks, but I don't need anything."

"No, I want to."

I shrugged. "How about a small ornament? It is the holiday season."

Jed agreed.

Looking back, I should have asked for a four-leaf clover. Or a life insurance policy.

SEVEN

LUNA AND TIGER POP were thrilled to see me when I arrived home. At least Luna was. Tiger Pop was lounging in front of the kitchen vent, preoccupied with putting the "fur" in "furnace" filter. I indulged both creatures in deep tissue ear and neck massages, then rinsed out and refilled their water bowls, piled kibble into their food dishes, and sieved Tiger Pop's litter box in search of treasure. Luna I let out just long enough to p and p, holding the door open so she could lope back in before her happy tongue froze.

After my roommates were tended to, I checked my blinking answering machine. Two messages, the first from Ron Sims.

Mira, your recipe column's overdue. Get me holiday food. By tomorrow.

Curse words! I'd never found anything weird enough to make it worth my time and had missed my deadline. Again. I couldn't believe I was still allowed to write that column. I made a mental note to uncover a recipe first thing tomorrow, even if I had to create it from scratch. I deleted the message, which cued the next one.

Mira, it's Johnny.

Nerve cells all over my body popped up to listen. His deep, throaty voice brought on spontaneous blushing. We'd gotten hot and heavy the week before, and since then, I couldn't hear his rumble without remembering the feel of his strong hands on the small of my back, pulling me in slow and deliberate for a kiss, his tongue parting my lips, his hips pushing hard into mine. After he'd melted my defenses, he moved from my bruised, open mouth and searched out my ear, gliding his tongue along its edge before kissing the curve of my neck, gently and then with more urgency, until he was pushing me against the wall with the force of his passion. Phew. I shook my head.

I'm calling to make sure we're still getting together this weekend, and to let you know I'm thinking of you. Nothing serious, I know the rules. He chuckled ruefully. *I'm looking forward to Sunday. Let me know if anything has changed.*

Not for the first time, I wondered how I was going to confine the both of us to third base for six months. It was just monthly luck that I'd kept my pants on last week. I tried to call on past experience. How had I hung onto my chasteness throughout high school? Ah, now I remembered: bad hair, cluelessness, and dry-humping. Since I'd sworn off claw bangs and discovered how fun sex could be nearly a decade ago, however, I'd need to improvise some other stopgap measure. I'd heard something about the virginity retention movement on *60 Minutes*. Maybe I could learn something about self-control from today's kids. I scratched "research purity pledges" on my kitchen notepad.

But man, it wasn't gonna be easy. For a flash, I allowed myself to envision a future with Johnny. We'd enjoy lazy Sunday mornings, him wearing nothing but cotton pajama pants hanging off of his slim, sculpted hips. He'd kick back at the kitchen table and sing silly love songs, an acoustic guitar in his lap. I'd be making us pancakes, flavoring them with love and happiness. We'd never get around to eating them, though, because he'd end up chasing me around the kitchen with the spatula, into the bedroom, and the pancakes would burn every time. He couldn't help himself, he'd say. He'd do anything to see me smile.

I caught Tiger Pop staring at me with disgust, so I wiped the moony expression off my face. It was a waste of time, anyhow. That future with Johnny was meant for some beautiful young blonde, free of neurotic baggage, who glowed like sunshine in the morning and always said the right thing, and whose breasts did not disappear when she laid on her back. That was who Johnny deserved, not messed-up me. The best I could do would be to string out this high school-ish honeymoon phase for a few months with my crazy rules. Then, with regret, I'd have to let Johnny go before he left me.

I finished my nighttime routine and climbed into bed with that cold thought for comfort.

———

"Central Minnesota continues to set records with its chilling temperatures. The high in Fergus Falls is not expected to top ten below zero today, making this the sixth day in a row of record lows. Combine that with 40 mph winds and it becomes hazardous to leave your home. If you live in these regions, the Minnesota Department of Transportation is advising you don't go out unless necessary."

I flicked off the morning news. When you can only tune in three channels, you expect better. I immediately regretted the silence, which emphasized the icy wind's raw howl. The scream of winter sliced across the thin walls of the double-wide, rattling the windows and shrieking, hunting for warm flesh to consume. I wasn't going down without a fight, however. Underneath my jeans and t-shirt, I was wearing tights and a thermal shirt. I yanked on monkey socks over that, then snowpants, mittens and a hat, my jacket next, and a scarf last. The order was important to seal any potential leaks.

I coaxed Luna to dash outside with me to start the car and fire up the fish house heater, though her eyes were pleading for me to teach her how to use the litter box.

"Ready?" Before either of us could change our minds, I darted out into the still-dark morning. As prepared as I was, the arctic force of the wind hit me like a snow shovel to the face. For a moment, I considered not opening the library. If that had been my only responsibility, I could have justified it, but I didn't have an Internet connection at home. I'd need to go to work anyhow to research and write the overdue recipe article. Besides, I wanted to stop by the Fortune today to see if I'd cross paths with the Battle Sacks HR lady, like Jed had. Some of my best information had been born of being in the right place at the right time.

Powering on toward the carport, Luna at my side, I pretended I was Pa Ingalls, braving the rabid jaws of winter to procure food and water for his family. "Dang!" I said, as the wind slipped through the weave of my scarf and kissed my lips with violent force. I half-expected my car not to start, but I had plugged it in overnight, and it was a Toyota. It took on the second pull. I cracked all the windows, set the fish house heater to low, stepped out to unplug the radiator block, and dashed back into the house. After rewarming myself and situating Luna and Tiger Pop for the day, I took off.

My driveway had drifted over in spots, but I maintained enough speed to break through the knee-high barriers. The portable propane heater kept the windshield clear and the inside comfortable, even with the windows rolled a quarter of the way down. I passed a few pickups on my way to town, but Battle Lake was otherwise desolate for a Friday morning. Once inside the library, I flicked on the lights, checked the returned books bin, and fired up the computers. It was going to be a slow day, so I got right down to finding the recipe I should have uncovered the previous day.

I am a fan of appetizers because you can eat a lot without looking like a pig, so I Googled "bizarre holiday finger food." This pulled up hits of actual finger/paw recipes, from jellied chicken claws to fried skunk paws, along with a killer pigs-in-a-blanket recipe that made the dough look like actual digits and the hot dog peeking out like a fingernail. Unfortunately, it was all too Halloween-y. I shifted gears and combined "Christmas" with "freshwater fish" and "appetizers," because nothing went over like a yuletide walleye recipe in the land of 10,000 lakes. The "freshwater" in the search didn't hold up, though, and I was inundated with salmon, shrimp, and oyster recipes.

Scanning the photos that appeared, I was drawn to a colorful shot of tiny slices of sushi decorated to resemble old-fashioned Christmas hard candy. A quick click on the recipe revealed it would be far too complicated to make and the ingredients impossible to obtain in the great Northwoods, but an idiot link on the bottom of the screen promised an easier version. I clicked on it and voila! My monitor was suddenly alight with a full-page shot of Twinkie sushi, like a gift from the trailer park adjacent to the North Pole.

I began furiously retyping the recipe, changing key points to adorn it with my own personal flair as well as to avoid copyright infringement.

Twinkly Twinkie Sushi

12 servings

- 12 Twinkies
- Two boxes green fruit roll-ups
- 1 5-lb. bag of Gummi Aquarium (assorted Swedish fish will do in a pinch)

Wrap each Twinkie in a fruit roll-up. Refrigerate in an airtight container for at least one hour. Remove fruit-rolled Twinkies from refrigerator and cut into 1-inch sections. Lay sections on their sides, not touching, on a serving platter. Insert one Gummi Aquarium creature into the white center of each flat Twinkie section. Make sure that the top of creature is flush with the top of the Twinkie so it resembles a roll of sushi cut into sections. Refrigerate at least one more hour. Serve with Zima martinis.*

*Recipe to come.

Talk about food representative of the Midwest. I zipped the recipe off to Ron and returned to my library duties, reshelving the returned books, organizing library bills to send to the city office, and completing various other tasks until lunch time.

When the clock struck noon, I covered myself in a thick coating of temperature denial, stuck the "Out to Lunch" sign on the door, and hoofed it to the Fortune. Once inside, I grabbed my favorite meal—toasted garlic bagel with Greek olive cream cheese, side of green tea accented with steamed soy milk—complimented Sid on her "Closets Are for Clothes" apron, and learned that the Battle Sacks' head of Human Resources was currently eating lunch on the far side of the restaurant. Apparently, the HR woman was a regular who always came at the same time, sat at the same table, and ordered the same food.

So sad, I thought, studying her as I bit into my third toasted garlic bagel with Greek olive cream cheese of the week. She sat with her back to the door, which was a pure survival move in this climate. She was wearing a red, green, and white sweater that had on its front the crocheted outline of two kittens batting around a Christmas ornament. Her stretchy pants were white, with the kitten pattern repeated on her top left thigh. She either sewed her own clothes or bought them at the same underground market that dealt in white purses, bolo ties, and stirrup pants.

I swallowed the rest of my bagel, grabbed my tea, and approached her. My plan was still a little baggy around the waist. I sensed that uncovering what was behind Jed's here-today-gone-tomorrow job offer might provide insight into what Clive and Tom had been fighting about the night Hallie had overheard them. The idea that the argument was over the line mechanic position

49

was a long shot, but if it proved true, it could provide Hallie with at least a measure of relief to know the fight had not been personal.

I was hoping the HR woman could enlighten me as to why Jed hadn't been hired, but I hadn't exactly ironed out how I'd convince her to cough up the information. HR people are notoriously tight with their information. Something to do with spending their days memorizing and enforcing rules, I guessed. Hallie could have ordered her to talk with me, but I'd promised to keep my employer as far outside of this investigation as possible.

"Hi." I stood over her, my tea in hand. She was reading the *Battle Lake Recall*, even though it was several days old. What luck! Here was my in. I nodded toward the article. "You check out the recipe column?"

She grunted and closed the paper. "I use recipes in that column as a warning of what not to cook."

Dammit, she was smart. This wasn't going to be easy. "Yeah, it's pretty gross stuff. Mind if I have a seat?"

She looked over her shoulder at the empty tables in our vicinity. "Do I know you?"

"No." I tried to think quick, but my brain had punched out to ponder the pros and cons of ordering another bagel. "I'm a friend of Jed Heitke's. He was wondering why he didn't get to keep the line mechanic job at Battle Sacks." Sweet Baby Jesus, I'd told the truth. That's what a lack of planning will get you.

She shrugged. "It's no secret. The job I hired him for was reclaimed. Union rules."

I leaned forward, my interest piqued. "Why was it reclaimed?"

Her eyes drew together and she set her lips in a firm line. "You'll have to ask Mr. None of Your Business."

Ah, I'd crossed paths with him on a number of occasions. He liked to play it coy, but I knew he enjoyed dancing. "That's got to be public knowledge, right? All I'm asking is why a person would quit their job if they actually wanted it. It makes it hard on the regular people who think they have a shot at the position."

"We're a private company. There is no public knowledge."

I forced myself to unclench. "I could find it out easily enough."

"Best of luck with that."

I wanted nothing more than to tug a loose thread on her kitty sweater, unraveling the whole works into a pile of sad, trembling yarn. She had the upper hand, however. I quickly shuffled the information I had in my head and played my wild card, the Ace of Hunches. "Look, I know you fired the chief line mechanic, and I don't care why he was rehired. I'm just trying to figure out why Jed couldn't be given some other job."

She shrugged, my flabby reasoning confusing her as to which information to protect. "I don't know who you heard that from, but we never fired Clive. He quit. Mr. Heitke is welcome to reapply for another position. We have a number of seasonal jobs opening up to accommodate our Christmas surge in business. You can't always rely on temp workers, though. I tell you, it gets to be so time-intensive to keep on top of them that I might as well join the factory floor myself."

She kept chattering, apparently more than eager to talk now that she could work herself into the story. I wasn't listening any more, not since she'd dropped her bomb. *Clive* had been the chief line mechanic, and more importantly, he'd quit his lifelong job right before he'd killed his best friend and boss in a hunting accident, and then he'd reclaimed it immediately after. I shivered involuntarily. Maybe Hallie was on to something after all.

EIGHT

THE FIFTH CHAPTER IN *Private Investigating for Morons* covered surveillance. In reading the book, I'd been disappointed to discover that the author hadn't taken into account how truly clueless some of us are—*The Marginally Ignorant's Guide to Private Investigation* would have been a more accurate title for the tome—but I was grateful that she was clear as to the basic rules of effective snooping:

1. Verify and crosscheck your subject's identity through various means, including photographic evidence, Internet searches, and firsthand witnesses. Consider subscribing to a public records directory to assist in this first step; any premium service will efficiently and accurately complete background checks, perform property searches, access criminal record databases, and search for tax liens, bankruptcies, judgments, and court records.

2. Once your subject's identity is established, familiarize yourself with his/her normal routine. Stay at least 400 yards distant at all times.

3. Create a cover story in case you're made, and always plan your exit. If your role is discovered, your investigation is compromised.

The records directory sounded like a great idea until I discovered it cost $49.95 a month. I'd deposited my $500 retainer the same day I'd received it. Then, I'd immediately written a check in the same amount and posted it to the student loan bank to keep my account from being sent to a collections agency. I'd have no more disposable income until I received my thin paycheck in a week or completed enough work for Hallie to justify a second installment on my services. I needed to up the ante and produce something on Clive.

Since I had number 1 covered—I knew Clive by sight already—I moved immediately to number 2. I called Jed to find out the schedule he had been hired to work. My call had woken him. Groggily, he'd verified that he was informed he'd be on call at all hours but that the regular shift was Friday, Saturday, and Sunday, midnight until noon. Once he explained that the line mechanic's main job was maintenance and that it made more sense to work on the equipment when no one was around, those inhumane hours made sense.

Today was Saturday, which meant Clive was currently at Battle Sacks, oiling the machines. I'd have plenty of time for light snooping before starting my busy workday at the library. On to number 3: I was a neighbor out walking her dog. What better cover story did I need? All that was left to do was bundle up and hoof it across the prairie to Clive's property to peek in the windows. I wasn't sure what I would find but figured it was a good place to start looking. Plus, since the temperature promised to crack zero today, I'd planned to take Luna for her first long walk since this steel-cold trap had seized the county.

Luna was a sweetheart of a dog, an orphaned German Shepherd-collie mix. Sunny, whose house I was sitting, had almost flattened the poor pup on a country road coming home from work one night. She'd scooped up the shaking puppy and brought her home. That was four years ago. Luna had come with the house-sitting gig, and I was happy for her company. She was loyal, smart, and put up with my cat. I grabbed the little-used leash before we left. She always stayed close by my side when we walked, but I figured leashing her would add credibility to our story. Plus, I knew Clive was an avid hunter, and I didn't want Luna accidentally stepping on any below-the-radar fox traps he might have set on his property.

The morning was beautiful, the promise of above-zero temperatures causing the snow crystals to reflect sharp rainbows of color back toward the bright yellow sun. The easing of the deep freeze released a range of smells, and I caught the keen scent of frozen trees and cold dust.

"Not too bad, eh Luna?" She wagged happily at me.

Clive's land was a two-mile trek through the woods on the southwest side of Sunny's property. He'd built his house on seven landbound acres near Whiskey Lake. I'd never had any reason to visit, but I passed his mailbox every time I drove Whiskey Road to work. His house and three outbuildings were far back but visible from the road, though you could only see the roof of the old barn when driving past. I'd never paid much attention, but I had noticed that he kept his house well-painted and didn't have any junk in his yard. I also didn't remember ever seeing a dog.

Luna and I crunched through the oak forest. Although she was initially annoyed by the leash, she got over it and we made decent time. Clive's red barn appeared through the leafless trees first. To the right stood two white sheds blending into the snowy landscape, and on the other side of the barn was his house. I ordered Luna to sit, and we both listened intently. The only sounds were the soft shuffle scrape of the rare dried leaf scratching against branches and the far-off hum of traffic.

I looked down at Luna, and she smiled back up at me. I knew our story depended on us walking together, but no one would believe we'd accidentally walked up to Clive's house, so I might as well let her loose in case we needed to make a dash for it. She wagged and licked my face when I bent down to unclip the leash.

"Just two gals out for a leisurely stroll," I told her. I wound the rope up and tossed it over my shoulder. Next, because though I may be dumb I certainly wasn't stupid, I yelled out. "Helloo! Anyone here? It's Mira, your neighbor." I was 99 percent sure Clive was at work, but 100 percent sure that if he wasn't, I didn't want to get accidentally shot.

When there was no answer, we took off toward the settlement. A well-worn path led the way. Given Clive's reputation as a devoted hunter, it was unsurprising that he'd spend a lot of time traversing his woods. I took care to keep my boot prints inside of his, though given the crusty consistency of the snow and the constant wind rearranging everything, I probably didn't need to bother. Still, I wanted to get in and out of here without a trace.

We were nearing the barn when Luna stopped, her hackles raised. A growl, scratchy and black, rumbled out of her mouth. The noise slipped like a wolverine's claw up my back. I'd never heard her make that sound before. I shot my eyes around the open yard but couldn't see anything out of order. That's when I caught the soft clicking sound, a repetitive snap that reminded me of sharp teeth on bone. It was coming from the barn. I sniffed the air and couldn't pick up a trace of farm animal musk or waste, but I couldn't help thinking of the town legend that Clive'd fed his family to the pigs. Had it been true? Had I stumbled onto an R-rated horror movie?

Luna's growl grew fiercer, more constant, and I reached for her collar to soothe her, my heart racing. She snarled at my touch but did not move her eyes off a spot just around the curve of the barn.

"Luna, come." I whispered, my mouth dry. Screw the investigation. This suddenly felt so very wrong. "It's time to go." I backed toward the woods, darting my eyes to the right and left but still not picking up anything. The tooth-on-bone click continued from the barn. Luna refused to budge. I was afraid to touch her again. I didn't recognize this feral side of her, but I couldn't leave her, so I tiptoed back, unwound the leash from my shoulder, and bent down to slip it through her collar. That's when a brown shape materialized around the corner, rushing toward us like a two-headed beast.

NINE

Luna leapt, and the creature held its shape long enough for me to realize it was an old boxer, so simultaneously scared and thrilled to have company that it was sidling toward us, head and butt moving forward at the same pace.

"Luna!" I yelled, but I needn't have bothered. She stood over the boxer, which had rolled immediately onto his back, and waited for me to reach her side.

"That's a good boy," I said, kneeling down to scratch the boxer's ears and the thin fur on his brown-and-white-speckled belly. As soon as I touched his tummy, his mouth opened up and a big tongue rolled out like a welcome mat. "You had us scared, doggie. But you're just doing your job, aren't you? What's your name?" I reached for the boxer's collar. Chuck.

"Well, Chuck, do you think you could show us around? We won't take anything." My body was still pumping thick adrenaline, but the flight or fight directive was easing.

I stepped back and Luna, proud of a job well done, sat on her haunches and stared self-importantly into the distance, too proud to acknowledge the fawning dog on the ground. She'd been spending too much time with Tiger Pop. Chuck jumped up as soon as I stopped petting him and wormed his way around my legs.

"What do you think, Luna? Should we see what's making that noise in the barn? Chuck, what do you think?" Chuck thought I should double-check his belly to make sure I hadn't missed a spot, and Luna was no longer in an aggressive posture, so I made my way toward the nearest window on the old barn. This required me to step off the trail, but the snow was hard-packed enough that my prints barely dusted the surface. The snow also raised the ground level so that I could peek into the windows without straining. I was initially confused by the black interior, but then I caught sight of a tiny scratch on the interior surface that allowed out some light, and I realized that the window had been painted black from the inside. I moved to the next, and the next, and found they were all the same.

Inside, the clicking continued with such regularity that I realized it must be mechanical. Maybe Clive had built a time machine, and that's what he didn't want anyone to know about. It was maddening not being able to see what was going on. At the front of the barn, I saw that the original carriage doors had been removed and in their place was a modern, windowless garage door. Above, the entrance to the haymow had been replaced by a beautiful bay window that let in plenty of light. Unfortunately, it was fifteen feet off the ground.

I glanced over at Luna and Chuck. All of the boxer's fear had been replaced by wiggle. He danced around Luna, begging her to play with him. She looked like she was considering it. Since the dogs were okay, I made my way to the house, where I peeked in all the windows just as I had done to the barn but with more success.

The inside of Clive's house revealed him to land somewhere between bachelor and hoarder in terms of cleanliness. His dishes were unwashed and pizza boxes and beer cans were piled around, which belied the cleanliness of his yard. Still, he had live plants clustered around the windows, so he couldn't be all bad. A circumnavigation of the house didn't turn up a ladder, and the other two outbuildings were also locked and had blackened windows. Frustrated, I returned to the barn and walked around it once more.

My second complete pass didn't reveal anything new, but on my third pass, I caught a scent that was distinctly out of place. I followed it to a warp in the wood between the windowsill and the glass. I put my hand up to it and felt a tropical heat even through my mittens. I leaned in and squinted through the crack with one eye and felt the heat on my face, followed by the unmistakable peppery green scent of growing marijuana. The size of the crack limited my view, but in my scope of vision was row upon row of lush and leafy pot plants, all of them at least five feet high and orange sticky on the ends. The clicking noise was louder through the crack, and I realized it was the sound of timed grow lights. The gardener in me envied the set-up. I could harvest fresh tomatoes and basil all year long if I had this going on in my barn.

I pulled back from the crack and leaned against the building. Both dogs had followed me, and Luna had dropped her cool nonchalance in favor of some mock-serious dog wrestling. Other than their play growls and the occasional car passing by a half a mile away, there was nothing to hear but the click click of metal halide high-intensity grow lights. If what I'd seen was any indication, Clive had tens of thousands of dollars of marijuana flowering in a very expensive environment. I whistled through my teeth. Though I wasn't personally offended by Clive's ventures, I knew the law would view him as a criminal. Was he also a killer? I strode to the front of the barn, ready to take my thoughts home to organize them.

A bird screeched overhead, an angry crow by the sound of it. Both dogs stopped tussling and shot a glance in the direction of the noise. I followed their sightline, but it wasn't the sleek black bird that caught my attention. It was the surveillance camera hiding just under the lip of the jutting roof, pointing directly at my face.

TEN

My first instinct was to shield my face with my hands, but it was too late. The placement of the camera suggested it was operative. If Clive had simply wanted to use it as a prop to scare off trespassers, he would have made it more visible. I cursed my idiocy. There was nothing to do now but hope. If the camera was recording, Clive would know I'd been here.

Chuck followed Luna and me most of the way home. He probably would have come to live with us if I hadn't made Luna ignore him after a while. Demoralized by our lack of attention, he eventually slunk back home. I felt bad, but I had already messed with Clive's boundaries enough without taking his dog, too.

I'd need to hatch a plan to cross paths with Clive in the next couple days and feel out how much of my visit he knew about. His camera could have been out of tape, or maybe he only checked it irregularly. If either was true, I was still undercover. Even if he saw the recording of me in front of his barn, the angle of the camera wouldn't allow for him to see the extent of my snooping. I could stick with my original story that I was out walking Luna and apologize for accidentally trespassing. It sounded logical, but I couldn't escape the chilly thought that I was dealing with a dangerous man.

The spy mission had taken more time than I expected, so I scrambled to get ready for work. I also wanted to make time to ask Jed if he knew that Clive grew and presumably sold weed. If anyone would know the dealers in the county, Jed would. I had only time to comb my hair, grab a change of clothes for tonight's library benefit, feed my animals, and snatch a banana and a can of Cuban rice and beans for lunch before dashing out the door.

Cursing, I remembered I'd also reluctantly arranged a book-signing for noon today. The author had recently relocated to Battle Lake and had introduced herself as a writer of inspirational religious aphorisms. If that description didn't make me want to take up drinking again, I didn't know what did. The woman—Peggy McMillian was her name—had built a thriving career as the writer of the little sayings that appear on church signs, like "Don't give the Devil a ride and expect him to wear his seat belt," and "The Ten Commandments are not multiple choice."

Her work was so popular that she'd been offered a book contract. *A Penance for Your Thoughts* had immediately gone into a second and then a third printing and was one of the most popular books in the Battle Lake library's collection. Spiritual soundbites weren't my cup of tea, but I was a librarian, and all books must be equal in my eyes. That didn't mean I had to like them all, just pretend equally.

I stopped at Larry's Supermarket to pick up assorted cookies and apple cider for the event. Today's break in the weather had people out laughing and stocking up on groceries before the next cold snap, but I managed to weave in and out of the giddy crowds. At the library, I had just enough time to fill the hot beverage tureen and arrange the cookies before the first knock came at the door. I looked up to see Peggy herself, a dark-haired, frog-shaped woman in her fifties who'd sported crumbs on her clothing both of the previous times I'd interacted with her. She'd also been twitchy and inclined to talking about her medical conditions. I didn't expect today to be any different. Her only apparent redeeming quality was her voice. It clicked and sang like a handful of glass marbles tossed up into the sunshine.

I strode over and unlocked the door. "Hi, Peggy. How are you?"

"Fine, fine," she said, stepping in and setting a box of books on the counter before removing her scarf. "This cold plays dickens on my joints, and I think my eyesight is going, though. I have a doctor's appointment on Monday."

I studied her for a second. Yup, only in her fifties. I wondered how long she'd been a hypochondriac. I tried putting a positive spin on the conversation. "At least you got nice weather for your book signing."

"Nice weather if you're a germ." She looked over my shoulder. "Are those cookies?"

I stepped to the side. "Help yourself. Do you want me to help you set up your books?"

"Yes, but make sure to arrange them spine out along the back of the table, leaving only enough room for me to lean forward to sign copies but not so much room that people can come around and stand close. The last thing I need is to pick up a flu bug. Then, display three books on each side, standing up and partially open but so that the cover can be read. You're very kind. Thanks for having me, too."

I mumbled something about it not being any problem and began unpacking her books and arranging them as per her instructions. I glanced at the spine of one. Her publisher was Inspiration Industries. How nice that capitalism and spiritual enlightenment had found yet another spot to merge. At the bottom of the book box, I discovered a hard-backed poster of Peggy, which I set at an angle. When I turned back around, she'd polished off three Oreos and a macaroon, judging by the crumbs on her chest and holes in the cookie tray, and was holding my copy of *Private Investigating for Morons* in her hand.

"This yours?" she asked.

"It's a library book," I said, evading the question.

"But are you reading it?"

"Yes."

"Oh, thank God." She fell into the nearest chair, an upholstered swivel computer seat, and moaned and swayed. She had sweat circles encroaching on the pinched white fabric under her arms. "Hallelujah! He always provides."

"Are you okay?"

She reached over for the *Morons* book and fanned her face with it, still humming and amen-ing in between her words. "My inspiration left me. It up and fled as soon as my book was published. It was pride, I know it. I wasn't humble, and I made money off my gift. Don't you see?"

I looked uncomfortably over my shoulder, smelling a freshly baked restraining order. I'd hosted authors before, and while they weren't a bunch you'd typically take life management lessons from, they seemed to play well with others and generally behave respectably in public. Peggy, however, was sweating like a Lutheran at the Inquisition, her glistening eyes staring greedily at me as she continued to fan her face.

"I'm afraid I don't," I said. "Do you need some fresh air?" I figured all I had to do was lead her outside, lock the door behind her, and call the police.

"Are you deaf? I lost my mojo. I can't write these any more." She reached over to a carefully arranged row of *A Penance for Your Thoughts* and shoved my display to the floor, where the books landed with a slapping thump. The effort slid her glasses down her nose. She pushed them back up with her pointer finger. "My greed got the better of me, and now I can no longer parse the words that inspire millions to seek the Light. They used to come to me as easily as breathing, right up until this book came out and I cashed my first royalty check. Once it was no longer a labor of love, the well dried up. Now I can't write anything more creative than my own name."

I relaxed a lick. What I was witnessing was writer's block with a splash of religious fervor, not a psychotic break. "Oh, you can't write your aphorisms any more?"

"They weren't *my* aphorisms. They belonged to the faithful. I was merely their vehicle." She reached for a fistful of cookies and popped them like aspirin.

I kneeled to pick up and reorganize the books. I paged through one as I stacked it. "Maybe there's enough here to last for a while?"

She talked around a mouthful. "There would be, if I hadn't signed another contract. I owe them a second book in a month.

That's why it's a sign that we've crossed paths! You are a detective. I am going to hire you to locate my mojo."

I shook my head. The woman was an emotional train wreck, and I liked drama a little more than pap smears and a little less than ill-fitting jeans. "It's just a book on private investigation. I'm not licensed, and even if I were, PIs don't look for mojo. You need a career change maybe, not a detective."

"No. This is a sign. I firmly believe in signs." She held up a copy of her book, which, in fact, featured a photo of a church sign on the front, the book's title inserted into it. "You'll help me, won't you?"

"Nope." I'd already taken on one too many cases for an unlicensed PI. Besides, this woman screamed high maintenance. I rearranged the cookies to cover the massive gap she'd created and began to switch on the computers. That's when I heard her sniffling and turned to see her batting her eyes like a toad in a hailstorm.

"I'm sorry," she said. "It's why I moved to Battle Lake, you know. I thought if I got away from it all, I'd find my way back into the Lord's good graces. When my friend Lynne asked me to housesit here, it was just the perfect opportunity. You know, a sign."

I felt the shot of premonitory fear and pity through my stomach. "You came to Battle Lake to housesit?"

"Yes." She blew her nose into a large purple handkerchief she'd pulled from her purse. "Just for a couple months. Then I return to Kentucky."

Just for a couple months. I knew how that story ended: six dead bodies, an overused detachable shower head, and a ring of belly fat shaped oddly like Tator Tot hotdish later, she'd still be here, maybe working for the newspaper, maybe at the library, possibly volunteering at the nursing home. I sighed from the depths of my soul, my cynical side warring with my human side. My human side won, but grudgingly. "Look, I'm not a detective, but I'd be happy to show you around while you're here. Maybe you can pick up some inspiration from the environment."

She became fidgety again. "Okay, that's a start. How much will it cost?"

"$49.95."

She nodded, suddenly distracted. "Do you have an air filter on the furnace in here? I think I'm coming down with something, and dirty air is the last thing I need."

The front door chimed, and in walked the mayor of Battle Lake. She was wearing a pink, fake-fur-lined ski parka, matching snow pants, and high-heeled boots, which I guessed were about as climate-appropriate as tiaras. Underneath a jaunty pink beret, she wore make-up that looked as though it had been applied with a spatula.

"There's worse things than dirty air," I muttered under my breath. Kennie had been my worst enemy when I'd moved to Battle Lake. She was a self-involved, calculating Mary Kay of a woman with no loyalties. Since May, however, the Fates had contrived to throw us together on more than one occasion, and she and I had struck an uneasy truce. She was now like the skin tag you couldn't afford to remove so made the best of.

Kennie sailed past me and held out her manicured hand to Peggy. "I hope I am the first one to welcome you to our lovely town." As always, Kennie's Southern drawl was out of place in the

Midwest, especially from a woman who'd never been farther south than Albert Lea.

Peggy recoiled. "I'm afraid I don't shake hands. Viruses, you know. I'd be happy to sign a copy of my book for you."

Kennie appeared nonplussed, but quickly recovered. "I get my inspiration from actions and not words, honey pie. Has it been a busy day for you?" She asked, indicating the empty library.

As if on command, a line of women burst through the door, each of them carrying at least one copy of *A Penance for Your Thoughts*. I stood aside so Peggy could begin her signing, her troubles lost for the moment amid the clamor of fame and attention.

"I come down here personally to welcome her to town and get pushed aside like day-old bread," Kennie grumbled, appearing beside me. "I could write a book too, if all it took was making up a sentence or two. How about this: 'a closed mouth catches no flies, and a closed fly catches no mouths.' Look, I'm an *author*."

"You'd be drawing on a whole different crowd with that one," I said, strolling away from her and toward the book return bin. "Sorry this was a wasted trip."

"Not a waste at all."

I recognized that tone of voice, and it struck a fear chord. Kennie fancied herself an entrepreneur and regularly invented new business ideas. Her scams were an eclectic mix, from home bikini waxings to coffin tables, and they never ended well for either of us. Usually, it was worse for me. "What do you mean?"

"Funny you should ask." Kennie strolled next to me, unzipped her coat, and flashed me, revealing a row of pills encased in light brown jars that were hanging off hand-sewn hooks like cheap Rolexes. "I'm selling good stuff."

"I can't believe it," I said. "Oh no wait, I mean the opposite of that."

"Amazing, right?"

"Tell me those are vitamins."

"Actually, they are." She plucked out a bottle of horse-sized pills. "See these? They make your skin as clear as a baby's bottom and your hair as thick as a lion's mane."

"When I think 'baby's bottom,' I don't think 'clear.'"

"What comes to mind when you see this?" And she plucked the pink beret off her head to reveal thick, wavy tresses where before had been over-dyed, brittle platinum hair.

"That's a wig."

"Pull it."

"But then I'd have to touch your head."

"Pull it." She grabbed my hand and stuck it to her head. At first repulsed, curiosity got the better of me and I tugged. No movement. I tugged again. It was real hair.

"The vitamins did that?"

"Yup."

"What's in them? Hooves and Rogaine?"

"Does it matter? They give you the hair of a Brazilian supermodel in under a month."

My mind raced. I'd always been cursed with thin hair, and I had a date with Johnny tomorrow. What if my hair was thicker by then? Even a little bit? They were just vitamins, right? God help me, I was considering it. But there was a catch. There had to be. "All over?"

"What?"

"Do they make you hairy all over?"

She paused. "No."

I knew that tone of voice. "Let me see your arm."

"No."

I put my hands on my hips. "I'm going to post a flier informing everyone that your vitamins make people grow nipples on the backs of their hands if you don't show me your arm."

Reluctantly, she doffed her pink jacket. Behind us, Peggy's line was growing longer as merry church ladies jostled for a chance to meet the new local celebrity. We could have been invisible for all the attention they paid us.

"It's not the hair and skin vitamins that did this," Kennie said, peeling away the gloves. "It was the Viag-min."

I leaned in close for a better look and couldn't silence my hoots of laughter. Although she had only a normal, modest dusting of hair on her arms, every single brown hair was standing erect, straining toward some unseen destination. "It's a hair army!"

She glared at me and brushed them down, but they popped right back up again. "It only lasts four to six hours. Then all the hairs lie flat again. Or if they don't, I have a 1-800 number to call."

I was still giggling. "A cold shower might be quicker."

She sniffed and pulled her gloves back on. "I guess you don't want to see what I have to offer."

"I was just teasing. Don't take it personally. I might want to buy the hair vitamins."

She was still miffed at me laughing at her hair-on. "I'd imagine so. I can see your scalp clean through your meager population up there."

"Now you're just being mean."

"All I'm saying is that there are plenty of women waiting in line to snatch up Johnny Leeson if you don't thicken your sparse offerings. You're one windy day away from a combover."

"Fine," I said, snatching the bottle out of her jacket. "I'll take your stupid hair vitamins, but not because I care what I look like. I'm just trying to get rid of you."

"Mmm hmm. Twenty dollars. And take one in the morning and one at night, with food. At least that's what the bottle says. I took a few more to get my hair to this state." She fluffed her waves, which was all the encouragement they needed to spring to attention like a fright wig. She must have felt the lightness because she hurriedly shoved her cap back. I handed her my last twenty, which had been earmarked for groceries and spent the next two hours forgetting about the vitamins as I helped Peggy sell her books and decorated the library for tonight's Love-Your-Library gala.

Peggy ended up staying much later than scheduled, right up until I closed the library in fact, because of all the people clamoring to see her. Her books were long gone and she appeared exhausted but content when I scooted the last fan outside and locked the door behind him.

"You're very popular," I said.

She nodded wearily. "That's what it's all about, you know. Inspiring the masses. Giving people hope. I need to get back to that." She reached in her purse for Purell and pushed up her sleeves past her elbows so she could douse herself.

"Let me show you out."

"Wait! Remember you promised you were going to help me find my … erm, show me around. When?" Those batting eyes again.

I glanced at the clock. "Can I call you? It's looking to be a busy week."

She returned the Purell to her purse and stood. "How about tomorrow?"

"It's my only day off."

"Monday?"

I sighed. I was suffering from empathizer's remorse. "Monday is the deadline for the local newspaper. I do freelance work for them, and I have a standing promise with the editor that I'll keep Mondays mostly free for last-minute articles."

"Tuesday?"

She was relentless. "When did you say your deadline was?"

"In two weeks."

"Fine. Tuesday morning. I'll pick you up before I open the library. How's 7:00 sound?"

She clapped her hands. "Perfect! And you'll take me to somewhere inspirational to look for my mojo?"

"I'll try." I was motioning her toward the door when the desk phone rang. "Battle Lake Public Library."

"Mira. It's Ron. I need you to write an article on the hunt club."

"Hi, Ron. How are you?"

"I need it by Thursday."

"Have I ever mentioned what a pleasure it is conversing with you?" He'd always been a terse man, but he was outdoing himself.

"Deer Valley Hunt, over by Millerville. The owner will be at the library tonight. He's rich. We're running a feature."

It took me a moment to locate the real meaning underneath his words. "Oh! He's a donor, and we want him to be more of a donor. You're having me write an article to benefit the library. Just when I thought you were nothing but a Scrooge."

"Don't get too happy. I didn't call with good news. Hallie Kicker is in the hospital."

ELEVEN

Ron didn't know the details, so I shooed Peggy quickly out the door, assuring her that we were still on for Tuesday, and strode back to the phone to call the Alexandria hospital, where Hallie'd been brought in by ambulance. After being assured that she was not in intensive care but also not available to talk, I requested the visiting hours, glancing at the clock and calculating as I scribbled them down. If I could get rid of tonight's guests by a reasonable hour, say eight-thirty, which was a half an hour after the Love-Your-Library event was scheduled to end, I'd have time to run to the hospital and make sure she was okay.

Unfortunately, there was no time to dwell on the details. The caterers were at the door. I held it open for them as they carried in the tables and began setting out the banquet pans and glassware. They were a local company, Food by Design, and this was the fourth year they'd catered this event. It was my first, so I stayed out of their way. I excused myself to the back room where I changed into my only winter dress, a navy blue number with a loose silk top that suggested I had boobs if you didn't know any better, an empire waist, and a swinging crepe bottom that fell just below the knee and suggested I had a flat stomach, if you didn't know any better. All in all, I considered it $29.99 well spent. I also wore nude nylons and matching navy blue flats. If you ever have to choose between being able to run from danger and looking sexy hot, you want to know you put your safety first.

My head didn't match the rest of my body, so I plugged in my curling iron and let it heat while I traced the upper lid of my gray eyes with dark blue liner, which brought out their hazel flecks, and slapped on mascara. I lightly dusted my cheeks with cherry-colored blush and glossed my lips. The curling iron put a nice wave in my long brown hair, but I felt too girly and so twisted it all up into a tight-messy bun and declared myself as pretty as I was gonna get.

When I returned to the main room of the library, the Food by Design people had rearranged it so there was a central visiting area circled by tables laden with hot finger food like chicken wings and mini-egg rolls, cheese, meat, vegetable, and fruit platters, sparkly nonalcoholic drinks as well as whiskey, vodka, rum, mixers, red and white wines, a selection of beers, and bite-sized dessert pastries. The deep burgundy tablecloths and the large leafy plants they'd arranged played off the twinkle lights, turning the library into a classy soiree spot. Strains of classical music complemented the feel. All that was left to do was wait for the company.

Love-Your-Library was started five years ago as a way to thank individuals and families who had donated $500 or more to the library in the calendar year. When I first surveyed the guest list that the city handed down to me, it looked like it was more of an opportunity for the town council to rub elbows with the wealthiest people in the county, but they signed my paycheck and I could give them two hours of schmoozing in return. Plus, I'd been promised that the city would mail out the invitations and pay the caterer, so there was little for me to do other than show up. My kinda party.

The first people to arrive were Bernie and Roy Nordman, the owners of the local hardware store. I was nervous and hung on to my clipboard containing the guest list like it was a security blanket. Probably sensing my discomfort in the hostess role, they made pleasant jokes about how hungry they were. I steered them toward the drinks, thinking everyone has more fun when they're liquored up, and checked them off the list. I was gratified when people began to stream in after that, and as the noise level grew, I made a note to push the stacks farther back to create more room at this event next year. Then I froze. Would I be living in Battle Lake next year? I'd moved here to get my head on straight and had only planned to stay through last summer. I pushed those thoughts down and continued to meet, greet, and check off my list, inwardly intimidated by the suits and the fancy dresses but outwardly confident. I hoped.

Sadly, as I checked off names, I realized Tom Kicker was on my list, which had been generated weeks before his death. I was just about to cross him off when Clive Majors strode through the door with Carla, a waitress I recognized from Bonnie and Clyde's, a bar in Clitherall, the next town over. Clive stared defiantly at the crowd, a tall, wiry scarecrow of a man with slicked-back hair. The chatter in the large room dropped an octave. My stomach followed suit. I hadn't yet hammered out the discussion where I conversationally led him to reveal that yes, he had a surveillance camera hooked up to his barn and no, he didn't regularly view his recordings. What was he doing here, messing up my lack of plans?

I quickly scanned my list. Nope. No Clive. This event was designed to be 100 percent Battle Lake bourgeoisie. I glanced around the room, but after a few uncomfortable stares and except for one guy who stared like Clive had antlers sprouting out of his head, most people went back to their conversations. Clive and his date beelined straight to the liquor table. I could tell by his sway that he'd already been hitting the bottle, and his bloodshot eyes suggested that wasn't the only self-medication he'd enjoyed tonight. He was wearing a suit at least—a worn, dark-blue polyester outfit with a clashing tie. There was something very sad about it. I was on my way to greet him when the front door opened to let in a freezing gust and the night's flashiest couple: Mayor Kennie Rogers and Chief of Police Gary Wohnt.

Gary had been demoted to deputy when he'd ended a purported affair with Kennie to follow a religious minx across the country a few months back. He'd returned to reclaim his job, no explanations or apologies. Kennie'd forced him to work as a deputy before fully reinstituting him as Chief of Police in October. He must have done something to return to her good graces, but I refused to imagine the details because I'd just need to wash my brain out later.

Frankly, it was difficult to be in the same room with Wohnt. He and I had always had a challenging relationship, with him consistently holding the information I needed and me always being in the wrong place at the wrong time. This dynamic, combined with his taciturn manner, should have been enough to make me permanently avoid him. Enter last month, when I realized that he exactly resembled Chief Wenonga, the super-hot, completely stereotypical but compellingly sexy 23-foot fiberglass statue that graced the northern edge of the town. I'd had a crush on the statue for an unhealthily long time. Wenonga was just my type—tall, dark, and emotionally unavailable. I'd never noticed the resemblance between the Chief of my heart and the Chief of Battle Lake because Gary had been doughy and a little greasy before he'd left to follow his woman who was following Jesus, but he came back to town taut and hot. And I didn't like it one bit.

In fact, it was physically uncomfortable to see him in the black dress pants and button-down white shirt with a commanding navy blue tie. I wanted him to be much more easily categorized as repellent lawman without the confusion of his new appearance. I scowled in his direction. I wasn't sure he possessed the muscles required for smiling, but without his usual mirrored sunglasses, he appeared relaxed. He helped Kennie with her coat, revealing a resplendent, white-sequined dress. If Mrs. Berns was here, she'd tell Kennie she looked like she'd been set on fire and put out with a shovel, but since she wasn't, I had to admit that Kennie looked pretty good. Her hair was pulled back in a tight bun revealing features as pretty as a porcelain doll's. Her make-up was thick but she made it work. The dress squeezed her in all the right places, highlighting a plush, womanly figure. Dang, I wish Mrs. Berns was here.

"Mira, come hug me!"

I looked around but didn't see any other Miras. I let Kennie approach me. "We don't hug," I whispered, so as not to embarrass her in front of the people nearest us.

"Of course we do." She wrapped me in a tight grip and leaned toward my ear. "Do I smell funny?" she hissed.

She needn't have asked. "You had me at 'of course we do,'" I gasped, covering my mouth. "What is that? It smells like the inside of a chipmunk."

"Holy hell. I thought only I could smell it."

"I *wish* only you could smell it."

"What am I going to do? Have you seen the Chief? He looks tastier than chocolate and wine. I can't make something of this night with my breath like this."

"Is it the vitamins?"

She considered this. "I suppose. I started on the de-wrinklers today. Do you have mints?"

"Lemme check." I waded to the back room to dig in my coat pockets and found a mint that was red, white, and fuzz. I brushed it off and brought it out to her with a warning. "It's a bit like expecting a tugboat to save the Titanic, you know. I think that odor is leaking out your pores."

"Shush. This will do just fine."

I wrinkled my nose. I couldn't quite place the odor, but it was powerful and familiar. "Wet chicken?"

She growled at me and left to work the crowd, which consisted of all the doctors, dentists, business owners, and heirs in the county. She seemed in her element, but I couldn't help but feel like my dress and my conversation were less then sparkly. I seized the moment to confront Clive. It would be better to meet this head on, I'd decided. I spotted him and Carla standing off to the side, looking sullen while eating manchego and membrillo mini-souffles, which was no mean feat.

"How are you two doing?" Carla had the decency to drop her eyes in party-crasher shame. Clive, on the other hand, looked like he was here to prove something, which made my stomach lurch.

"I don't want trouble," he said, reaching for the cocktail he'd placed on the table at his side. He emptied it in a gulp.

"No trouble." I smiled queasily. I didn't know whether he was referring to crashing the party or to my trespassing. I chose the safer focus. "This event is technically open to the public, but only the bigwigs get invited. It's nice to see some commoners besides myself."

He shot me a glance that I swear was grateful but then turned dark. It was now or never. "Say, I accidentally stopped by your place yesterday. I was walking my dog and got lost. We're neighbors, you know."

His jaw clenched, but he didn't respond. The silence between us created a buzzing tension that I couldn't stand. I turned to Carla. "How're things at Bonnie and Clyde's?"

She took a swallow of her glass of white. "Better than you'd think. People get cabin fever in this weather and treat a bar like their second home."

"Yeah," I said wistfully, remembering the days I drank. "Well, thank you both for coming. All the food and drink has to go, so don't leave hungry."

I walked away and felt a stare aimed at me. It was the same guy who hadn't pulled his eyes from Clive when he'd entered. The ogler was average height, in his mid-to-late 60s, and sporting a thick but well-groomed mustache that for some reason made me think of small penises and Hawaiian shirts. He had me locked in his sights and didn't look away when I met his gaze.

He was a stranger to me, but as the donors could be from anywhere in the county, it was no surprise that I didn't know everyone. I strode over with my checklist because there was no way I was going to let this googler creep me out. This evening I'd allowed formal wear to intimidate me, but I'd spent enough years waiting tables that I couldn't let an eye pirate steal my power. When he registered that I was moving toward him, he broke eye contact and leaned in to whisper conspiratorially to another man I didn't recognize and a third I did—Mike Ramos, Otter Tail County's recently retired sheriff.

I held my hand out to the guy modelling the Tom Selleck lip warmer. "I'm Mira James. I run the library." It would have been more efficient to call myself a librarian, but that would have been a lie without a clear benefit.

He shook my hand firmly. His was cool and dry, and his eyes were now aloof. "The name is Frederick. You know Mike and Mitchell?" He indicated his conversational partners.

"Mike and I have met, but I'm afraid I don't know Mitchell." I shook their hands in turn.

"Mitchell Courier," said the second stranger, a guy built like the Brawny man with an aggressive smile. "I own Deer Valley Hunt Club. I believe we were destined to meet tonight."

His smile was meant to put the humor in his words, but I didn't like his eyes. They were dark brown and watery and looked like they preferred laughing at rather than with someone. "Nice to meet you, Mr. Courier. Ron said you'd be here tonight. We need to schedule an interview."

"That's right. And I'll do you that favor if you do me this one." He handed over a pile of fliers he'd been gripping in his hippopotamic fist. Each page was bordered in Christmas trees framing an ad requesting temporary wait staff for the Christmas Hunt a week from this Wednesday, the inauguration of a five-day hunting blow-out, according to the copy. "I need about a dozen single-day waitresses, and I pay well. Can I leave these fliers on your counter?"

"I don't see why not." And I wished I did because I liked him less the more I talked to him. I accepted the fliers. "Are you free for lunch on Wednesday?"

"For the interview?"

"Yes."

"Why don't you come by the hunt club and I'll lay myself open."

I wrinkled my nose. "Or you can just answer a few questions."

"A woman who knows what she wants. I like it. Wednesday at noon it is."

I nodded, wishing I could spray him with some Kennie breath. I changed the subject instead. "Are the three of you enjoying your-selves?"

"It's very nice, every year it is," said Mike. "Thanks for inviting us."

We all knew it wasn't up to me, but hey. Mike had a reputation in the area as being a fair sheriff. I wondered what he was doing with these two creepers. I wasn't sure what he'd been up to lately but knew he'd retired his star shortly after I moved to town, and not because of me. I swear. "You're welcome. How's retirement treating you?"

He chuckled ruefully. "I'm getting fat and lazy."

Frederick and Mitchell matched the laugh. "That's not new, Mikey," Frederick said, clearly comfortable ribbing the former sheriff.

I glanced over at Clive, who was stumbling over to the make-shift bar for yet another cocktail. I didn't want to reveal my motive to Tom Selleck and the Brawny man, but I had a question I needed answered. "While I'm here, can I ask something?"

"Sure," Mike said amiably. I noticed Frederick and Mitchell exchanged a glance, but it meant nothing to me.

"Have you heard about any drug problems in the county?"

I suddenly had all their attention, and I wished I had phrased the question differently. "What kind?" Mike asked.

"I dunno," I said, thinking quickly. "I just read an article in the *Star Tribune* about the drug problems in the state. I wondered if it'd be worth my time to research and write an article on our area. I've heard there's a lot of marijuana in the county."

"I wish it was just pot," Mike said. "Since meth has hit the area, that's taking up most of the force's time. We no longer have the manpower to bother with small-time marijuana dealers, as long as they keep their noses clean." He glanced toward Clive and back at me.

I didn't know if it was coincidence or purposeful, but he'd per-fectly answered my indirect question. It was time to get while the getting was good. "Thanks. And thanks again for coming, all of you."

I walked the fliers over to the front counter and unloaded them before glancing at the clock. It was only 7:00, and the hors d'oeuvres table was still half full. Dang it anyways, I wanted to make it to the hospital in time for visiting hours. I strolled over to the food to do my part and was happily munching when I smelled Kennie approach. "Need another mint?" I asked without turning.

"Hair a little thin?" she shot back.

I swiveled to stick my tongue out but saw that she was standing behind me with a tense-looking Gary Wohnt. He was awash in almost enough cologne to mask her odor, something musky that reminded me of hormones and high school. Paco Rabanne? I reached for a holiday spritzer to cool myself. "What can I do for you folks?"

"I'm here to tell you what I can do for you, actually."

"Again?"

She ignored me. "I am giving you the opportunity to give back to the city. Battle Lake was recently awarded a state development grant, and I need a committee to look into the best way to spend the $15,000. You and Gary have volunteered to be on that committee."

My eyes shot to Gary's. His were inky and unfathomable, but the clench in his jaw indicated he wasn't any happier with this than me. "I unvolunteer myself from this opportunity that I never knew existed."

"That's not an option."

"Why not? Can't you get some patsy from the city council to do it? That's why they all joined, for gosh sakes. They love this kinda stuff."

"And they couldn't organize their way out of a kiddie pool. Besides, if you do this, you can make sure a chunk of the money goes toward the library and Gary can direct some toward the police department. You just entered a request for three new computers, didn't you?"

I made a noise like a fifth-grade girl who'd just discovered that life isn't fair. "But you can't blackmail me to get them! The library's main computers are so old they take five minutes to open the Internet."

"That's not blackmail, sugar, that's simply asking you to take responsibility for the library's needs. Same for you and the police department, Chief."

Cripes, it was hard to swallow, but she was right. "Fine. Tell me exactly what we have to do."

"I already did. You have $15,000 to spend, and it all has to go toward the city. I want a full report in two weeks that outlines where each penny will go and how it will be spent. Gary has offered to collect all the requests early this week. Thank you." She spun on her heel in a glittery wink and left me and Gary alone.

"I think this is a bad idea," I said.

He only raised an eyebrow. That's how he'd goaded me to admit to all sorts of things in the past, by the way, from the Sno-Balls I stole from John Fuchs' lunchbox in kindergarten right up to the last dead body I'd found, the one with a bag over its head in room 19 of the Big Chief Motor Lodge. I wasn't going to let it work this time. I was strong. "I took a box of pencils home from work yesterday, but it's only because I also work at home and so I use the pencils there. To work." Dammit.

He said nothing.

"I'll bring them back on Monday." My shoulders slumped. I was weak, and I just wanted him to go away. "How about we meet here Tuesday at noon. Any requests for the grant money we have by then, we fund, splitting what's left over between the library and the police station. Deal?"

He nodded, once. "You look nice tonight." And then he turned to follow Kennie.

I stood there, stunned, parsing his words. Had he put the emphasis on "tonight," suggesting that I'd looked like a red monkey butt during all our previous encounters? Or had he put more weight behind "nice," meaning that I looked generally dull and inoffensive? I glanced over at the wine table. In the past, liquor had helped me to clarify these questions, or at least render them irrelevant. Crap, it was hard being dry. I forced myself back into the crowd, asking questions and talking to people I'd only known by name as the clock crawled toward 8:00.

I was peripherally aware that the crowd was growing louder as the wine bottles emptied, but it wasn't until people began to dance the "time to go" shuffle that I realized that Clive was responsible for a lot of the noise. He was gesticulating and arguing with the hardware-store-owning Nordmans, who were gazing hopefully toward the door. I also noticed Mike, Frederick, and Mitchell staring across the room at the situation with steely eyes, and Gary on the other side of the front desk doing the same. Intending to head off an uncomfortably dramatic intervention, I made my way to Clive's side.

"Hey, Clive. Thanks again for coming. Say, can I ask you something about cars?" I knew how to deal with a drunk man. I'd trained for it the first 17 years of my life. You start by distracting them by making them feel smart, and then you lead them away like kittens.

"I'm no car mechanic," he slurred.

"No, but you're handy. And this is important. My car runs great, but there's no heat in it. I'm afraid to bring it in because I can't afford to fix anything expensive."

"It's your thermostat," Carla said. The Nordmans had seized the opportunity to grab their coats and exit, leaving only the three of us in this corner.

"But what if it isn't?"

"Only one way to find out," Clive mumbled. "And it isn't by talking about it."

I studied him. I'd witnessed him making six runs to the liquor table in the past hour, but except for his slurred words, I wouldn't have called him drunk. "Carla, I think we're closing up here. Can you get Clive home?"

"It's what I do for a living," she said. "You ready to go, honey?"

Clive threw off her arm and raised his voice so it carried to the far reaches of the library. "What, they don't want no murderers here?"

My skin grew icy. All conversations in the room stopped.

Carla said, "Clive, this isn't the place."

"If you don't want a killer here, then you should just say so. It was an accident! A goddamned accident!"

Mike made his way over. "You've had too much to drink, buddy. It's time to go." He put his hand firmly on Clive's and guided him toward the door. Carla trailed behind. Clive began to struggle, but Mike tightened his grip.

"Wait now, I got something to say."

"You've already said enough."

"But I got something here." Clive reached into his inside jacket pocket with his free hand, and out of the corner of my eye I saw

Gary move in from his back-up position. Before he arrived, Clive produced a checkbook. "You gotta be a moneybags to come, right? Pay to play. Well, I'd like to donate some money to the library. Just so I feel bona fide." He laughed. It was a melancholy sound.

I walked over and made sure he was looking me in the eyes. The look he shot me was belligerent but not mean, the pleading glance of an over-disciplined dog. "That's not necessary."

Clive dug in his heels, and Mike reassessed his grip. "I think it is," Clive said, any hint of reasonableness gone from his voice. "You gonna stop a man from donating money to the library?"

Mike and Gary exchanged glances. Mike spoke. "You write the check, and you go. You understand?"

"Yessir." Clive leaned clumsily into the nearest table, yanked a pen from his pocket, and began scribbling loudly on the check. He ripped it out with a flourish and handed it over to me.

I glanced down. It was made out to the Battle Lake Public Library in the amount of $5,000. This hefty donation created three possibilities. Number one, Clive had been squirreling away honest cash for a while and was overcome by the season to show his admiration for the public library system. Two, he was as good as declaring to the world he was a pot dealer. Or three: someone had recently paid him a hunk of hot cash, possibly in the form of a bribe, and he'd rather donate it publicly than hang onto it one more minute. The third option suggested Hallie's intuition had been dead on.

TWELVE

THE ANTISEPTIC HOSPITAL SMELL immediately curled my ovaries. It reminded me of the fear I'd felt when I'd arrived here last October, not knowing whether or not Mrs. Berns had survived her car crash. I shoved that thought down and asked for Hallie's room.

I found her in a private wing on the second floor, reclining in bed and watching a rerun of *The Golden Girls*. Her face and hands looked swollen and her eyes were grayish and bagged. "Hallie?"

She turned slowly from the TV, and it took her a moment to register who I was. "Mira? What are you doing here?"

"I hope I'm not bothering you," I said apologetically. "Ron Sims at the paper said you'd been hospitalized, and I was worried."

She clicked off the TV and pushed herself up in bed like she was made out of glass. "I'm fine. This is nothing new. Meet my good friend, Fresenius 4008." She motioned toward the machine next to her bed. It was taller than I was, boxy, and on wheels. Red lights flashed sleepily on the front. A screen on the top third scrolled information I couldn't decipher, and a bag of clear fluid hung off an antenna-like structure on the side.

"What's it do?"

"Dialysis."

"Oh. Your kidneys are bad?"

"They've been better, but not for a while. I have diabetic keto-acidosis. It's treatable, but stress exacerbates it. I guess it's been a pretty stressful week."

I sat heavily on the chair next to her. "I guess. You're going to be okay?"

She smiled reassuringly and made an "x" motion across her chest. "I'll be fine, cross my heart. I'm used to this. Sorry to worry you."

I tried to return her smile and made a weak attempt at a joke. "Can't have anything happen to my only client."

I immediately regretted my words because her eyes sparked. "Have you found something? You have, haven't you?"

Clive's indoor field of thick green mary jane flashed in my brain. I'd found something, but I couldn't be sure it was related to Tom's death, which made it probably none of her business and for sure none of mine. As to the big check he'd written at the library tonight, I wasn't certain I wanted her to know about that just yet. It might cause stress without purpose. "I only started looking, and it doesn't help that I don't know what I'm looking for."

"You're trying to find out why Clive killed my dad."

I envisioned Clive swaying at the library, yelling. *It was an accident! A goddamned accident!* "Could there be more reasons than whatever they were arguing about?"

"What do you mean?"

91

"I'm just brainstorming. We know that Clive shot Tom, or has at least taken responsibility for it. If the shooting was intentional, could there have been other reasons for Clive to have killed your dad, other than a little fight?"

She pursed her lips. "I'm not sure what you're getting at."

I sensed a latent diplomacy gene trying to spark, bless its soul. I ignored it and laid out what I'd been thinking ever since I'd spotted that pot in Clive's barn. "What if the shooting isn't as direct as you think? Maybe someone had something on Clive and talked him into shooting your dad in exchange for their silence."

"What?" She rubbed at the IV needle taped to the back of her hand and began coughing. "But that would mean someone else wanted my dad dead. He was a wonderful man. Wonderful! No one would ever want to hurt him."

I placed my hand over hers to calm her. "Everyone who met your dad thought he was wonderful. You can't walk through Battle Lake without people talking about what a nice person he was. It's just, don't you want me to look into all the possible angles?"

"I suppose," she said shakily. Her coughing fit had passed, but it left her looking and sounding like she'd run a marathon.

"Then I need you to give me the full background on Clive and Tom's relationship and any other relationships your dad had, suspicious or otherwise. I should have gotten all this from you right away."

I pulled a notebook and pen out of my shoulder bag. She seemed reluctant but plowed in, beginning with her earliest memory, that of her dad taking her on a business trip to Orlando.

"I was maybe four years old. I got to sit in on sales meetings with him, and at the end of the day, he took me to Disney World. I felt like a princess."

I glanced up from my note taking. Her skin was still gray, but her eyes had the sweet joy of a well-loved child sparkling in them. I was ashamed at the sudden wash of jealousy I felt and pulled my eyes back to the notebook in my lap.

"He took me on most of his business trips after that, even when it meant pulling me out of school. Catherine didn't like to travel, not at first, but she learned to love our trips."

I paused in my writing. "Catherine?"

"My stepmother. My dad married her when I was little, still a toddler."

"What happened to your mother?"

"She died in childbirth."

"I'm sorry."

Hallie shrugged. "I never knew her."

"Your stepmom was at the funeral?"

"She was. She and dad divorced about ten years ago, but they stayed friends."

I nodded. I'd heard of stranger things. "Do you happen to have her contact information?"

She pointed an unsteady finger toward the address book in her purse and returned to marking off Tom's life with landmarks that she remembered as his daughter—holidays, graduation, milestones in the business. When I asked for more detail on Tom and Clive's relationship, she reiterated that Clive had been working at Battle Sacks for as long as she could remember and that he and her dad had always been friends, though other than hunting, they rarely socialized outside of work.

"They'd never had an argument before that night?"

"None that I knew about. Neither of them was aggressive. My dad was too easy-going, and Clive, well, Clive didn't care enough about anything to fight for it."

"Is that why he was still a line mechanic? Given his relationship with your dad and the number of years he'd been at the business, I'd think he could have advanced to an office position."

"Not Clive. He liked to work with his hands. And believe me, he got paid well for what he did."

I scribbled that fact and asterisked it. Maybe Clive did indeed have enough money to legitimately donate some to the library. "During the fight, you heard Clive say he didn't want anyone to find out for a week?"

Hallie studied her hands. "Yes. I think so."

"You *think*?" I looked at her incredulously. "That single dis-agreement is the whole reason you believe your dad's death wasn't an accident, right?"

"Right," she said. "I still believe that. It's just, I'm not so sure exactly what Clive said anymore. I don't know if he was talking about himself or my dad not wanting other people to find out."

I thought about that. "Does it make a difference?"

"I don't know," she said simply.

"Where in the county was your dad shot? I'd heard it was a local hunt club, but if anyone mentioned the name, I don't re-member it."

She winced. I didn't know if it was the question or her medical condition, but she was appearing paler than when I'd arrived.

"Deer Valley Hunt Club. It's out by Millerville. My dad and Clive hunted there all the time. It was owned by a friend."

Well, I could cross one item off my list. I already had a visit out there planned to interview Mitchell. I leaned in. "Can I ask you something?"

"Of course."

"Why didn't you tell me Clive had quit?"

She looked genuinely shocked. "He didn't. I saw him at work just yesterday."

"He quit right before your dad's death and reclaimed his job right after. Why would he have done that?"

"I don't know. He was impetuous, but that job was his life. How do you know he quit?"

"I have my sources." Luck, Chance, and Serendipity were their names. "What else can you tell me about your dad? Any enemies you can think of? Anyone he unintentionally upset?"

"This is confidential, right?"

"Absolutely."

She glanced over my shoulder like she wanted to shut the door all the way but settled for lowering her voice. "Battle Sacks wasn't entirely my dad's idea."

"What do you mean?"

"I mean there was another guy in town who had a similar business making hunting packs. He didn't have a catchy name for them and was never much of a businessman. My dad saw one of these backpacks and decided he could do better. He made some improvements and started marketing his version. I don't think the original guy made any profit at all. That's how capitalism works," she said a little defensively. "You have to be quick to make the money."

"Is that guy still around?"

"I'm not sure. He'd be pretty old. Last I heard, he was living in a nursing home in Fergus Falls. His name is Julius Mertz."

I wrote down the name. "Can you think of anything else worth mentioning, anything that seemed a little off?"

She returned to studying her hands. "There is one more thing. A mechanic. Over in Parkers Prairie. That's the only place my dad would ever bring his cars to get fixed."

Parkers Prairie was another small town about a half an hour southeast. There were twenty mechanics between here and there, most of them reliable. "He couldn't get it fixed any closer?"

"Exactly."

"Do you know the mechanic?"

"I never met him. One time I asked my dad if I should bring my car there because the guy must be a magician with cars. It was one of the only times I've ever seen him angry. He wouldn't even tell me the name of the mechanic."

"How do you know where it is, then?"

"I'm his bookkeeper, remember? I pay the bills. It's Lyle's in Parkers Prairie."

I scribbled that information in the notepad. "Anything else?"

"That's it, I think."

I finished jotting down notes and looked up. Her eyes were closed. In the restful position, with her cheeks puffy and innocent, she looked much younger. "Thanks, Hallie." I whispered. "I'll take it from here."

She didn't stir.

I let myself out and drove home. The weather was still holding above freezing, which meant I could keep my fish house heater on its lowest setting. Maybe, I thought as I drove, this whole case was a cosmic Rube Goldberg designed to force me to a mechanic through the most circuitous route possible. I would call Lyle's tomorrow, but I wouldn't commit to more than an oil change. And in the meanwhile, I had some vitamins to ingest and some hair to grow in time for tomorrow's date.

THIRTEEN

THE NEXT MORNING, I awoke feeling oddly jumpy, like I had a bug crawling on me that I couldn't locate. Shrugging it off, I hopped in the shower, scrubbed with sandalwood-scented body cream, and washed my hair and shaved my legs in anticipation of tonight's date. I toweled off outside the shower and stood naked in my foggy bathroom, twining my hair into a dozen braids so it'd be wavy when it dried. After applying body lotion to my winter-parched skin, I pulled on a pair of Levi's, a thermal undershirt, and my favorite roller derby t-shirt.

My list for my day off included calling three people to see if they'd answer a few questions: the mechanic, the possible real creator of the original Battle Sack, and Tom's ex. I also wanted to talk with Jed to see what he knew about Clive's pot farm. In addition, I planned to bake fresh bread and whip up some clam chowder from scratch for my date with Johnny tonight. I had told him I'd do the cooking, and I didn't want to let him down.

I loved to cook in the winter. It took the place of my gardening obsession, which wasn't an option in the icy months. Sure, I had my miniature indoor greenhouse where I grew fresh herbs, and my orange and lemon tree that were both laden with babyfist-sized ripening fruit, but it wasn't the same as digging my fingers in the dirt and yanking weeds. Kneading bread dough, however, or mincing spicy fresh thyme and chopping sharp onions, felt real and soothing. And the aromas of my kitchen as a pot of homemade soup simmered and I pulled a loaf of crusty brown bread from the oven was as satisfying as surveying an immaculate garden.

I grabbed a handful of granola, washed it down with some rice milk, and considered starting a pot of coffee. Caffeine was a Sunday morning treat for me, along with the *New York Times* crossword puzzle, but I felt too jittery and so passed on both. I wondered, as I downed a quadruple dose of the hair and skin vitamins, if I was nervous about tonight's date. I was looking forward to it, and I knew Johnny'd respect my boundaries, but dang if I didn't feel like something big was about to happen.

I shrugged it off and settled for a mug of herbal tea. Tiger Pop twined herself around my feet when I plopped down by the phone. Hallie had provided the phone number for Tom's ex, Catherine, who'd kept her married name. I couldn't remember if my phone book covered Parkers Prairie, though, so I'd stopped at the library on my way home from the hospital last night and retrieved the number for Lyle's. I made a copy of the yellow pages devoted to all the Fergus Falls nursing homes while I was at it so I could track down Julius Mertz.

Looking over my list, I figured I'd start with the ex. What I would say to her, I still didn't know. I dialed on my old black rotary-dial phone. I loved the whirring sound of the dial swinging back between each number, the sharp click as the dial found its home, the crackly trill of the ring on the other end. It took five rings to get her answering machine.

Hi, thanks for calling! This is Catherine. I'm not in. Please leave a message.

Her voice was husky, either naturally deep or she was a career smoker. I hung up before the beep. Most everyone but me had caller ID, so she'd likely know that a Miranda James in Battle Lake had called her. She wouldn't know what I'd called about, though, not until I'd decided if I was going to be straight with her or skew the facts a little.

I debated whether or not to call the mechanic next. On the one hand, I didn't want to bring my car in. On the other, it'd be the easiest call to make because I wouldn't need to make up my story yet. In the end, I went for easy.

Lyle's machine picked up on the third ring. Not surprising that no one was there, given it was Sunday. I took note of the business hours and hung up without leaving a message. That left only Julius Mertz.

I used to be afraid of nursing homes as the result of a poorly thought-out eighth-grade field trip. Each student was paired with a "grandma" or "grandpa" from the local nursing home with which to spend the afternoon. Although my lady was nice and mostly remembered my name, my general impression of the place was that I'd rather go to school naked for the rest of the year than grow old and get shipped off to a nursing home. Turning 30 and spending time with the sassy crowd at the Senior Sunset in Battle Lake had changed that viewpoint, fortunately.

I reached for the handset and called all the Fergus Falls nursing homes, asking for Julius Mertz. The first four did not have a resident by that name, and I was starting to feel desperate when I struck gold on the fifth try. My call was transferred to his room.

"Hello?" The man's voice was quavery and brittle, like a sheet of paper blowing down a street.

"Mr. Mertz?"

"Yes. Who is this?"

"My name is Mira James. I'm a reporter for the *Battle Lake Recall*, and I'm doing some research on Tom Kicker." That was only a lie if you assumed one fact was tied to the other, and I can't be responsible for other people's assumptions. "Mind if I visit and ask you a few questions sometime this week?"

The other end of the line was quiet, and I was starting to wonder if Julius had decided to punch out for a nap. Then he coughed, a polite and thoughtful sound rather than an old man rasp. "I heard Tom passed."

"Yes. Last week, I'm afraid."

"Terrible sad. A hunting accident."

"That's right. Do you think you'd have some time to talk to me? I heard you were instrumental in developing the Battle Sack."

I heard more coughing on the other end of the line, then realized it was laughing. "I guess you could say that. Sure. I don't ever turn away company. Do you want to come by for lunch on Tuesday? The food here tastes about as good as most of us look."

I smiled on my end. "I'm afraid I don't have time to drive there and back for lunch. Could I take you out for coffee Tuesday morning?"

"I'm too old to leave. I wouldn't object to you bringing in a cream-filled Long John Tuesday morning, however. If you're so inclined."

"Looking forward to it." We said our goodbyes, and I wrote him into my Tuesday calendar. That's when I saw Peggy's name written in already. Shoot. Well, we'd double up and look for her mojo in Fergus, I guess, which was a little bit like looking for your common sense in a strip club, but hey. The world can be a peculiar place.

Luna and I stepped outside to play a little fetch. The sky was deep-water ice blue with wisps of clouds gathering and breaking apart. The air stung but did not bite my cheeks. An out-of-stater might believe that the cold snap had broken, but a native would know that a break of this color and temperature meant only one thing: a big heap of snow was heading our way. Nothing could be done about that, so I finished up the game, herded Luna back into the house, and made my way to Jed's.

I was beginning to like the fish house heater in the car. It was a dry heat. I hummed along to the Air Supply song floating out of my tinny radio as I drove. I used to have musical standards before I moved to Battle Lake, but you spend enough time in a county where the radio stations consist of new country, Christian, pop, and classic rock, you begin to appreciate a truly magniloquent rock anthem. Come to look forward to it, in fact.

The roads were drivable all the way to town. They were coated with the solid gray blanket of ice-mashed snow and Mn/DOT-sprayed sand that would remain until spring, when the mess would melt away and we'd remember again that roads came in black. I parked in an empty spot half a block from Jed's new studio and let myself in the front door.

"Hello?" I didn't hear an answer and made my way to the back room. The massive glass-firing furnace Monty had been working on looked fully functional and hungry, with its wide front door gaping like a sooty mouth. Something about it gave me the shivers, some buried childhood memory in a scary basement or an amalgamate of horror stories that featured the burning of human flesh. I turned away to silence my silly phobia. After all, I loved glass creations, and the furnace was the medium for them. The array of tools and bent glass figurines sprinkling the workbench suggested Monty and Jed were making progress on their business. But I still didn't see anyone. "Jed?"

One of the three doors off the back room led outside, the other led to an empty bathroom, and the third looked like it went to a dark basement. I returned to the front room and walked to the slightly ajar door on the far wall. "Anybody home?" Jed's winter apartment must be up the stairs, but I didn't feel comfortable intruding. I should have called before I came, but where else would he be?

"In the workroom."

The voice coming from the rear wasn't Jed's. I strolled back and found Monty with his arms stacked full of canisters.

"Where'd you come from?" I asked.

"Basement," he grunted. "Care to help with these?"

"Sure. I thought the light was off down there." He didn't respond as I grabbed the canisters out of his hands and stacked them in a pile on the nearest table. After I'd lightened his load, I held up a can. "What's iridizing spray?"

"That particular one will create a mother-of-pearl sheen on torch-worked glass."

"Torch-worked?"

"Yeah." He organized the canisters by the color dots on their covers, following the rainbow pattern of red, orange, yellow, green, blue, violet. "Jed and I decided it'd be best if he worked on making beads at first. They're hard to mess up as long as they've got a hole all the way through them, and they're a nice way to get used to the rhythm of hot glass. Once he's comfortable with that, he'll graduate to bigger stuff. He's a smart kid, but it takes time to learn glass blowing."

"I can imagine. Where is Jed, anyhow?"

Monty walked over to mess with the gauges on the furnace. He still wore his pompom cap though it was warm in the room. He was down to a white t-shirt and a worn pair of blue jeans. "Got a job at Battle Sacks."

I whipped around. "What? He got the line mechanic job back?" My mind raced with the implications.

"No. Got a temp job in the mailroom for the busy season. Figured he'd need some form of steady employment until we got this business off the ground."

"Oh. I see. What time's he get done?"

"Not sure. I'm not his mother."

I studied him for signs of sarcasm but saw none. He'd stated a fact. I glanced over at the ashtray, which had a nice cache of roaches. "Can I ask you something?"

"Shoot."

"Ever buy weed from Clive Majors?"

He paused his tinkering and shot me a look over the top of the furnace. "You lookin' for some?"

"Nope. Just want to know if Clive is selling."

He wrinkled his brow and kept me square in his gaze. I imagine he was wondering why the hell I wanted to know and how well Jed knew me. He must have decided pretty well. "Clive sells. Always has. Everyone in the county buys their weed from him."

"So he's got a big operation?"

"I don't know about that. I know the law leaves him alone."

"Why?"

He returned his attention to the fiddling. "You'd have to ask him that."

"Can I ask you something else?"

I saw a smile tug at the corner of his mouth. "Can I stop you?"

"Did you know Tom Kicker back when you lived around here?"

He cranked the knob so far to the right that it came off in his hand. "Damnation. I knew that was a rotten one." He held the knob up to the light and studied it, replying in a far-off voice. "Tom Kicker? I suppose you could say I knew him. I was a few years younger, but we were both on the football team in high school. I remember him being decent. Haven't crossed paths with him since I got back and don't suppose I will now that he's feeding the worms. Anything else you wanna know?"

"Nope. Will you tell Jed I stopped by?"

He nodded and I let myself out, feeling only slightly wiser. I'd discovered that I was the last person in the world to learn Clive was a successful pot dealer, that Tom had been nice back in high school, and that Jed had landed a temp job at Battle Sacks. I couldn't see how any of that information would help me. I stopped by Larry's to pick up ingredients for tonight's date and went home to start cooking.

———

The loaves of French bread came out lusciously golden and crusty, filling the double wide with the comforting scent of home and hearth. On the stove top, a kettle of creamy clam chowder bubbled softly, full of chunks of potato and carrots and slivers of clam. I had a bottle of white wine chilling for Johnny and was flirting with the idea of sharing a glass with him. I'd quit drinking in August because it'd caused me to make a really poor decision, but it turned out I did that just fine without alcohol and was exactly half as much fun. I marched to the bathroom for the tenth time to make sure I didn't have a peek-a-booger or something in my teeth.

In the mirror, I fluffed my dark hair, and then leaned in to plump it up again. Then I angled in even closer, not believing what I was seeing. I had new little hairs sprouting up, baby-fine but still there. The vitamins were already working! I ran to the kitchen to down another handful while I considered how to hide the new growth until they were long enough to blend in with the crowd. I settled on a black beret that I'd bought in a moment of weakness about five years earlier. I'd been peddling batik sundresses and Bali hoop earrings as a low-wage counter girl at an import store on the West Bank of Minneapolis to supplement my waitressing income. As it happened, I was scheduled to work every Wednesday with a performance artist named Riva. She was a stunning woman, exotically sloe-eyed. I developed a lady-crush on her, entranced by her worldly travels, her self-confidence, and the bevy of men who regularly stopped by the store to bask in her presence.

When Riva offhandedly told me she thought I'd look great in a cap, I'd let her audition a whole selection from the back room on me. She settled on the beret. "Une belle femme!" she'd exclaimed, clapping her hands together. Two weeks later, she booked an overseas gig, and I'd never seen her again. I'd put the cap into storage. I knew in my heart I wasn't a hat person, but I couldn't let go of the hope. Maybe tonight was the night to live that dream. I dusted off the beret. It was shaggy with age but looked better than my eager baby hairs fighting for attention.

I stirred the soup, stirred it again, and went back to the stereo for the fifth time to send the Norah Jones CD to the first track so when Johnny arrived, the environment would seem effortlessly jazzy and smooth. Where was he? He was supposed to be here three minutes ago. Had he gotten in an accident? Forgotten we'd had a date? Decided it'd be easier to date a neuroses- and battle scar-free twenty-year-old? Luna began whining at my side, looking at me funny, like she'd seen me sprout antennas. I felt self-consciously for the beret. None of the hairs were poking through.

"It's just a hat, puppy. No worries."

She cocked her head, studying me sadly. Dogs could read the thought bubbles above our heads, and mine currently didn't much impress her. Fortunately, the crunch of footsteps in hard-packed snow outside the bay window saved her from having a talk with me.

"It's Johnny!" I raced to the front door before I realized what I was doing. Not only was I wearing a beret, but I was acting like a teenager. This was embarrassing. I forced myself to calm down and waited for him to knock. When he did, I opened the door slowly, as if I had plenty better things to do.

"Mira." He held out a bouquet of grocery-store wildflowers.

I was fighting so hard to stay cool that my face twitched. "Thank you. Come in." I turned to place the flowers in water and to hide my face. Man, talk about a natural hat person. Johnny could even work a ski cap. I tried not to stare as he stepped in and pulled off his jacket, but I couldn't help but notice that the form-fitting blue sweater he wore underneath would have popped my panties clear off, if I'd been wearing any. It wasn't an erotic choice, for the record. I just didn't like the bunchy diaper feeling of underwear beneath jeans.

"How can you be so hot?"

"Excuse me?"

Jesus. I'd said that out loud. My face flushed a deep scarlet. "I said, 'how much time do you got?' You know, just planning ahead. 'Cuz I got lots of food if you got lots of time!" Probably the exclamation point on the end was too much, but I was embarrassed, which feels that much more acute when you're wearing a hat.

He walked over, confusion warring with hope on his face. "I have all night."

"Great! Let's get eating." Damn, I needed to ease off of the exclamations. I let him peck my cheek before ushering him to the kitchen. The double wide was too small to house a dining room, so we ate at the glass-topped table situated between the refrigerator and the living room. I walked the steaming kettle of soup to the table and stuck a ladle in. "Help yourself while I get the bread."

I tore one of the loaves into crusty chunks, my mouth watering at the sound of fresh bread ripping. The inside was snowy white with beautiful air bubbles, and golden crumbs fell into the sink.

"It smells delicious, Mira. Thanks for cooking tonight."

I smiled over my shoulder. "You cooked last time."

Before I knew it, he was behind me, one arm wrapped around my waist. He used the other to push my hair off my neck and kiss softly at the point where it curved into my shoulder. I leaned back into him and was gratified to feel a hard push at the base of my spine. "I like the beret," he whispered into my ear, licking softly at the edges of it. "It makes you even sexier."

When his hand moved up from my waist, I turned to kiss him face on. Or at least I intended to, until the burp bubbled up my throat. It was soft, so quiet only I could hear it, and I was confident I was the only one who knew I'd had the poor manners to belch. I was confident, at least, right up to the moment when the smell hit my nostrils and burnt the hair off. The odor reminded me of methane gas and lawn. I cursed Kennie's name. It wasn't the anti-wrinkle vitamins that had given her breath like a swamp monster, it was the hair vitamins.

"Luna," I scolded, trying to pass the blame to her. She raised her head from her spot on the kitchen floor and shot me the same sad look as before. *You're just making it worse for yourself*, it said.

Meanwhile, Johnny played the situation like a champ. He wrinkled his nose and his eyes watered a little, but after an involuntary recoil, he came back at me with the kiss. Grateful, I leaned in ready to give it my all when another gas cloud burbled up. The smell was so bad I saw beads of sweat form on his temple.

I watched him struggle to maintain a shred of passion and distantly considered whether the vitamins should have been billed as birth control instead. I wished I could make a joke of it to ease the tension, but there was no way I could claim the stench, not after I'd fingered the dog. I'd have to live the lie. "Um, maybe we should eat," I offered. "Sure. Sounds good. Can I help with anything?" He hurried to the table so fast he left a cartoon outline of his body behind.

"I got it covered." I poured him a glass of wine, which he spent the next half an hour pretending to drink from but really using it as a glass shield whenever a poof of air left my mouth, a harbinger of the green and gray gas cloud to follow. It got to the point where he knew I was going to burp before I did and up that glass would go, guarding his mouth and nose as the wine beat ineffectually at his lips.

I was equally as miserable and wondered if I should ask him to pull my finger to seal the deal. I felt like a four-legged creature putting on airs and was grateful when the meal was over. Johnny had said he didn't have any plans for the night besides me, but I mercy-killed the date for both of us. "You know, I'm not feeling that well. I might need to turn in early."

A shadow of relief colored his face but since he was a much nicer person than I could ever dream of being, he refrained from saying *You think? Because it smells like your insides are becoming your outsides*. Instead, he did what he does best and treated me like a queen. "I'm sorry, honey. Do you want me to stay and make you some tea?"

"No, I'll be fine. Just a little stomach bug. Probably something I ate at the library party last night." Or got from a witch who decorated her gingerbread house with hair-growing vitamins to lure in mildly vain 30-year-olds who were dating men way out of their league.

"You sure? I don't mind staying."

His eyes told me that he knew exactly what sort of a smell-fest he was signing up for, and I'd never cared for him more than I did

110

in that moment. So I set him free. "Thanks. I'm fine. Really." I smiled as warmly as I could without unclenching my teeth and dashed in for a quick peck on the cheek before the next green monster surfaced. "You should probably go."

"OK," he said reluctantly. "I'll call."

I smiled for real this time. "I know."

FOURTEEN

"Lyle's." the voice was gruff but not unpleasant, and I imagined I could smell motor oil and Lava soap through the phone line.

"Hi. I'm wondering if I could bring my car in this week. There's something wrong with the heating system." There. I'd said it. I'd committed to having her looked at, and the rest was in the Fates' hands.

"What kind of car is it?"

"Toyota Corolla."

"Don't really fix imports. The dealership in Fergus is your best bet."

The Fates had spoken! My car must be fine. "How about an oil change?"

"I can do that. When would you like to come in?"

"Are you open evenings?"

"Until six, later if I need to be."

"How about Wednesday at 5:30?"

"Can't do it. Got an engine replacement that'll take all day. Thursday work?"

I checked my packed calendar. When had I become so popular? Actually, judging by my other commitments this week, "dim-witted" was probably a better adjective. "Thursday works great."

He took my name and number. "See you at 5:30 on Thursday."

"Thank you!" One down. I hung up the phone and dialed the number of Tom Kicker's ex. I heard five rings, and then her answering machine.

Hi, thanks for calling! This is Catherine. I'm not in. Please—

I hung up before the greeting finished. Maybe she was a serious screener who didn't answer the phone unless she recognized the name and number. I needed to work up a story so I could leave a message. My morning chores done, I tended to my furry companions before making my way to the library.

The nice people from Food by Design had cleaned everything before they'd left and mostly put stuff back where it belonged. I only had to realign a few tables and redistribute the library literature. I was grabbing a stack off the front desk when Mitchell's fliers requesting temporary waitstaff fluttered to the ground. I gathered them up, wondering if I should apply. I wasn't too proud to waitress and could sure use the money. The $49.95 from Peggy covered the database I intended to sign up for today, but I was still in the hole because of the vitamins and needed to round up another payment for the student loans.

Walking over to the computer with flier in hand, I Googled "Deer Valley Hunt Club." When several hits came up, I added "Millerville" to my search terms and was immediately rewarded. The web page featured a camo theme punctuated by a loop of a duck call followed by a gunshot. I turned off my sound and checked the links: News, Deer, Fowl, Shooting Range, Lodging, Dining, Staff, and Contact. After exploring all of them, I was left with the impression that the hunt club was catering toward an out-of-towner with more money than time. Basically, a person paid $10,000 annually for a membership, and that money went toward "wildlife preservation," which I suppose was a nice way of saying replacing the animals that you shot. That fee also bought members the opportunity to use the shooting range whenever they wanted and to engage in four hunts throughout the year. The shooting range was free with membership, but the hunts cost more, dependent on tag fees, trophy and disposal costs, and other Orwellian-sounding services.

On top of that, a member could reserve the Trophy room at the lodge, was guaranteed premium seating in the restaurant, and could have the animals they bagged "dressed," and I don't think they were talking about a tux. The language overall seemed aimed to sanitize the hunting experience. I'm not a big fan of guns, but I respect people who have the skill and the patience to get their hands dirty and take down their own meat. This hunt club struck me as more of a rich man's zoo with the hunters in possession of long rifles and short skill.

While I was on my computer, I completed a basic search on Clive Majors. Not a single hit appeared. I don't know if I was more surprised he'd kept clean or that a person could live in this era without popping up on the Internet at least once. I read this as a sign that it was time to join the database service. Twenty minutes later, I was in. First, I searched for myself and found that I looked like a pretty decent person from a distance. Next, I dug deeper on Clive, but never uncovered a single mention of him besides a copy of the title on his car and his property.

The same couldn't be said of Tom Kicker, whose name was World Wide Web wallpaper. A series of articles had been written about his business, but he'd also been an active philanthropist who'd donated to many women's and children's organizations over the course of his life. The more I read, the more I understood the far-reaching effects of his loss.

I figured this was as good a time as any to check in with Hallie at the hospital. I'd decided early this morning that I should tell her about Clive's check to the library. She'd hear about it eventually given the rate of gossip dispersal in a small town. She took the news well, so well in fact that I thought she must be on mood-enhancing drugs.

"Doesn't it upset you?" I asked. "Clive was throwing his money around like it was on fire."

"Sure, it upsets me," she said, her voice growing heated. "But it also means that I'm right. My dad's death wasn't an accident. It's just like you said. Someone paid Clive to kill him."

"Whoa. That was just one possible theory. We don't know anything for certain right now. There's a lot of different ways Clive could have come into money. You yourself said he was paid well."

"Well enough to live decently in a small town, not to donate thousands of dollars to a library. And most of what he made went straight into a liquor bottle. You don't need to be a detective to know that. So where else could he have gotten the money?"

I still wasn't ready to rat out Clive's pot business. Forget that it labeled me a trespasser. I had a hunch it wasn't relevant, and I wasn't going to turn him in without certainty. "Maybe he's been saving his whole life. Maybe he feels guilty about accidentally shooting your dad and it's making him behave irrationally with his savings."

"You don't believe that, do you?"

I pursed my lips, refereeing my options. In the end, there was only one honest answer. "No, I don't."

FIFTEEN

"GET IN," I ORDERED Peggy. She was standing next to my car, letting all my valuable warmth escape as she gaped at my fish house heater in the back seat. Her eyes appeared particularly wide-set this morning, and her green parka and hunched posture made her look downright amphibious. I was in a crabby mood anyhow because I'd woken up remembering I needed to figure out some way to get her mojo back while simultaneously visiting a nursing home.

"Is it safe?"

"It's not a bomb."

She looked hesitant. "I don't know."

I let up on the clutch and pushed on the gas a little so the car crept forward. "If you have better things to do, I'm fine leaving you here," I called out.

She ran forward as quickly as her short legs could carry her and threw herself in the front seat, her flowery perfume thick enough to slice. She reached immediately for the seat belt. "Does this thing have air bags?"

"More like air pockets. It's a ten-year-old car. Safety wasn't a priority then. Anyhow, if we need to stop quickly, your main concern is going to be that heater in the back seat flying forward and beaning you on the back of your head. The seat belt it's wearing is more for decoration."

She squished her eyes tightly shut. "I think I feel my vertigo coming on. Let me know when we're there. Where are we going, anyhow?"

"Fergus Falls."

"What a beautiful name! Is it an inspirational town?"

Sunny, a lifelong resident of the area before heading to Alaska and who'd earned more than her share of speeding tickets before going, claimed that Fergus had three things to offer the world: geese, police, and cheese. I would argue that its library and historic downtown offset that somewhat, but she wasn't far off. "Lots. Piles of inspiration."

"Great," she said. Without opening her eyes, she reached into her purse and pulled out an inhaler. She took a quick puff, returned it to her purse, and came out with a Nut Goodie candy bar. I'm not even lying.

"Where'd you get that?"

"This?" She held it up blindly. "I always carry a couple Nut Goodies in my purse."

I groaned a little, softly, so she couldn't hear over the wind whipping through my cracked windows. I like Nut Goodies like you like oxygen. They're a Minnesota original, smooth milk chocolate poured over nuts and a maple nougat center, a blob of lusciousness as big as the palm of your hand. A Nut Goodie resembled what happens after you eat food more than it resembles actual food, but what it lacked in aesthetics it made up for in a perfect harmony of sweet taste and complex texture.

"Are you okay?"

I glanced over at Peggy, wiping the drool off my chin. Her eyes were still closed. "I'm fine. Why?"

"You're breathing heavy."

"Your imagination." I turned on the radio, but she must have sensed my need, one junkie to another, because she handed over the Goodie.

"Here you go. I've got more."

"I didn't have breakfast," I said lamely, as I tore into it. I specifically did not keep Nut Goodies in my house because they eroded my self-control.

"I did." She pulled out another bright red-and-green wrapped candy mound and dug in. I found a little room for her in my heart at that moment.

"What do you think of old people?" I asked between bites.

"I'm not sure what you mean."

"Do you find them uplifting? Inspiring?"

She seemed to ponder as she ate, chocolate-covered peanut bits raining down on her lap. "I'm sure some of them have led inspirational lives. Are you taking me to a nursing home?"

"I am." I thought as I talked. "I'm meeting a friend for coffee this morning, and he lives in a home. I thought you could interview some of the residents while I hang out with him."

Her eyes flew open. "What? Do you have any idea how many illnesses exist in a nursing home?"

I rolled my eyes. "No more than in a library. But if you don't want to go in, you can stay in the car. I'll leave the heater on."

She glanced worriedly into the back seat and clutched her purse tighter but didn't say anything.

We stopped at a gas station so I could pick up the cream-filled Long Johns I'd promised Julius. I wasn't sure about his preferred topping, so I chose chocolate, maple cream, and sprinkles. All three looked like lovely, corn-syrup laden gut torpedoes. I wondered idly who I could convince to smuggle me in Nut Goodies if I was ever institutionalized.

The streets of Fergus Falls were icy, but the traffic was light. I drove down Lincoln Avenue because I loved the old brick buildings with shops on the bottom floor and apartments above. The Kaddatz Gallery was closed, but I'd read in my own newspaper that they were having a sculpture exhibit next week. I'd have to check it out. As much as I liked to think of myself as cosmopolitan, the truth was that I geeked out over all sorts of statues. Don't tell Chief Wenonga. I turned right at Victor Lundeen's print shop and bookstore, pointing it out to Peggy as a possible spot for a future signing, and continued the last mile to the nursing home. We made it there in record time, and Peggy reluctantly agreed to go in with me as long as she didn't have to touch anyone. I told her I thought that was an awesome life rule when encountering any strangers.

Unfortunately, according to the door, visitors weren't welcome until 8:00 a.m. Probably a staffing issue. "OK, here's the plan," I said, as we shivered outside the front entrance. "We walk in like we know what we're doing. Don't stop at the front desk, don't look guilty, and don't make eye contact. You just walk confidently beside me and let me do all the talking. Got it?"

She giggled, the first time I'd heard laughter from her, and it was even more melodic than her voice. "This is exciting."

"Yeah, we're a regular James Gang, busting into the Fergus Falls Nursing Home and Assisted Living Facility. You with me?"

"Yes, ma'am!" She saluted, and we walked in like we owned the place.

Immediately to the left of the door were residents watching TV in a bland alcove off the lobby. The walls were cream-colored and hung with colorful abstract paintings, the kind where you wondered if the artist laughed whenever she found out someone paid money for them. The front desk was not personned at the moment. Four doors led off the lobby, not counting the one we'd walked through. Two were clearly marked restrooms, one led off the front desk, and the other was a set of double-doors that guarded a long hall. The clink and chatter of a cafeteria breakfast hour tumbled out of the crack underneath that door, and the air was distinctly scented with an odor of eggs, coffee, analgesic heat rub, and if I wasn't mistaken, dusty, hand-crocheted afghans.

My brain working with jet speed, I strode over to the brightest-eyed oldster parked in front of the TV, a dapperly dressed gentleman barely this side of 100. "Can you tell me which room Julius Mertz is in?"

He didn't respond. I tried it again, louder. Still no response. "He only talks during commercials," whispered the white-haired woman to his left. "If you show me what's in that bag, I'll tell you what room Julius is in."

It ended up costing me two Long Johns, but I got the room number. "You wait here for me, Peggy. I'll be back in half an hour."

She glanced worriedly toward the front desk. "What if the receptionist comes back?"

"Play old." I slipped back into my confident posture and strode through the door to the main part of the home like a gunfighter at high noon. I caught the back end of a uniformed nurse slipping into the cafeteria, but otherwise, the hallway was clear. Julius' room was the fifth on my right. I knocked.

"Come in."

Inside, the room was small, maybe 10 feet by 15, and it consisted of a bed, a TV mounted on the wall, a dresser, a bedside table, two chairs, and a huge window whose ledge was stuffed with glorious green plants. I felt immediately comfortable and approached the wizened man sitting in the chair by the window. "Hi, Mr. Mertz? I'm Mira."

He stood, even though it took him great effort. He was stooped, his thin white hair was combed back in an old-fashioned wave held in place with pomade, and his brown eyes were rheumy. His smile was brighter than the light shining in, even though I'd bet dollars to donuts he was sporting dentures. Speaking of, "I hope you like sprinkles on your Long John. I had a wider selection when I first walked in, but it's a tough crowd in the lobby."

He chuckled his dry, staccato laugh. "I should have warned you. We don't get much sugar in here. We're liable to jump any good-looking donut that drops by."

"Well thank you," I said, making him laugh again. "Can we sit? I think it'd be more comfortable."

"Can I get you a cup of coffee first? I have some instant decaf."

"No, thank you. I'm good." I really wanted him to sit before he toppled over, but he was too much of a gentleman to go down before I did. I plopped myself into the hard-backed plastic chair so he could have the recliner. "Thank you so much for seeing me."

"Not at all. I'm happy to have visitors. Thank you for the donut."

"You could eat it right now," I said, sensing that he wouldn't in front of me. When he politely declined, assuring me he'd enjoy it later for a snack, I jumped right in. "How well did you know Tom Kicker?"

An emotion passed behind his watery eyes. "Less and less, the past few years. He'd become a busy man. When we first met, he was my neighbor. His parents lived right next door."

"You lived in Battle Lake?"

"I surely did. Right over by the Brown Bat. You know where that is?"

I did. The gorgeous, cedar-shake home on the shores of West Battle Lake was a throwback to the 1930s when wealthy industrialists from out East vacationed in the area during the summer. I had no idea how it'd earned its nickname, other than its color. "I've driven past it."

"Beautiful home, that. My house was not so nice." He chuckle-rasped again. "It had four walls and a roof, however, and I had a decent business going as a fishing and hunting guide. Tom sometimes worked for me, cleaning equipment, taking out the occasional fishing group when I had another obligation, odd job tasks like that."

"Do you mind me asking if you two got along okay?"

That emotion again. "You're writing an article, you say?"

He was sharp, his aging body be damned. And I liked him too much to lie to his face, even though I doubted I could have gotten away with it had I tried. "I said I work for the newspaper, but I'm actually asking about Tom because his daughter Hallie thinks his death might not have been an accident."

The coughing started again, and it was ten seconds before I realized it was real distress. I rushed to get him some water from the yellow plastic pitcher at his bedside and helped him to drink. His coughing stopped, though his hands were shaky.

"I'm sorry. I could have worded that better."

He held up his hand, and the skin looked as dry and fine as paper. "I'll be fine. This old heart and lungs just can't take it like they used to. I'll tell you this, and I want you to listen. Tommy Kicker was as true blue as they come, and if he's been murdered, that's a crime for not only his family but his community."

"So you weren't mad that he stole the idea for Battle Sacks from you?" I lowered my eyes apologetically. "Hallie told me that was the rumor."

His shoulders relaxed, and he looked out the window, a sad smile replacing the tightness in his lips. "Just like any rumor, that's about 10 percent truth and 90 percent bull waste, excuse my language."

"Battle Sacks weren't your idea?"

"I suppose, since I'd mentioned to Tom about thirty years ago that I'd sure like to own a sturdy bag with the right-size pockets to fit all my gear in. I also told him I'd like my outgoing letters to walk themselves to my mailbox, and do you suppose he'd have been stealing from me if he'd thought up email?"

"That's it? You just mentioned it in passing?"

"Well, I had these little bags that I made from canvas, but they weren't very good. Tom made them better and asked me to try one out. I did, and I told him what else I'd like to see in the perfect hunting satchel, and he sewed that in, too. In the end, it was all his hard work, and he still paid me a good lump of cash for my help once he got the business off the ground."

"Wow." I sat back in my chair.

"That's right, miss. He was a good person." Julius reached a trembling hand toward his glass of water and brought it to his mouth, spilling some in the process. "And I was happy to see him get his feet back on the ground after the scandal. That bad business threatened to take down more than one decent boy before it was over, but Tom walked away clean, and I was glad of it, almost as glad as his parents. That's how much I loved that boy."

SIXTEEN

My pulse picked up a beat. "Scandal?"

He waved dismissively. "That's in the past. No use talking about what we can't change."

"I wouldn't mind."

"I won't say another word on the subject."

He looked like he was getting agitated again, so I changed rather than let go of the topic. "When was the last time you saw him?"

That was the right question because Julius smiled. "Well of course he always sent me a birthday card. My birthday is the week before Christmas, so I get used to being forgotten. Not Tom, though. He never forgot to drop me a birthday note. As for seeing him, the boy came to visit me once a year every year at the beginning of muskie season. That was one wily fish we were both fond of catching, so he'd stop by to hatch a plan. Well, he knew with me stuck in here I didn't have much to offer, but he'd come by anyways. Looked forward to it every year." He brushed one hand over the back of the other and gazed out the window again, a lost look taking hold on his face. I wanted to smuggle him home with me and feed him donuts every day.

"When does muskie season usually start?"

"Early June, every year."

"So the last time you saw him was this past May?"

"I'd guess so."

"Did you two come up with a fishing plan?"

"Oh yes. We have the whole county mapped out, you know. Best time of day, best water temperature, honey spots only we know about. I bet he was here four or five hours." I let Julius reminisce for nearly forty-five minutes. Peggy was probably doing shots of Purell in the lobby, but the more Julius talked about fishing, the more his eyes sparkled. He could have gone all day, I'd wager, if his body hadn't betrayed him. His words started coming fewer and far between, and his eyes grew heavy, until he drifted off in the middle of a sentence.

I patted his hand, and his skin felt like warm parchment. "Julius?" I whispered. No answer. I checked his pulse, just to be sure. It was light but steady. I grabbed a quilt off his bed and tucked him into the recliner. I considered leaving the donut within easy reach but I didn't want a nurse to walk in, spot it, and confiscate it. I settled for placing the box in the top drawer of his nightstand and slipping a note in his robe pocket so he'd know where to find it. I patted his hand once more, thanked him in a whisper, and let myself out.

A nurse built like a bulldozer walked past me in the hall and then turned to scowl. "What were you doing in there?"

"I went into the wrong room." I felt it a moral obligation to lie to petty tyrants. We must be within the official visiting hours by now, so she had no right to question me.

"What patient were you trying to visit?"

"I was actually trying to leave."

"You're not supposed to be here without signing in, and I just checked the visitor sheet at the front desk. It's blank."

"That's why I was leaving." Before she could argue that logic, I took off down the hall and through the doors into the lobby. I was surprised to find Peggy involved in a heated card game with six animated residents. The receptionist was at the counter but didn't seem to mind Peggy's presence.

"Time to go," I whispered in her ear.

"Time to go *fish!*" yelled a sweet little wrinkle of a woman in an inappropriately loud voice. "Who has a six?"

"You're playing Go Fish?" I asked Peggy.

"It's the only game we all could agree on." She indicated the other six card players, all of them with hair as white and thin as dandelion fluff and beautiful wrinkles lining their faces. "Sure I can't stay a little longer?"

"If you want to walk home. I have to open the library in thirty minutes and it takes twenty-five to reach Battle Lake from here." It wasn't the time crunch that was making me tense, though. I kept wondering about the scandal Julius had referred to. Tom had been young when it'd happened, that much I'd gathered, and he'd said that it had affected more than one decent boy. Was it old news, or relevant to his death? Probably the former, but I didn't know who I could ask. Hallie was the last person I'd pose that particular question to.

Peggy's face fell, but she stood and slid on her jacket. "I'm so sorry I have to go. This is more fun than I've had in weeks. Mind if I come back?" After assurances that she'd be welcome but they'd be playing for money next time, Peggy followed me out the door.

"Get any inspiration?" I asked as we got into the car.

"I'm not sure, but they had such amazing stories. Did you know that Wallis' grandparents were one of the original Minnesota homesteaders? And Magdelene's family lived right next to an Ojibwe tribe growing up?"

"You don't hang out with the elderly much, do you?"

"Not nearly enough." She blew her nose and looked out her window. "Not since my mom passed, that is."

"Oh. I'm sorry." I stopped firing up the portable heater to give her my full attention. "Was it recent?"

"Six months ago."

"Crap. That's awful. How're you holding up?"

"Some days are better than others."

I was debating whether or not she'd appreciate a hand on her shoulder when she began to twitch in the passenger's seat, as if she were suddenly crawling with ants. "What is it?"

She began wailing softly, and I leaned slightly to the right to offer a hug neither of us likely wanted when she grabbed my arm in a vise grip. "It's here."

"What?"

"My mojo. I can feel it."

I looked around. "You've got it back?"

"No, but it's close."

"What the hell does that mean?"

"You wouldn't understand. You're not an artist." She opened her eyes and sniffed.

I was too curious to be offended. "Try it."

"What?"

"Try your mojo. Produce an inspirational soundbite."

"What if I can't?"

"Nothing ventured, nothing gained." Since we were short on time, I started my car and pointed it toward Battle Lake. "We'll consider it the first gunk that comes out of a water pump you haven't used in awhile, in case it's not your best work."

"OK, here goes: 'If at first you don't succeed.'"

I waited. And waited some more. Finally, I couldn't stand it. "Yes?"

"That's all I've got."

I widened my eyes. Wow. This was going to be difficult. In fact, it gave every indication of blowing. "Try harder."

She rubbed her nose, squinched her eyes, and made noises like a slot machine about to produce big winnings. "'God's last name is not dammit.'"

A dud. There was no way I could put a nice face on that. "I'm sorry."

She slumped in her seat. "See? That's why I need you. I still don't have my mojo back inside me."

She looked almost ready to cry, and I'd already met my emotion quota for the day. I tried to soothe her. "But it visited you at least. It's circling. We'll get it back."

"Do you really think so?"

"Absolutely," I said, wondering if she knew how well I could fake confidence. She began humming and looking peacefully out the window, so my guess would be no. I dropped her off at her home and made it to the library one minute before opening time. The two patrons waiting outside weren't nearly as impressed as I was.

The morning flew by as I caught up on the book returns and ordering duties I should have completed before the library opened. My stomach was the only reminder I had that it was lunch time. I herded the patrons out so I could take my lunch hour and was about to lock up and seek out sustenance when a police car pulled into the library parking lot, as sleek and affable as a shark.

SEVENTEEN

IF I'D JUST MOVED a little faster, I could have killed the lights and disappeared before the bad news exiting the cruiser spotted me. And if my aunt had been born a man, she'd be my uncle. As it was, Chief Gary Wohnt leapt out of his car and marched toward the door before I could figure out if I was scared or confused. I decided to play it safe and selected both. I tugged the front door open. "Library's closed."

He yanked the door free of my hand and stalked past me, spraying testosterone on the way. "I know. That's why I'm here." He wore his mirrored sunglasses and a winter police cap that made him look both warm and capable, something I'd have a hard time pulling off even in the high heat of summer.

Scared and confused consulted one another. Both agreed this situation would be better handled by confused. "What are you talking about?"

He had his back to me, surveying the empty library. He set down the bag he was carrying, removed his glasses and his cap, and placed them on the counter. His police-issue jacket came next. Underneath, he was wearing a fitted black sweater and blue jeans. I couldn't help but notice that he filled out both nicely. My type was long and lean, but I couldn't argue that his thick and muscled form had an appeal. What was happening to me? "It's weird that you're here and have your back to me while you're silently taking off your outerwear," I blurted. When in doubt, state the facts.

He turned. "We have a grant to write for the city. I've got a half an hour break today, and this is the last place I want to spend it, so let's get to work."

His icy mood set me back a pace. We weren't friends, but I'd always imagined he deep-down respected my sass and my creativity. At the least, he could remember that I hadn't invited him. "What'd you have for lunch, crabby cakes?"

"I didn't have lunch yet. I brought sandwiches for both of us so we could work." He indicated the bag.

I squirmed. I was hungry, but his offer was uncomfortably generous, like when a clown gives you a balloon. "What kind of sandwich? I don't eat red meat, you know."

He cocked his head, and his eyes traveled up and down my frame. I forced myself to be still and keep my eyes on his face. When his inky black stare returned to mine, I couldn't help but blush. I wasn't sure exactly why.

A corner of his mouth twitched. "Peanut butter and jelly."

"White bread or wheat?"

"Wheat."

"Fine." I stomped over to a table, more to break the tension than with a purpose. He brought over the sandwiches and unwrapped them. I noticed with no small satisfaction that he hadn't spread the peanut butter all the way to the edges. He wasn't nearly as perfect as he pretended to be. When he pulled out a water bottle for each of us, and then a bag of dill pickle potato chips, though, I went a little weak at the knees. Good thing I was sitting down. I got down to business to distract from the awkwardly personal feeling of sharing food. "We have fifteen grand to spend, right? The library computers will cost $2,900 with all the necessary software and a new color printer." It would take weeks for the city to process the donations from the Love-Your-Library event, and they'd disappear into a secret kitty before I could ever use them.

"You didn't ask for a color printer."

"I didn't before. I am now." I silently dared him to challenge me. He didn't.

"Get a pen and paper."

"Why?"

"To outline our requests."

I wrinkled my nose stubbornly. "Why can't you?"

"I don't know where they are." His eyes glittered. "And I brought lunch."

After retrieving a notebook and pencil—because he had asked for a pen, and I wasn't going to completely follow his orders—from my desk, I sat back down across from him. "How much does the police station need?"

"Our communications system is a decade old. We need four new Vertex/Yaesu VX3000 systems, waterproof, four double FT23R battery units, and eight Kevlar-reinforced professional grade QDs."

"I don't understand so I disagree."

He ignored me. "The department also needs a new surveillance camera and two full surveillance kits."

I perked up. "Now you're talking. How do the kits work, and who're you going to surveil?"

He finished his sandwich, folded the wrapper neatly into a small square, and returned it to the bag. "The total cost will be $3,700."

"And if I okay that, you okay the library computers and printer?"

"Yes."

I licked the dill pickle powder off a chip and then popped the remaining crunch in my mouth. Tangy goodness. "Deal. That's $6,600 total between the library and the police department. Who else needs the money?"

Fortunately for me, Gary had all the town's requests in hand. We ended up allocating $3,200 of the state grant to the municipal liquor store—the town's biggest source of revenue— for three new end caps and an industrial wine cooler, $4,000 to the city for solar-powered Christmas lights to decorate the Main Street trees and streetlights, and the remaining $1,200 went to the fireworks fund. All in all, it seemed like a fair and worthwhile distribution. I agreed to write up the report and email it to Kennie before the end of the day. I thought that would conclude our meeting, but Gary took one last opportunity to lock me in his steel-trap stare as he donned his coat.

"You're doing detective work for Litchfield Law Firm."

It wasn't a question, so I didn't feel it required a response.

He zipped his jacket without looking away from me. "You're familiar with Minnesota licensing guidelines for private investigators?"

"Yes."

He nodded thoughtfully and pulled gloves out of his pocket. "PI work can be dangerous sometimes."

"So can life."

He tugged on his cap and began walking toward the door. "Let the Tom Kicker issue drop."

My heart picked up speed and weight. "What?"

He didn't answer. "There's nothing to find there. Nothing you want to find, anyhow. Nothing that will help Hallie. The best thing for her is to let it drop."

My face felt hot and flushed. How did he know I'd been looking into this at all? I puffed myself up. "Are you threatening me?"

He stopped at the door and shook his head. "Just offering friendly advice." Unexpectedly, he spun on his heel and returned to our worktable, where he grabbed the sack of garbage and half-empty bag of chips. On his way back out, he stopped uncomfortably close to me. "Your hair looks nice, by the way. Thick." And he forged out as macho-ly as he'd entered.

My brain fluttered against the inside of my skull like a trapped bird. As of right now, only Julius, Mrs. Berns, Hallie, and her attorney knew what I was up to. Which one had ratted me out? Did that mean others knew, and how would that affect my investigation? Why hadn't he left the chips for me to finish? And what in the hell did that comment about my hair mean?

I dealt with the one point I could immediately address by scurrying back to the restroom to check my hair. Did it look unusually voluminous? I couldn't tell. All I could be sure of was that the new little hairs were long enough that they were no longer sticking up. To be on the safe side, I popped a handful of vitamins from the bottle in my purse and prepared for the post-lunch rush. I had intended to stop taking the evil pills after my swamp monster incident with Johnny but hadn't gotten around to it. I had no plans to see him for a few days and didn't care how I smelled to anyone else, so what could it hurt to finish off the bottle? If I only took a few a day instead of slamming them like I had earlier, I might even avoid the whole toxic burping problem.

As soon as I got a break in the day, I tried Tom Kicker's ex-wife on the phone again. Again, I reached the answering machine. A little worm of worry wriggled in my brain. I had her address. She lived in Underwood, a town of about 350 people nine miles up State Highway 210. It wouldn't take much effort to drive past on my way home. Besides worrying about her, I'd already decided she'd be my best bet for uncovering the scandal Julius had referred to, on top of possibly shedding some light on his relationship with Clive.

I settled in to write the grant report and dispatched it to Kennie. I also helped a middle-aged library patron research start-up costs for opening an already-ran movie theater in Battle Lake, ordered home wine-making instruction books for a woman from Henning who requested them over the phone, reviewed my December budget, and watered all the plants. I put the finishing touches on a flier for next Monday's children's hour ("Bring your used socks and buttons! We're making hand puppets!"), reshelved books, and got caught up on my "Ask the Librarian" emails. When 5:00 rolled around, I felt I'd more than earned my pay. I ushered out the senior high kids researching GMO food production for a persuasive essay, locked up, and pointed my Toyota toward Underwood after the fish house heater had generated enough warmth to keep the windows clear.

Catherine's address put her on the north side of town, directly on the shores of Bass Lake. The lake had enough ice to support a sprinkling of portable fish houses, and by January, this side would be cleared for a skating rink. The far side, with the prefab houses and seasonal cabins, would be set up for ice-racing old beater cars. Catherine's house was unassuming, a 1950s one-level box bungalow that looked like a retro servants' quarters next to the McMansions around it. This surprised me. Tom had been a wealthy man. Had she gotten screwed in the divorce?

Her driveway hadn't been plowed since the last snowfall, which had been almost two weeks earlier. My worm of worry grew. I parked my car on the street and grabbed boots from my winter survival kit. I yanked them on and checked for lights in neighboring homes. While they all had their yard lights on and a few shone with interior light, I didn't see any movement. I slogged through the knee-high drifts until I plowed my way to her front door. It was snowed shut. I pushed the doorbell and heard an accompanying trill inside, but no movement. I pushed it again and waited a full three minutes.

"Haven't seen Cathy in a couple weeks."

The voice made me jump. I turned to see a woman approaching my car about 300 yards away, pulled by an eager Golden Retriever. The sun was beginning to dip below the horizon, but I could make out her friendly smile.

"You live around here?" I asked.

"Five houses up. The blue one." She pointed behind her, toward a nouveau riche castle.

"Does she usually tell you when she goes out of town?"

"No. The Conrads would know. The first house on your left."

"Thank you." There are some benefits to being female in this society. People usually assume you're not a criminal, or at least not a threat.

She waved and continued on. I stepped off the stoop and leaned over scraggly bushes to peek in Catherine's front window. The main room looked like a perfectly clean den. One doorway led into the kitchen, another door looked like a closet, and an opening led down a hall. I saw no signs of a struggle or unexpected flight. I considered leaving a note but wasn't sure what it'd say. Instead, I retraced my foot-holes back to the car and drove home.

After feeding and affectionating Luna and Tiger Pop, I called Catherine's answering machine and deposited the words I'd decided on during my drive home. "Hi, my name is Mira James. I'm the Battle Lake librarian, and I have a couple questions for you. Call me when you get a chance." It was an odd communiqué, but I figured my librarian status was the most innocuous of the four I had to choose from, reporter, underqualified and unlicensed PI, and stranger being the other three.

I microwaved a bowl of popcorn and constructed a cheese and pickle sandwich for supper, popped a handful of vitamins, and realized I was exhausted. Tomorrow was going to be another long day. I had an interview with Mitchell over lunch and a subsequent article to write on top of my regular library shift. I also had a hunch that the universe was ready to reveal more about Tom Kicker's death, but the feeling came with an icy edge.

EIGHTEEN

LUNA AND I TRUDGED a quarter mile through the woods to the sledding hill and started our frigid morning with some downhill action on a green plastic toboggan. The first few runs were sketchy as we forged a trail and she debated between riding with me and running alongside and barking excitedly at me. She finally decided both had their selling points and alternated between them. The daybreak was gorgeous, a frosty three degrees above zero with the rising sun sparkling tangerine and violet off millions of snow crystals. The air smelled pure, cleaning out my lungs in great visible puffs. Only my eyes were naked to the glacial licks of air, and my winter gear kept the rest of me warm. Luna and I traveled up and down the hill a dozen times before she plopped down at the top and began chewing at the ice clumps dangling off her paws.

"You ready to go back?"

She wagged her tail in the affirmative. Back at the house, Tiger Pop allowed me to feed her catnip and scratch her ears and the bony spot right in front of her tail. I toasted and buttered two slices of multigrain bread, swallowed three of Kennie's vitamins, watered my plants, and drove to work. The bog burps started on the drive, but I now had them scheduled. The first one erupted 20 minutes after taking the vitamins and lasted one to two hours, during which time I was toxic, but I swear I could actually feel my hair growing. Then, magically the burps would disappear. Right on schedule, by the time I closed up early to drive to the hunt club, I smelled like a rose. The plan was to interview Mitchell and return before 1:00.

I'd passed the Deer Valley Hunt sign a hundred times on my way to Alexandria but never had a reason to pull in. Now that I did, I was impressed by the enormous log structure that served as the main lodge. It looked straight out of a photograph, constructed of gorgeous buttery logs and as big as a hotel. Several outbuildings looked well used, judging by the tracks in and out of them. A wide-open garage featured an army of four-wheelers and snowmobiles. I pulled into the nonhandicapped spot closest to the entrance, the one marked, "Whitetail," and made my way indoors.

The main lobby featured a crackling, three-story fieldstone fireplace that gave the whole space the warm scent of pine and community. The far wall was made up almost entirely of glass and overlooked sweeping hills and into a hardwood forest. I sauntered to the front desk and helped myself to a perfect red apple tempting me from a beautifully arranged bowl of fruit. I stuffed it in my shoulder bag and dinged the bell. I was rewarded almost immediately when Mitchell popped out. "Right on time. That's what I like."

"This place is beautiful," I said. I wasn't a fan of all the stuffed animal carcasses decorating the walls, but the cathedral ceiling, glossy maple floors, lush Persian rugs in deep jewel tones scattered around, and handcrafted furniture made for a decidedly masculine but impressive interior. The glittering Christmas tree must have been three times taller than me, and it was decorated top to bottom with twinkle lights, tinsel, and tastefully muted red, green, and blue ornaments.

"Thank you. Mind if I show you around while we talk?"

"Not at all." I took out my pad and pen so I could take notes while we walked.

Mitchell rolled out his rehearsed pitch for me, explaining how the hunt club had been handed down to him by his father who had inherited it from his father before that, and how it had always focused on animal conservation. I considered suggesting that no longer shooting the creatures dead might be instrumental in conserving them but didn't want to interrupt his flow. His grandfather had built the lodge from the ground up with hand-hewn logs, he revealed, and his father had created much of the furniture.

"You've got a talented family. Do you work with wood yourself?"

It was the first question I'd asked since the tour began, and he seemed irritated by it. "Too busy running the place to get creative. These are different times."

I wanted to ask him to elaborate, but he stayed on-message, lecturing about the various animals that could be hunted in this area and the famous people who'd visited the lodge, like two former Minnesota governors and a very famous shipping family from the West Coast. As he talked, we strolled the premises, and I was shown the fully furnished guest bedrooms, the kitchen, the full-service bar, the elegant, cavernous dining room lined with windows and dark-paneled wood, and ended the tour at what he called the Men's Smoke Room, a library almost as big as the main lobby.

"No women allowed?" I asked, semi-jokingly. OK, defensively.

He laughed off my concerns. "The name's a carryover from my grandpa's time. The men would come to the room to smoke while the women stayed behind in what is now the lobby. They'd have tea, but the men would prefer something a little stiffer."

"I bet the women would have, too."

"Different times."

"But you let women in here now, right?"

"Absolutely." He winked at me. "You're in here, aren't you?"

I paid him back with a reluctant courtesy smile and made my way to the nearest shelf of books, sagging under the weight of Shakespeare, Hemingway, and Dickens. "The classics. Very nice. Who chose the books?"

"My father, I believe."

I pointed toward a floor-to-ceiling panel in the far bookcase that looked off-kilter. "And he built the shelves?"

Mitchell glanced at me sharply and hurried across the room to push on the angled case. It slid easily back into place. "Him or my grandpa. Either way, this place is nearly a century old. I've been meaning to shore that one up but haven't had the time."

I ignored his lame attempt to cover up. "That's a secret room back there, isn't it? An honest-to-goodness, behind-the-bookshelf, hidden space!" I couldn't hide the joy in my voice. I'd uncovered a similar room at a local mansion-turned-bed-and-breakfast this past summer, and it had stored some pretty cool secrets. Apparently, the hidden "rum rooms" were common in the nicer houses in this area that were built right before or during Prohibition. I started walking toward the panel when he physically stepped into my path.

"That's private."

I peeked around his shoulder. Up close, he was even brawnier, a little thick around the middle but carrying at least six feet worth of ass-kicking, if he had a mind to. "It *is* a secret room!"

"We're done in here." He stopped short of putting his hands on me, but he inched in close, his eyes narrow and snapping sparks. I backed away, and he came at me again, holding his angry face within inches of mine. My arms were crossed, and his were fisted at his side.

"Who built the secret room?"

He pulled in a deep breath and unclenched his hands in a visible attempt to get a grip on his temper. "My grandpa did. It's just a storage room now, but I imagine he had some liquor stills in there back in the day. Don't put that in the article."

"If I can look in the room."

"I'm afraid I can't let you do that. It's not safe. A section of the floor has already given way."

He was still standing uncomfortably close, and so I did the only thing I could: I made him uncomfortable back. "It's very sad that Tom Kicker was shot here. Has that hurt business?"

His face turned an angry red and he seemed to grow several inches taller. I was weighing whether I'd have better luck running or yelling for help when a woman appeared at the entrance to the Men's Smoke Room. She was in her late fifties, by the looks of her, and she spoke familiarly to Mitchell. "Phone call, honey. It's Frederick."

"That was an unfortunate accident," he said to me, his voice low and lethal. "Tom was on the edge of the property on his own time, however. It had nothing to do with the hunt club, and I don't like your question." He pointed at the door. "After you."

I had no choice but to walk in front of him, my danger spikes on full alert. I followed the woman who had delivered the message. When we arrived at the lobby, he shook my hand, squeezing it painfully in his meat hooks, his message clear. *I'm stronger than you and I can hurt you.* "Too bad there wasn't time to bring you to the shooting range. I'm a pretty good shot. Next time, maybe." He laughed, and it contained the echo of an animal baring its teeth.

I had the willies, but I didn't show it. I even held on to his grip for another second after he released mine, though my hand bones felt crushed. Then I thanked him for his time and walked out. And you better believe that before I reached my car, I had formulated a plan for how I was going to sneak into that hidden room.

NINETEEN

I KNEW THAT CLIVE and Tom had argued before Clive shot Tom to death. I knew the police had ruled it a hunting accident. I also knew that Tom had been involved in some sort of major scandal in his younger days, that Clive sold pot and the law looked the other way, and that Clive had played his cards close to his chest until recently, when he made it publicly known that he had cash to spare. Finally, I knew that the creeper who ran the hunting lodge where Tom had been shot was unpleasant, to say the least, and had a secret room. Not a whole lot to go on. If information was coolness, in fact, I would not register on the Fonz end of the spectrum. I was barely a Potsie.

The lead on my pencil cracked as I tried to draw some connections between my isolated bits of information. I was pushing too hard. I dropped my head in my hands and moaned. Hallie was right about there being more to her dad's death than we knew, I was convinced of it, but I'd be danged if I could figure out what was really going on.

The pleasant ping of the library's front door opening made me drag up my head. My jaw dropped when I saw what was walking in. "What the helicopter?"

"It's bad, isn't it?" Kennie stood just on this side of the door in her pink winter getup. Her skin was the color of Fanta, and she seemed to have a smear of chocolate above her lip.

"Not if you're trying to infiltrate a citrus fruit Mafia ring," I said. Then, in case my initial comment had been too cryptic, I added, "Because you're orange and you have a mustache."

"I can't keep the dang thing off my face! I shaved right before I came here." She scuttled to the front desk, peering around the library for any unwanted witnesses to her transformation.

"Have you always had that?" I asked, pointing at the Gene Shalit homage gracing her lip.

"God, no. Have you ever seen it on my face before?"

I had to admit that I hadn't. And then an icy bath washed down my spine. "Sweet Jesus, it's the vitamins, isn't it? Which ones have you been taking?"

Her eyes stopped darting around the empty library and tractor-beamed on mine. She spoke slowly and succinctly. "There *is* only one kind. There's ever only *been* one kind. They have different labels, but it's always been the same goddamned pill, do you understand me? Every one of them will turn your skin orange and grow monkey fur on places the sun don't shine, if you take them for long enough!"

Her voice was reaching a high pitch, and I put a hand out to soothe her but was stopped short by the Frodo patches on her knuckles. "OK, we'll figure this out. Did you call the vitamin company?"

"I tried, but no one is answering the phones."

"All right." I wheeled over to my front desk computer. I had visions of Kennie turning into a werewolf while my back was to her. "What's the name of the company?"

"Triggaz Vitaminz 4 U."

My heart dropped to my toes. "Tell me I didn't just hear the number 4 being inserted for the spelled-out word just now."

"And a 'z' at the end of 'Triggaz' and 'Vitaminz,'" she added helpfully.

"You ordered medical products from a company that can't be bothered to spell words properly?" Now my voice was reaching the high keen. "Off the Internet?"

She nodded.

My voice continued its ascent. "Perfect. You sold me vitamins that some basement-dwelling, who-knows-what-ingredients-using freak created in his free time?"

"He's no freak. His name is Triggaz." She pointed over my shoulder at the screen that had popped up while I'd been typing and screeching. Triggaz was a white male wearing a lab coat, thick glasses, and no pants.

I cried. "I'm going to look like a Mediterranean fishwife by tomorrow, aren't I?"

"How many vitamins did you take?"

I reached toward my purse and yanked out the brown bottle. Three vitamins rattled around the bottom. I looked at her hopefully.

"It wasn't until my second bottle that my skin changed," she offered. "The hair was a problem earlier, but I've been able to keep on top of it until today. It seems like the more I shave, the faster it comes back."

"You stopped taking the vitamins, didn't you?"

She hesitated. "Yes."

"What aren't you telling me?"

"I've stopped taking the vitamins. You're going to stop taking the vitamins. We'll be fine."

I gasped. "Who else did you sell them to?"

"Not very many people," she said defensively. "This weather's kept most folks at home. Just a handful bought vitamins from me, really."

"Their names?"

"Unh unh." She crossed her arms. "There's a little thing called patient confidentiality."

"There's a little thing called the FDA, too, and I bet that didn't slow Triggaz down."

"Ethically, I can't tell you who else has purchased the vitamins. They're a medicinal product, and I promised the buyers absolute secrecy."

I was poring over my arms. They looked normal, but I knew that the hair on my head had been multiplying. Could the rest of it be far behind? "Then you better inform them on your own. And give them a full refund. You can't make people pay to be turned into circus freaks."

"Ok." She began to back away toward the door.

"Kennie?"

"I said okay! I'll do it. I just have to run home and shave first." She darted out the door.

I cursed her retreating back. Then I hurried to the bathroom to check for extra hair. The hair on my head looked darker and thicker than usual. My eyebrows, too. Very Brooke Shields in that department. No mustache, though, and from the neck down, I couldn't tell much difference except that my legs were due for a shave. I returned to the main room of the library, tossed out the remaining vitamins, and made a deal with the gods: if I got through this experience without turning into a neon furball, I'd never give in to vanity again. Part of me realized that if you ever find yourself in a position to make a deal like that, you probably deserve whatever comes your way. I ignored that part.

I immersed myself in library duties, not slowing down until it was time to lock up and head home. I had my glove on the door handle of my car when I heard Peggy's crystalline voice.

"Where are we going today?"

A wave of bummer washed over me. I'd promised I'd help her look for her mojo again today. I turned to look at her. Her face was half-covered by a scarf, but I could still see her nose was red and running from the cold. Her green winter jacket appeared to have a chocolate smear down the front and she hadn't taken her mittens off yet, but her eyes were hopeful. "The animal shelter," I said, using a vision of furry Kennie as inspiration. "If that doesn't stir your soul, I don't know what will."

She nodded, her face covered by a scarf, and hopped in the passenger seat. I figured I could get her in and out of the Tri-County Shelter in under twenty minutes and be home in time for supper. I was wrong. She treated every single animal she saw as if it were her own child. She petted each kitten, from the wheezy tortoiseshell with runny eyes to the super-fat tabby that had been found in the worst of the snowstorm two weeks earlier. She played with the dogs, offered to clean the hamster and rabbit cages, and even let the one boa constrictor sit on her shoulder. I was a great admirer of animals, but she made me look like puppy Hitler. I had no choice but to dig in and help her to attend to every living creature. We were finally kicked out at 7:00 p.m. so they could close up.

Peggy's expression was beatific as she walked to the car. "That was amazing."

I smiled back at her. "That was pretty cool. I keep forgetting how much help they need. I should volunteer more."

"I'm starting tomorrow," she said.

We got in the car. "That's great! You got inspiration?"

"I meant I'm volunteering there, starting tomorrow. I don't think it helped my mojo, but it sure helped my soul."

I flicked on the fish house heater and cranked the engine. We shivered while the heat dispersed. "That's a good thing, no doubt about it. But you're sure you didn't find any inspiration?"

She squeezed her eyes shut and tried a practice wail. Then silence. She squirmed in her seat and tried another warble. Nothing followed it. I was about to pull away when she held up her hand. "It's here."

"Your mojo?"

"Yes! It's here!"

"That's awesome," I said. "What's it got?"

She kept her hand in the air. "A bird in the hand is worth two in the bush."

I raised an eyebrow. "Been done before."

"A catechism has nine lives."

"That doesn't even make sense."

She cleared her throat and began swaying. "You can teach an old dogma new tricks."

I considered that one. "You know, that's not half bad. Which means it's only half good. But you're on your way! I think."

"Really?" She turned like she was going to hug me, and I pulled away.

"No need for physicality. It's not my thing." I put my hand over the back of her seat so I could see behind me as I pulled out. I made a little brushing motion over my mouth as I did so. "You have some dog fur on your lip, too."

She immediately pulled her scarf over her nose. "Thanks."

A suspicious thought knocked on my skull. I slammed on the brakes. "Peggy?"

"Yes?"

"Did you buy vitamins from Kennie?"

"The mayor? Yes, why?"

"How many did you buy?"

"Just one bottle. The one that's supposed to bring you serenity, naturally. It worked so well that I bought two more. Why do you ask?"

"Those vitamins turn your skin orange and make you as hairy as a spider monkey. She didn't tell you that, did she?"

Peggy gasped and covered her mouth. "Good heavens, no! Is that why I have this on my lip? I would have stopped taking them if I'd known."

"Now's a good time to stop." I drove her back to her car, feeling more than a little self-righteous for all the good I'd done the world today. It was too late to go home and make supper, so I grabbed some turkey chili to go from the Turtle Stew and stopped by Jed's to eat it. Fortunately, he was home, working in the back room with Monty. Monty was dipping a molten blob into gray crystals, and Jed was watching.

I was amazed by the glittering menagerie on the rear room's worktable. The early works were apparent—poised horses with misshapen legs, apples the color of eggplant, globes with cracks in the side—but the evolution was also laid out, and at the end of the table was a series of glorious glass ballerinas, each perfectly delicate and balanced in various positions on a single, fragile toe.

"Monty, did you make these?" I set down my Styrofoam package of comfort food and reached for one of the dancers. "They're amazing."

Jed turned down the music and loped over to where I was standing. "The dude's incredible, isn't he? Go ahead and touch 'em. They won't break. At least, not if you don't drop them."

I was already there. I held a dancer up to the light, amazed at the way her slippers appeared to be tied around her ankles, and the delicate depth of her frilled pink tutu. "Monty, you're a real artist."

Monty only grunted. He grasped a second set of tongs and was pulling the blob apart like taffy. What I'd thought was a sprinkling of gray powder was warping and melting and transforming into a jeweled green as deep as a pine forest. I watched, and he pulled and yanked and prodded until the blob became a beautiful little swan, its long neck as graceful as a curtsy. He set it down on a sheet of metal on the table.

The process took my breath away. "Are you learning how to do that, Jed?"

He scratched his head ruefully. "Trying. Most of the leroys on the end are my handiwork," he said, pointing to a pile of warped and misshapen figures. "But I'm getting really good at beads! Check it out."

He led me to the table nearest the back door. It was half the size of the front table and covered in beads of all colors and shapes. Some were long, some were short, some had patterns, and others were navy, plum, lemon, and garnet red. "These rock! It looks like a pirate's treasure. You two are doing great work."

Jed wagged his head happily. "I love it. Tomorrow's our grand opening. Can you come?"

"I can sure try. Will you have enough to sell?"

Monty pulled off his gloves and used a dental-pick type tool to texture the swan's wings. "We've got this much and more downstairs. The trick'll be to get it all out front before tomorrow night."

"I can help."

Jed smiled. "Thanks, Mir, but we got it. Johnny's coming over tonight, along with some other friends. You're welcome to stay, though, if you want."

The mention of Johnny's name sent a jolt through me, half shame as I remembered my odor production and half pure hot tension. I hadn't been vitamin-free long enough to risk an encounter. "I can't, not tonight. I'll definitely be back for the grand opening, though."

"OK, Mir. Hey, before you go, Monty mentioned you might want to buy some pot."

I glanced over at Monty. He was intent on his work. "Not exactly. I was just asking about Clive. He's my neighbor, you know."

Jed smiled his puppy smile. "He's a good guy. Just ask Monty. They go way back, don't you guys, Monty?"

"Sure, I suppose."

I tilted my head. "You didn't mention that."

Monty shrugged without interrupting the motion of his work. "Clive grew up here and so did I. Besides, you didn't mention anything about investigating him for Hallie Kicker."

I made an involuntary noise. "Who told you that?"

Jed looked abashed. "I might have. Everybody's talking about it at Battle Sacks."

"How do they know?"

He held up his hands. "It's like a small town within a small town there. People know what you're doing before you do."

"Well, that blows pretty hard."

Monty put down his tool. "I wouldn't worry about it. By all accounts, no one's taking Hallie's concerns seriously. You should know, however, that although Clive isn't a choir boy, he's no Charles Manson, either. He was dealt some bad cards in high school, got shot up in Vietnam, and came back home to do the best he can with it. You should meet him before you judge him."

"I have met him."

"I mean make an overture. You said he's your neighbor. You ever stop by?"

"I'm not a 'stop by' kinda gal."

"You stopped by here."

"You ever give up?" I asked.

He shot me a smile. "Probably before you do, but not by much."

"Fine, I'll stop by and say hi to my neighbor. Anything else?"

That was all Monty had to offer, so I said my goodbyes and crossed the street to grab a dozen sugar cookies from the Fortune Café and took those and my cold chili back toward home. It was pushing 9:00 when I pulled into Clive's place. His yard light was on, and the barn leaked slivers of grow light, but his house was dark. Just to be sure, I climbed out and knocked on his door. Chuck started barking and came to the window to pretend like he was fierce, but as soon as he saw me, he melted into a wiggle. I tapped the glass and left. I'd tried.

Tiger Pop and Luna were happy to see me. I shoved the chili in the fridge, fed them, and then ate six sugar cookies while I checked my messages.

Hi, this is Catherine Kicker, returning your call. Call me when you get a chance.

How about that. She was alive. I was beginning to wonder. I saved the message and played the next.

Mira, it's Johnny. Hope you're feeling better. I'm playing at Bonnie & Clyde's on Friday and am hoping you can stop by. Only if you're free. Take care.

I inhaled deeply. I should try to be free that night. I really should. But I couldn't commit yet. I also couldn't call Catherine to set up a meeting or Hallie to let her know I'd been ratted out, because it was too late in the evening. I deleted Johnny's message and played the last one on the machine. I was popular today, I was thinking, as the unfamiliar voice came on. Then, as I listened to the growled warning, all thoughts fled:

If you don't stop asking questions, you'll be next.

TWENTY

My heart thudded in my chest. Suddenly, I felt like someone else was in the house with me, hiding, watching me, waiting until I fell asleep to slip his hand over my mouth and neck.

I didn't want to, but I had to play the message again. There was no preamble, no background noise, just nine nasty words, uttered in a baritone. The voice sounded a little altered, as if someone had deliberately lowered his tone, but only slightly. On the third play, I thought I heard the sound of a dog bark once as the speaker said "next," but I couldn't be sure. When I began to play it a fourth time, Luna whined at my feet.

"You're probably right," I told her. The more I played it, the more scared I was, but I didn't learn anything new. "Think we should tell the police?"

She whined again, but when it comes to strategy, it's better to consult a cat. I looked over at Tiger Pop, who was stretching on the kitchen floor. She gave me a bored glance and stalked away. "I don't think so, either. Wohnt will use it as proof that he was right about me looking into this case. Hell, it might have been him who left the message."

I didn't believe it, but it gave me cold comfort as I tried to stay awake in front of the TV, too tired to concentrate and too scared to doze off.

———

The next morning, Catherine answered her phone on the second ring. Her voice was cheerful and smoky, a marked contrast to my grumpy rumble. I'd stayed awake until 3:00 a.m., when I fell into a fitful sleep peppered with dreams of hunting dogs chasing me through a dense forest, their angry jaws snapping at my heels. Four hours later, I dragged myself off the couch and to the coffee maker. This day called for a strong black shot of caffeine. Fortunately, in the light of day with a mug of dark roast in my hand, the message didn't sound as frightening. The call was most likely made by a friend of Mitchell's. He struck me as the kind of guy who didn't know when to quit.

"Hi, this is Mira James. Is this Catherine?"

It was, and when I explained why I was calling, she said she'd be happy to stop by the library the next day to talk about Tom. She said she'd been meaning to pick up some new books anyway, since she'd just returned from visiting relatives in Florida and needed something new to read. That piece of business resolved, I voted for visiting Hallie at the hospital instead of calling her to deliver the bad news about our mole. Peggy was on my calendar to "seek inspiration" that morning, anyhow. I'd dump her in the pediatrics wing while I touched base with Hallie.

Although I didn't comment, Peggy's face looked clean-shaven when I picked her up. Thankfully, my hair growth had confined itself to my head, though I'd gotten in the habit of feeling for a beard. Peggy spent the ride to Alexandria worrying about how she was sure she had recently contracted strep throat and a foot fungus, but she'd packed two Nut Goodies for each of us, so I let her talk. The hospital now seemed easier to visit. Immersion therapy. Inside the main doors, I directed Peggy to the second floor maternity wing and marched toward Hallie's room. I passed by the gift shop and bought a happy, silly bunch of brightly colored gerbera daisies to cheer her room.

My mind was on my visit with the mechanic after work. What answers would he provide? Would he treat my Toyota well? I almost walked right past her room. I backed up, and peeked in.

"Knock knock."

A curtain hid the bed. Over it, another *Golden Girls* rerun was playing. I tiptoed toward her, in case she was sleeping, and peeked around the corner of the curtain. "Hello?"

An elderly woman looked up from the bed, a pleasant but confused expression on her face. "Are you the nurse?"

"I'm so sorry! I thought I was in my friend Hallie's room."

The woman's face drooped. "Oh, that poor dear from Battle Lake. She's not with us any more."

TWENTY-ONE

I PUT MY HAND against the wall for support. "What happened to her?"

"Discharged, I believe. They moved me into here just as she was leaving. I was sharing a room with another woman, but she was too noisy. Jabber, jabber, jabber. Always talking. It gets on a person's nerves. Do you know what I mean?"

I was pretty sure I did. "You know, the way you phrased that comment about Hallie made it seem like she was dead."

The woman put her hand over her mouth. "I suppose it did. She's not."

"I'm just saying, 'not with us anymore' is a pretty common euphemism for 'dead.' You might want to update that portion of your vocabulary. You almost gave me a heart attack."

"I'm sorry, dear. Were those flowers for Hallie?"

I looked at the bright vase of daisies in my hand and around at the impersonal, gray space. "Nope, they're for the room. Should I just leave them here?"

She smiled from cheek to cheek, exposing brilliantly white artificial teeth. "You're a sweetheart. I really am sorry about giving you a scare."

"It's all right." I set the flowers on the table nearest her bed so she could admire their spring-like colors. "Will you be in here for long?"

"Not too. Just getting over a bad case of flu with a dash of pneumonia."

"I hope you feel better soon." I left the room and confirmed with the nurses that Hallie had been discharged before I tracked down Peggy.

I'd often thought a visit to the maternity wing of a hospital should be a mandatory part of sex ed, starting in sixth grade. Sure, the newborn babies in the big incubator room were cute in a red and vulnerable sort of way, but the primal screams of a woman giving birth were guaranteed to haunt your dreams. I always thought it was weird, too, how women had babies at all hours of the day. It seemed like it should be a nighttime thing, but at this very moment I could hear at least one poor soul cursing her partner's existence, and another begging for an epidural, whatever that was.

"It's a war zone in here," I whispered to Peggy. She had her nose to the glass of the baby display case. As far as I could tell, it was a zoo room for humans, with two rows of six infants each, every one of them swaddled in pink or blue like bawling cocoons.

"I'm in love."

"You met someone?"

"The babies. Aren't they beautiful?"

I cocked my head and considered the evaluation. "They look like a lot of work."

"Shush," she said gently. "I can't have a child, you know. I had so many cysts, the doctors decided it would be best to take out my uterus rather than put me through surgery after surgery to remove them. I'm too old now, anyway, but I love kids. They're life itself. And they only get better. I just got to play with two brothers, four and six, over there in the waiting room while their dad visited with their mom and their new baby sister. The stories they told me."

"Did they inspire you?"

Her eyes lit up. "I do feel close to God here."

"Then let her rip."

She clenched her fists, shut her eyes, and began vibrating and moaning. I glanced at the nurses in the baby zoo, but they were too intent on their gurgling bundles.

"I feel it," Peggy sang. "I feel the power!"

"Should I have pen and paper handy?"

Her voice came out in an ethereal wave. "My savior has a first name, it's J-E-S-U-S, my savior has a second name, it's C-H-R-I-S-T, I love to praise him every day and if you ask me why I'll say … Jesus Christ has a way with a C-R-A-Y-O-L-A." She opened one eye and peeked at me hopefully.

"Did you color with those boys?"

"Maybe. Not so good?"

I shook my head. "You've got me thinking of bologna and God."

"How's this? 'Incredible Hulk questioned. Heathen lent Christ hymn faith.'"

"Wow."

"Good?"

"Yes. If it's opposite day," I said sarcastically. "I'm sorry. I think it's back to the drawing board."

Her shoulders sagged. "You're right. I'm never going to get my mojo back, am I?"

Against my better judgment, I put my arm around her and led her out of the maternity wing. "Maybe we're focusing on the wrong approach. Maybe we shouldn't try for a product and instead you should just keep appreciating the experiences."

"How will that help me to meet my deadline?"

"I don't know. Sometimes things come easier if you don't force them." That had never been my experience, but it seemed like an appropriate comment to make.

"Maybe." Her voice came out small and sad. "But you'll keep taking me to inspirational places, right? Just in case?"

"Right. But for now, I need to get back to Battle Lake and make a phone call."

———

Hallie didn't pick up right away. Her answering machine clicked on, and I was about to leave a message when her voice cut in. "Hello?"

"How're you feeling?"

"Mira, good to hear from you. I'm fine. I got out of the hospital yesterday. There's still tests to run, but there always are." Her breath sounded labored on the other end. "Do you have any news?"

"Yes, but I'm afraid it isn't good. It seems that your employees know I'm investigating Tom's death."

A long pause on the other end of the line. "I might have something to do with that."

"What do you mean?"

"I mentioned it to Jean in HR. I've just felt so isolated. I needed to reach out to someone, and she and I have been friends for years." She continued, her voice contrite. "She might have told a few other people since I've been in the hospital."

I bit my tongue. "You know this'll make it harder for me to find out anything."

"I'm sorry."

I sighed. "There's nothing to do about it now. Is there anything else I should know?"

"Not that I can think of. Let me know the minute you discover anything, okay?"

"You're the boss."

I hung up and got to work. The first half of my library shift was a maelstrom of activity. I attributed it to the nice weather that was still holding. The blue skies felt so plump and close that they reminded me of a dam wall about to break and unleash a frozen flood on us. I wasn't the only one muttering about an impending snowstorm, either. I overheard patrons second-guessing the weatherman, who'd claimed we were in for a week of above-average temperatures and no precipitation. A storm was coming, no question. We just didn't know when.

I nuked last night's untouched chili for lunch and ate it while I dialed the hunt club.

"Deer Valley."

I was glad it was a woman who answered instead of Mitchell. She was probably the person who had saved me from the worst of Mitchell's wrath in the smoking room. I'd guessed from the intimacy in their interaction that she was either his longtime employee or his wife. It didn't matter. "Hi. I'm calling about the temp job. For the Christmas banquet?"

"Do you have banquet experience?"

"No, but I do have five year's waitressing experience."

"That'll do. You'll need to bring black nylons and heels. We'll supply the uniform."

"Gack."

"Excuse me?"

"Heels? To waitress in?"

She harrumphed. "It's tradition. Our wait staff wears Santa baby outfits. It's not as bad as it sounds. Your top is covered and the skirt comes to just above your knees. Plus, you get to keep the hat."

I glanced at my "to do" list that I'd slid next to the phone. "Break into secret room at hunt club" was the next item. Damn, curiosity is a tough mistress. And I didn't own a pair of heels. As a matter of fact, wearing cobbling, uncomfortable shoes went against everything I respected about myself. Still. We were talking about sneaking into a secret room. "What do the male wait staff wear?"

"We don't hire any."

"Perfect," I said dryly. "Where do I sign up?" As she filled me in on the details, I scratched off "break into secret room" and replaced it with "buy heels." I hung up the phone. While I was on the topic, I decided to write my hunt club article, since the deadline Ron had set was approaching.

DEER VALLEY HUNT CLUB CELEBRATES
TENTH ANNUAL CHRISTMAS HUNT

Deer Valley Hunt Club, located just south of Millerville, is celebrating its tenth annual Christmas Hunt on Friday, December 15. "There won't be any reindeer," joked Mitchell Courier, third-generation owner of the hunt club, "but we'll do our best to provide a good time. The event is open to the public, and food, drinks, and entertainment are included in the price of the ticket." The humiliation of female wait staff comes at no extra charge.

Mr. Courier's grandfather, Tobias Courier, built the hunt club's main lodge in 1923 out of hand-hewn white pine. The structure was initially intended as a summer home for the mining family from Duluth. However, when their mines went dry, Tobias relocated his family to the summer "cabin" and turned it into an operable hunting lodge. Tobias used his connections in the mining industry to quickly establish Deer Valley Hunt Club as the go-to getaway for the post-World War II upper-crust.

Tobias' son Michael picked up where his father left off. He purchased an additional 100 acres on the west side of the existing property and added hand-carved wood furniture to the décor. When Mitchell took over the family business in 1988, it was the largest wild game hunt club in the Midwest, and it remains so to this day.

"We offer our guests a unique experience," explained Mitchell. "They can escape their hectic lives and return to an easier time, when men hunted what they ate to provide for their family. We have deer, grouse, turkeys, and pheasants, and even ducks on the private natural lake on our property. It's a true haven here."

Unless you're a deer, grouse, turkey, pheasant, or duck. More information on the Christmas event is available on the Deer Valley Hunt Club website (www.dvhc.com) or look for their ad in this edition of the *Recall*.

I figured Ron might edit out a sentence or two, it was hard to say. That's why he earned the big bucks. I saved the file and emailed it to him as an attachment just in time to lock up the library and head to my appointment with the mechanic.

The roads to Lyle's paralleled the roads to the Deer Valley Hunt Club, only instead of turning right on County Road 87, I kept the Toyota pointed east on County Road 38 toward Parkers Prairie. Man, that town needed an apostrophe.

The bitter cold followed by a relative warm-up gave the roads a black ice frosting. I took the curves slowly. I'd already kissed enough ditches in my life. The trick, if you ever find yourself careening into one, is not to stop, by the way. The same undirected power that pulls you in can boomerang you out, if you keep your wits about you.

Lyle's shop was on the north side of town. It consisted of a green and white-striped metal pole barn with a little wooden hut marked "Lyle's—Office" attached to it. The parking lot was home to cars in various stages of de- or reconstruction. I couldn't tell for sure which, but the healthy dose of snow covering all of them suggested it was the former. I parked my girl in front of the garage door, turned off the fish house heater, and entered the office. The unmanned room was a mess of dot matrix-printer paper under which was hidden a metal desk, the world's oldest computer, a front counter, two musty candy dispensers—one half-full of peanuts and the other topped off with Mike and Ike's cheerful sugar suppositories—a pop machine that dispensed glass bottles of soda, and a row of plastic chairs. I dinged the bell and glanced at the pile of papers nearest me. They were bills for work done two years ago.

"Just a sec!" The door to the shop was half-open, and by craning my neck, I could see legs sticking out from under a Dodge Neon.

"No hurry." I slipped around to the desk behind the counter and rifled through some more papers. Just bills, a lot of unpaid, outgoing bills. At the bottom of the stack was a desk calendar surprisingly open to December. Of this year. Today's date featured a scribbled shorthand of times followed by letters. My initials served as my Rosetta stone: 5:30/MJ-OC. Oil change for Mira James at 5:30. A whir of dolly wheels alerted me that the mechanic was on his way. I scurried back to my proper location in front of the counter.

Lyle, according to the namepatch sewed on his jumper, appeared, wiping his oily hands on a rag. He was in his late fifties, with salt and pepper hair and a pleasantly creased face. "Can I help you?"

"I called the other day. I've got the Toyota needs an oil change." I bent my head in the direction of my car.

"Keys in her?"

I liked that I felt comfortable in a small space with him. "Yup."

"Shouldn't take more'n a half an hour. There's magazines." He indicated the stack of *Outdoor Life* on one of the plastic chairs.

"Thanks." I sat and pulled out my copy of *Private Investigation for Morons* while he left to drive my car into the open stall of the garage. I was on the chapter covering online research. I skimmed it, happily realizing that I already knew all of it. I closed the book and reached for an *Outdoor Life*. The pictures were nice.

Lyle poked his head in the office. "Your thermostat is bad. I have one'll work. Want me to change it?"

I drew in a sharp breath. "I thought you didn't work on foreign cars."

He shrugged his shoulders. "A car that old is easy to fix. No computer to worry about."

"How much is a new thermostat?"

"The part is three bucks. Labor'll run you another $10."

My eyes were watering. I'm sure it was just the accumulated fumes of years of automotive work and not gratitude-coated relief. "Yes, please."

He disappeared back into the shop. Fifteen minutes later and my car was ready to go. The total bill was $43.95.

"You're not going to get rich charging people those prices."

His lips moved, but I wouldn't call it a smile. "I'm not one who was meant to be rich."

I pulled out my checkbook. "I make it out to Lyle's?"

He pushed a stamp and a pad over to me. "Use this."

"A person would drive a long way for prices like that. Is that why Tom Kicker always brought his car here to get fixed?" I risked a glance at Lyle. A nerve in his jaw jumped but his eyes stayed easy.

"Who's asking?"

"I'm a friend of the family." I finished the check and ripped it out so he could see my name. "I knew Tom always brought his cars here and figured I'd find out why. Now that I see the prices and service, I think I know."

Lyle didn't even look at the check. His eyes were fixed on a far-away point over my right shoulder. "He won't be coming here any longer, will he?"

"His funeral was last week."

"I read about it."

"Did you consider going?"

He ran his hands through his hair. A chunk stayed pointed in the air, giving him a strangely vulnerable look. "We weren't friends, no offense to you or his family. It was a business relationship. He had a debt to pay off, and it could only be paid with time."

"What do you mean?"

Lyle focused his eyes and locked them on mine. "I did time for him, and then I made him do time for me."

TWENTY-TWO

THE MOOD IN THE office grew distinctly chilly after that. When it became clear Lyle wasn't sharing any more details, I thanked him for his work, took my keys, and left. I reached for the fish house heater's "on" dial out of habit. Realizing what I was doing, I yanked my arm back and kept my eyes on the road. Dare I try my heater? It'd been a couple weeks since I'd considered it. My breath was starting to fog the windows, so I needed to make up my mind soon. If it didn't work, I was no worse off than before. No biggie, right? Before I could talk myself out of it, I shot my hand to the heater fan dial and turned it up full bore. Blessed heat poured forth from all the vents, clearing the fog from my windows with bionic force. And unicorns everywhere kicked their heels and fairies wept with joy.

"I love you, Lyle Christopherson!" At least for his automotive skills. His comment about doing time for Tom raised other concerns. He'd suggested jail time was involved, and that he believed he'd taken a fall for Tom. I wondered if that jail time was tied in any way to the scandal Julius had mentioned, and what kind of time Lyle made Tom do for him, other than bring his car out there. The new information made it all the more urgent that I uncover some facts from Tom's ex tomorrow. I was tempted to stop by the library on my way home to research Lyle Christopherson's criminal past in my schnazzy new database, but it was already late, and I had promised Jed and Monty that I'd stop by the grand opening of the Glass Menagerie tonight.

On a whim, I picked up Peggy on my way. I found glass figurines captivating; maybe she would, too. If nothing else, she'd appreciate the significance of me having normal heat in my car again. I found her home and wearing the largest pair of footie pajamas I'd ever laid eyes on. It took some coaxing, but a half an hour later, we found ourselves in the Glass Menagerie.

The place was packed to the rafters with what seemed like every citizen of Battle Lake, the sound of their combined conversation a constant roar. It was crazy to have this many people gathering this time of year—the weather lent itself to hibernation for all but the hardiest—and the air had a celebratory, slightly manic feel. Peggy backed toward the door, but I pulled her off to a less noisy corner so I could steal a better look at the figurines.

The center of the main room held two large tables. People set their drinks and finger food on these, but respectfully, for the most part, because Jed's beads and abstract shapes filled both tables. They'd also built shelves to display their wares and lined the walls with them. Monty's delicate dancing creatures and multicolored vases owned the shelves. I walked to the nearest one and touched a pea-sized fish, its body clear, its fins blue-tipped, and its face dominated by sweet pink lips. Next to it was a larger version, and then a larger version, until at the end, there was a kissing fish as big as a cantaloupe. I wished I could buy everything in this place.

"Partial to the aquatic life?"

I spun around. "Hi, Monty. These are gorgeous. Did you make all of them here?"

He adjusted his rainbow cap. He'd thrown on dress slacks and a button-down shirt, but the hat, apparently, was non-negotiable. "Most of the ones on the shelves, though Jed is getting good at puffer fish, so he made those on the bottom shelf."

"They're lovely," Peggy said in a hushed voice. She looked enchanted by the glass magic, and her childlike focus made me smile.

"Thank you. Jed has a present for you, by the way. He's back in the work room."

I left Peggy to ogle the art and threaded my way through the crowd. I found Jed waving his hands animatedly in a conversation with the Nordmans. When he saw me, he rushed over.

"Mira! How totally sick is this? Do you see how many people are here?"

"Yeah, it's pretty cool. I saw your puffer fish, too. I like them!"

"Oh." His eyes fell. "Then you probably don't want this." He reached into his low-slung jeans and pulled a plum-sized ball of wrinkled paper wrapped with cellophane tape out of his deep pockets. When he handed it to me, I realized it had a solid center. I peeled back the paper gently, revealing a lopsided orb shot through with waves of burgundy and deep blues. It looked like a precious gem and fit perfectly in the palm of my hand.

"I love it."

"Naw, it's all googly. It was my first ornament, you know. It's not any good."

He reached to pluck it out of my hand, but I closed my fingers firmly around it. "I'm honored that you gave me your first ornament. If I could pick one thing in this whole store, I'd pick this."

He blushed and pushed a straggly hair back from his face. "You mean it?"

"Yup."

His smile was dazzling. "Whoop!"

I let him return to his conversation with the Nordmans and held my treasure close. I was happy for his and Monty's success, but I'd had enough human company for the day. I tracked down Peggy with the intention of bringing her home. She was in a conversation with Monty about his travels to Turkey.

"Hey, Peggy. Sorry to interrupt, but it's been a long day. Mind if we head out?"

She pushed her glasses up her nose and took a messy bite off the tray of cheese and crackers Monty had brought over. "I suppose."

"Monty, thanks for having us. You've really got amazing work here." I offered my hand, but before he could take it, another guy butted into the conversation.

"Did I hear her call you Monty? Monty Dunham?"

"That's me."

"We went to high school together." The interrupter tapped his chest. "Phil Kramer. We graduated the same year. How long have you been back?"

"Not quite half a year."

"I remember reading that your mother passed. Damn shame. She was a good woman. Have you hooked up with the old gang since you got back?"

I inserted myself back into the conversation. They could reminisce all they wanted once I was out the door. "Like I was saying, Monty, thanks. See you later." I shook his hand and led Peggy out.

———

The sky was gray and overcast the next morning, which made for even warmer temperatures. I slept in and skipped breakfast to play snow Frisbee with Luna before cruising to town to grab Peggy for her morning's inspirational retreat. Nancy and Sid had mentioned in passing last week that their church was having Friday morning services in the weeks leading up to Christmas. When I remembered, I slapped my forehead. Why hadn't I taken Peggy to church already? What a perfect place to find her brand of inspiration.

"Actually," she said, blushing, "church never has done much for me. In terms of inspiration, that is. At the end of a service, all I can write are limericks."

"You're serious."

"Don't tell the pastor. And while your car's heat is lovely, I hope it doesn't dry out my sinus cavities and make them more vulnerable to infection."

I rolled my eyes, but quietly. We both sat through the service, and afterward, I introduced her to Pastor Harvey Winter. He was a generous man with white hair and smile crinkles all over his face. He was Sid and Nancy's spiritual leader and had helped me uncover a murderer in August. Peggy was immediately enamored of him, I could tell, and he also informed her that he was a great fan of her work. After they got their mutual praise fest out of the way, I pulled Peggy away so I could open the library.

"Get anything?"

She nodded tentatively. "There once was a pastor who was blunt, and he had a female parishioner who was a real—"

"Stop. Stop it." I shoved my fingers in my ears. "That's a little messed up, you know. You'll want to make sure your readers don't find out about this limerick affliction of yours."

A fat tear rolled down her cheek. "I'm a terrible person."

"Argh." This was at least partially my fault, I was certain of it. I wasn't sure exactly how, but I felt responsible for her feeling lousy. "You're not a terrible person. We went to the old folks' home and you made friends. You helped animals at the shelter and reminded me that I want to help there more. We went to the maternity wing at the hospital, and the kids loved you. At church, Pastor Harvey hung on every word you said. You do have a gift. You make people feel inspired."

"But I can no longer inspire myself."

"Here, I'll try to help." I scrambled for the most anti-limerick subject I could think of. "You finish this phrase: 'Noah's Ark—'"

"OK." She slammed her eyelids shut tight and started to squirm.

I put a hand out to still her. "Eyes open, no moaning or wiggling."

"I don't know."

"It's worth a try."

She put both hands on the wall of the church foyer. Beads of sweat appeared on her forehead. Her nostrils flared. Sound burbled from her throat. "Noah's Ark. A boatload of fun."

My left side twitched involuntarily. Fortunately, she couldn't see it. "It's not a limerick. That's progress. Let's quit while we're ahead."

She drooped. "I need a break. No more inspirational field trips for a little bit, okay?"

I felt awful for her. She'd come to town for inspiration, figuring she'd be able to leave again unscathed. No one leaves Battle Lake unscathed. "All right. But when you want more help, I'm here for you."

I dropped her off at her temporary home with enough time to stop by the offices of the *Battle Lake Recall* before I opened the library. I figured the database service I'd subscribed to could give me the hard facts about Lyle's criminal background, and I intended to check as soon as I got to the library. However, the *Recall* had been running the "County Crimes" column since its inception, right next to "The Tattler," the column that covered who had eaten dinner with whom or brought what hotdish to which local event, and other riveting small town news. If Lyle had been arrested locally, I'd find a lot more from a newspaper article than a line in a database.

Mrs. Sims was working behind the desk. She was Ron's trophy wife, gregarious and ten years his junior. The two of them were locally famous for their habit of making out in public, which is why I was glad only half of the couple was present.

"Ron covering a story?"

She shook her head. "Dentist appointment. He's getting a crown on one of his wisdom teeth."

"Mind if I check the archives?"

"Knock yourself out. And I was supposed to email you a reminder about your next 'Bites' column, but since you're here, I'll just tell you. Ron needs the article by this afternoon."

"It's almost done." I'd completely forgotten. Thank god for the Internet.

In the back room, I sat down at the research-dedicated Mac. The *Recall* had been around since the early 1900s. Three years ago, Ron had paid big bucks to have a California-based, document-scanning business convert all the microfiche archives to searchable PDF files. I had my complaints about the balding, taciturn little man, but lack of organization wasn't one of them.

In the end, Lyle's criminal record was disappointingly easy to find. He hadn't been assigned a passing mention on "County Crimes." He was the headlining story of the July 9, 1962, edition.

DOPED-UP BIKER ASSAULTS LOCAL WOMAN

Lyle Richard Christopherson, age 19, roared into town on his motorbike, bringing with him corrupting drugs and the community's worse nightmare. Originally from the Duluth area, Mr. Christopherson claimed he was passing through Battle Lake on his way to a motorbike rally in South Dakota. He was initially stopped by local police, who could not find a reason to detain him.

It is believed that later that day, Mr. Christopherson returned to Battle Lake to sell marijuana, an illegal intoxicant, to local youth. What is certain is that on the night of July 4, Mr. Christopherson sexually assaulted a local girl, whose name is not being released because of her minor status. Mr. Christopherson is scheduled to appear in court on August 2 on charges of drug possession, intent to distribute, and statutory rape. If convicted, he faces up to 15 years in prison.

My blood ran as cold as the Minnesota wind.

TWENTY-THREE

I COULDN'T IMMEDIATELY SORT out what was more confusing. Was it how drastically I'd misread Lyle, or was it how drastically everyone else had misread Tom? Because according to Lyle, he'd been sent up the river for a crime that Tom had committed. I couldn't imagine either him or Tom as a rapist, however. I checked various spellings of Lyle's name in the newspaper's files to see if there was any other mention of him. The only other appearance he made in print was the coverage of his sentencing. He received the full 15 years.

I searched for Tom Kicker's name, and found more articles than I could possibly read in a day. Skimming the titles revealed them all to be positive, detailing his involvement with local and state charities. I logged off and reached the library just in time for opening, my mind reeling. No one was waiting to get in, so I accessed my criminal database service. I was correct that it provided a brief version of what I'd read on Lyle, but the essential facts were the same. I hoped none of this was somehow related to Tom's death. It would break Hallie's heart to find out her dad wasn't the white knight she believed.

My mind was still fuzzy with too much information when Catherine Kicker, Tom's ex, arrived. I recognized her as an older version of the woman in Hallie's family photos. She was dressed sensibly in snow boots and a red down jacket, with a matching red cap and gloves.

I left my post at the front desk to greet her. "You must be Catherine. Thanks so much for coming."

"Not at all. I needed some fresh reading. I intended to stop by when I got back from Florida anyways. Now tell me why you want to know about Tom."

I led her to a quiet corner of the library, where we both took a seat. Since Hallie'd already let the cat out of the bag, I saw no harm in explaining my mission.

"Ah, well you'll have a hard time uncovering any dirt on him. He was a good man, top to bottom."

Of all the questions that comment raised, this one rose to the top: "So why'd you divorce him?"

She made a sad, dismissive gesture. "Different interests, mostly. It turned out later in life that we switched roles. I became the one who loved to travel and he became weighted to his business. Sun up to sun down, there was nothing for him but Battle Sacks. I imagine we could have stayed married. He didn't mind me gallivanting around on my own. But I was looking for passion and partnership in the last third of my life. Selfish, I suppose."

"Have you found it?"

She chuckled her smoky laugh. "Not yet. But I haven't started looking too hard. Right now, I'm just visiting friends and family I've fallen out of touch with."

"I have a rude question. Did you do okay by the divorce?"

She raised her eyebrows. "Money-wise? Yes, I did just fine. You're probably referring to my house. My car's not much nicer. I prefer to spend my money on non-material goods. Plane tickets, for example."

I nodded. "I have another difficult question. You know that mechanic, the one in Parkers Prairie that Tom always brought his car to?"

"I think so. Lyle's? I tried to bring my car there once. Figured it must be the best service this side of the moon for Tom to drive that far. Tom wouldn't let me. What of it?"

I explained the crime Lyle had been convicted of and his belief that Tom was somehow involved.

She looked confused, and then angry. "Everyone in town knew about that rape. A biker came into town, crashed a party, and took advantage of that poor girl. She was just 16, if I remember correctly. That was the same man who fixed Tom's cars?"

I nodded.

She pursed her lips. "There's no way Tom was involved in a rape. I can swear to that 100 percent. He was the kindest man on this earth. He'd sooner get out of his chair to release a spider outside than to squash it. No, I can't believe it. That Lyle person must be wrong. If he's a criminal, he wouldn't have any trouble lying."

"It would explain why Tom drove out there regularly."

"So would good prices. And if Tom was guilty, why wasn't he accused? You said he wasn't even mentioned in the newspaper article."

"I don't know." I drummed my fingers on the tabletop. "Can you remember anything else about the attack?"

"It was so long ago." She'd taken her gloves off when she entered. She now pulled her hat off. Her gray-streaked blonde hair crackled with static electricity. She smoothed it with her hand. "I know the girl was local, though I was from Fergus at the time so didn't know her personally. She was too ashamed to stay around afterward, I think I remember hearing. Rumor had it she was pregnant from the incident. Probably smart that she left. The whispers and judgment would have been brutal. Not right, certainly, but brutal. I can't remember her name." She tapped her chin. "Kay? Clair? Hmm. Carla, maybe? Yes, that sounds right. My mom had a cat named Carla, that's why I remember. A hairy old thing. Had to put her down when my mom passed."

She kept chattering in the background, but I could focus on only one point: Carla. That was the name of Clive's girlfriend.

TWENTY-FOUR

CATHERINE HAD NOTHING MORE to reveal, other than more details on what an amazing man Tom had been. I gathered that she missed him, first as a result of the divorce and now since she'd never see him again. I thanked her for her time and helped her find a nice blend of nonfiction and novels to keep her company the next few weeks.

It was hard to concentrate while I helped her. I was trying to recall how long Carla had been around, and how long Clive had been dating her. She'd been working at Bonnie & Clyde's since I'd moved to town last spring. Was she the Carla who had been raped forty years earlier, and had Clive killed Tom when he found out about his friend's involvement? There were far too many ifs. It made me crazy. I planned to return to Lyle's tonight to get more information, and stop at Bonnie & Clyde's on my way back to talk to Carla. Of course, that meant I also might run into Johnny, whose band was playing at the bar tonight.

The ticks on the clock ached by. I had book orders to look through and shelves to organize, but I couldn't focus. There was too much I needed to know, and I was trapped at work so I couldn't find it out. I decided to churn out a recipe column instead of getting real work done.

While I Googled "Minnesota Christmas recipes," I considered what my home economics teacher would think about where I'd ended up in life. Her name was Mrs. Davidson, and she was the spitting image of Julia Child, but shorter and more motherly. When I was in seventh grade, a budget crisis forced the administration to lay off the health teacher and formulate the brilliant idea of combining Mrs. Davidson's cooking class with sex ed. The kitchen was close to the bedroom, right? The new class was called "Family Sciences," and from this fertile pairing sprang a generation of kids who would forever associate spinach quiche with the reproductive system. Mrs. Davidson would understand "Battle Lake Bites," I decided.

Unsurprisingly, all my Minnesota recipe hits were for white food—lefse, lutefisk, potato klub. You'd think a snowbound people would make their food easier to locate were they to drop it while walking outdoors. Finding no tasty hits in the web, I went old school and browsed the Battle Lake section of the library. As far as I know, the Battle Lake library was the only one in the state to house a whole area dedicated to the history of the town, including yearbooks and original plats. I'd skimmed the yearbook section back in May when I'd needed to find some info on Kennie and Gary, both BLHS graduates, and I'd remembered seeing church cookbooks nearby, but for the most part, library patrons didn't check out these books so I didn't handle them much.

Sure enough, there were nearly two dozen spiral bound recipe books donated by various area churches over the years. I reached for the thickest, titled *Corn of Plenty*. It was published in the eighties, back before corn wasn't oversubsidized, transformed, and injected into everything from orange juice to shoes. The book contained only corn-centric recipes and was divided into appetizers, salads, main dishes, and desserts. On the bottom of every page was a "Corn Fact." *Did you ever wonder how they make that yummy jewel-like gravy in restaurants? The secret is cornstarch!*

I flipped first to desserts, thinking they would be a challenge to work corn into. I was disappointed to discover that they all simply used high fructose corn syrup, before that was a dirty word. I flipped next to appetizers and felt immediately transported to the 1950s, where men wore hats and drank highballs and women curled their hair and donned full-skirted dresses to vacuum the house. And from that vision, my first Minnesota Multicourse column was born.

STILL TASTY AFTER ALL THESE YEARS

Turn up the Sinatra, fix yourself a scotch on the rocks, and slip into your party clothes, ladies and gentlemen. "Battle Lake Bites" is taking you back to a simpler time, when your meat was canned and your vegetables creamed. Welcome to the first installment in the Themed Menu series. This one is titled "Dragnet Dinner," and it's perfect for a romantic night with your lover or a dinner party with your closest friends.

Company Ham Spread with Ritz Crackers

1 can deviled ham

½ can corn

2 tablespoons Thousand Island dressing (Wishbone brand is the best!)

2 tablespoons chopped pimento-stuffed green olives

¼ teaspoon Lipton's Onion Soup mix

1 sleeve Ritz crackers

Combine everything but the crackers. Chill for two hours (can be made a day ahead of time). Spoon topping onto crackers. Garnish each with an olive.

Chilled Ambrosia Salad

1 can Del Monte peach slices in heavy syrup, undrained

1 can Del Monte sliced pears in heavy syrup, undrained

1 can mandarin oranges, drained

¼ cup maraschino cherries

1 container Cool Whip

4 tablespoons sweetened shredded coconut

Mix all but coconut and Cool Whip in a bowl. Spoon into individual serving ramekins. Top each with two tablespoons of Cool Whip, sprinkle with coconut, and chill one hour before serving.

MAIN DISH

Card Club Chicken Hotdish

1 package Rice-A-Roni Chicken Flavor

2 tablespoons corn oil margarine

2 cups cubed, cooked chicken

1 can Campbell's cream of chicken soup

1 package frozen chopped broccoli, cooked and
   drained

1 can corn

¼ cup slivered almonds

Cook Rice-A-Roni according to package instructions. Combine in large bowl with remaining ingredients except for almonds. Pour into a greased, microwave-safe casserole container. Microwave on high for seven minutes or until bubbling. Sprinkle with almonds and serve.

SIDE DISH

Creamed Corn

2 cans Green Giant Creamed Corn

Open cans, pour into microwave-safe bowl, and microwave on high for two minutes before serving.

DESSERT

Annette Funijello's Christmas Treat

1 cup water
1 teaspoon corn syrup
¼ cup Brach's cinnamon imperials
1 package strawberry-flavored gelatin
1 jar Musselman's applesauce
1 teaspoon lemon juice

Combine water, corn syrup, and candies in saucepan and heat until boiling. Stir as needed to dissolve candies. Place gelatin in a mixing bowl. Pour boiling water and candy mixture over gelatin. Stir until gelatin is dissolved. Cool slightly. Stir in applesauce and lemon juice. Pour into Christmas-themed mold. Chill until set.

Phew. I'd given it my best. If Battle Lake didn't have the most smashing Christmas ever, it wasn't my fault. I sent the column off to Ron just in time to close. My car felt a bit lonely without the fish house heater, which I'd removed before I left for work today, but I had a feeling I'd get used to it. I let the Toyota warm for a couple minutes while I scraped my windshield, and then hopped in to head to Parkers Prairie.

———

The traffic was heavy, for a small town, and it took me nearly 45 minutes to arrive at Lyle's. My heart was knocking some in my chest. I was jazzed at the possibility of finding answers, but I didn't imagine the social etiquette for asking a man about his criminal background was completely outlined, even in my *PI for Village Idiots* book. How would Miss Manners handle it? *Never wear a hat*

when indoors, turn off your cell phone when entering a restaurant,
and make sure not to speak with your mouth full when inquiring
about a person's past rape conviction. It didn't make it any easier
that the guy was single-handedly responsible for the fact that I
could see out of every window in my car without the aid of a fish-
house heater.

No point in worrying when I could be doing. I screwed up my
courage, parked my car in the spot directly in front of the office
door, and marched in. I was greeted by a wall of Jimi Hendrix
wondering if I might be experienced.

"Hello?" No way was he going to hear me in the shop over the
blaring music. I looked in vain for a button that might be connected to a light in the back. "Hello?"

I waited nearly two minutes before letting myself into the shop.
The music was louder back here, and the oil-heavy air was laced
with the distinctly sweet smell of marijuana. All the lights were on.
An old Ford pickup was hoisted in the air, and some poor sedan
had its engine cherry-picked right out of it and dangling over the
open hood, ready for surgery. The third stall housed an SUV. I figured Lyle must be under there because I couldn't see him anywhere else. I marched over, the loud music making me tense. I
walked around the vehicle and didn't see him. Getting down on all
fours, I peeked underneath. Still no Lyle.

As I stood, a hand grabbed my shoulder. I squealed and turned.
Lyle stood there in his dark blue jumper, his eyes bloodshot, smiling a crooked smile.

"You scared me!"

He shrugged.

"Care to turn the music down?" I yelled.

He shrugged again, but pointed toward the back of the shop. I found the stereo console and turned the music to low. My ear drums throbbed. "That'll make you go deaf."

"Aren't you a little young to be my mother?" he asked.

"You're high."

"You're low." He smiled again, but it had a dark underline. "Something go wrong with your car?"

"I'm here to talk to you about what you said about Tom. You said you'd done time for him, and then he did time for you. Were you referring to the rape charges?"

He turned abruptly and strode toward a tool bench, where he began noisily pawing through the wrenches. "I never mentioned a rape," he said over the noise

"No, you didn't. I found it in the records of the Battle Lake newspaper."

He came up with a crescent wrench. "Sure going to a lot of trouble for a friend of the family."

It was my turn to shrug.

He sewed his lips, then thought better of it. "If you read it in the paper, then you know all of it. I was arrested for rape. Sentenced to fifteen years, did ten."

"That's all there is to it?"

"I suppose, if you look at my record."

"Records don't always tell the truth. What would a fly on the wall have witnessed that night?"

He chuckled. The sound made the back of my neck cold. "A fly wouldn't'a wanted to be there, birdie. But I'll tell you the same thing I told the police because it doesn't make any difference anymore, does it? I was passing through Battle Lake a long time ago, doing carpentry work here and there. I got a gig helping out a big-shot business owner upgrading his summer place. That was my first mistake. His son was a member of this lily-white, country boy gang that called themselves the Four Musketeers. They knew I had weed and invited me to a barn party. I went, and that was my second mistake."

He polished the wrench as he spoke, his voice hard. When the metal of it caught light, it shone like a diamond. "It was the four boys there, the Musketeers, and me. We got high. A girl showed up, and we started drinking. We drank too much. The barn was full of hay, and it was warm, and I was tired, so I fell asleep. I woke up to that pretty little thing crying, hay all in her hair and stuck in her yellow party dress, and I knew what I was up against. The Musketeers had all left, and the police were on their way. Who called them, your guess is as good as mine. I never touched that girl, I never did, but she was a local and protected her own. I was hung out to dry."

"Tom Kicker was one of the Four Musketeers?"

Lyle leaned under the hood of a two-door sedan and continued as if he hadn't heard me. "I did my time, and when I got out, I opened up this here garage and didn't much look back. Though, if you're wondering, I believe Tom's patronage spoke for itself, in terms of his guilt. That man never could handle guilt well."

I digested that information. "Who were the other three?"

Outside a car door slammed. Lyle released the hood on the car he was working on and turned on me. "I've talked enough."

"I could find out who they were. I can go back to the newspaper archives."

He laughed, a sound as cold as a December whistle. "You won't find out who they were. Not in the newspaper, anyhow. Every town protects its privileged sons."

He was moving uncomfortably close to me, the glittering wrench still in his hand.

"Why'd you come back here after you got out?"

"I called in favors to get this business going," he said darkly. "And I might have an ironic streak. If I don't get to forget that night, neither does anyone else."

We both heard the door in the office open. "Hello?"

The voice was male, and it gave Lyle a jolt. He strode the last three feet to me and gave me a push. "You should leave through this side door."

His unease was contagious. "Why?"

Instead of answering, he pushed me toward the door. I craned my neck but at this angle couldn't see who entered. Outside, I jogged back to the front of the business, where a black Jeep was parked next to my Toyota. I walked to the office entrance just in time to see the door to the garage slammed shut. I returned to the Jeep and peeked in the windows. A couple jazz CDs were spread out on the passenger seat. The inside was otherwise clean. I slid into my Toyota and drove to Bonnie & Clyde's to ask Carla if she was the girl in the yellow dress.

TWENTY-FIVE

THE UGLINESS OF WHAT I was dealing with was undeniable. In the 1960s, a girl had been raped. According to Lyle, the Four Musketeers were responsible for the attack, and Tom had been one of those Musketeers. They had framed Lyle. That corroborated Julius' suggestion that a scandal in Tom's past had threatened to take down more than one "good" boy. Either Julius was mistaken in his assessment of the men or I was misjudging Lyle as a rough but basically decent person. He truly believed he'd been done wrong. It might not have happened exactly like he remembered, but his conviction convinced me that the newspaper didn't have it right, either.

Fast forward to today. Tom is murdered at the hands of his friend Clive, who is currently dating a woman who may have been the rape victim. Had Carla let slip the story of her past, and Clive avenged her? That seemed far-fetched, but I didn't have anything else to go on until I figured out if Carla was the rape victim, and who the other three Musketeers were.

It was not yet 8:00 p.m., and Bonnie & Clyde's was sparsely populated. Ruby was behind the counter, smoking and watching the tiny color television. Carla was dispensing golden mugs of beer to a group of four drinking near one of the two pool tables. They were young, early twenties tops, and were likely here for the two-band lineup. Johnny was nowhere in sight. I sidled to the bar.

"Hi, Ruby."

She didn't look away from the TV. The bar was hers. She'd inherited it from her late husband, and she was a character. She wore jeans with 1970s patches and had the appearance and mien of Flo from Mel's Diner. "You still not drinking?" she asked me.

"I drink water."

"Not in Clitherall you don't." She was right. There was a sign on the bathroom taps informing clients that the water was not potable, and the bar purchased their ice from Koep's gas station up the road. I'd heard it had to do with all the pesticides from the potato farms circling the town.

"True enough. Could I have a Diet Coke?"

She hung the cigarette from the corner of her mouth, grabbed a glass and a scoop of ice, and filled it. I slid her two dollars and looked away. She had this neat trick where she'd take your money and leave you change without you noticing. I preferred not to watch. I didn't want to discover her secret. I turned back, and the money was still there.

"This one's on me. You're covering the bands tonight?"

I thought about it. "I could try. It's up to Ron if he wants to run the story. Who's the opening band?"

"Iron Steel," said a hot voice in my ear.

I grimaced and pulled away. "Hi, Brad. I didn't see you here." Brad had been the boyfriend I'd left behind in Minneapolis, the one who looked like a blonde Jim Morrison, conversed like a kindergartner, and screwed like a mime. Unfortunately, the same vortex that had relocated me to Battle Lake had also caught him in its trap. We crossed each other's paths on occasion, but otherwise, I avoided him. I'd made peace with his cheating ways, but there's something about running into an ex that reminds you of every bad decision you've ever made.

He ran his fingers through his feathered hair. "I was tuning my bass. You here to check out my new band?"

"What happened to Not with My Horse?"

"We broke up. Creative differences."

"Uh hunh. Did they get tired of the techno polka fusion?"

"Doesn't matter." He pitched his voice so he sounded like a big-hair '80s radio dee jay. "I am now Iron Steel. Twice the metal."

"Where'd you find the new band?"

He looked around at his feet, the ceiling, the wall. He'd never been a good liar. Even when he'd cheated on me. "You know. Around."

"It's the same band, isn't it? Just a different name."

He appeared chagrined, then must have decided the expression was too much work. "Yeah. But we've reinvented ourselves. Totally different."

"Can't wait. If you'll excuse me." Carla was back at the bar and had lit a cigarette. I peeled myself away from Brad and sat next to her, and he returned to the stage to finish setting up his instrument. "Hi."

She glanced at me, looking bored. Her dishwater blonde hair was pulled back in a low ponytail. She'd made time for eyeliner, mascara, and lipstick, but they only served to accent her washed-out color. In general, she looked like life had rode her hard and put her away wet. "You know the band?"

"No," I lied. "Remember me? I was at the library the other night. When Clive came in and wrote the check."

"I remember you." She took a deep drag off her cigarette.

"I cashed Clive's check. It didn't bounce."

She raised her eyebrows. "Clive is a man of surprises."

"How long have you two been dating?"

"A couple months, maybe. It's not serious."

In the background, Iron Steel began to tune up. It sounded like scissors being sharpened. "The dating pool is pretty shallow here. But you probably know that better than me. You're from Battle Lake, right?"

"I lived here for awhile, went away for awhile, been back for a while." She looked around me at a group of twenty-something women who had just entered the bar, laughing loudly and made up for a night of fun.

"Yeah, I've only been in Battle Lake since last spring. I'm house-sitting for a friend. I'm actually neighbors with Clive."

"Excuse me." She stabbed her cigarette into the ashtray. As she walked off to take drink orders from the new arrivals, I noticed she was wearing elastic-waisted blue jeans, their waistband almost invisible under a baggy t-shirt. Despite the aura of exhaustion she emanated, I could tell she had a naturally trim figure under her shabby clothes. Maybe they were all she could afford. Her newest customers had seated themselves in the only large table in the room, off to the immediate right of the stage. I predicted they'd be asking for sweet and pretty drinks and settling for Malibu rum and diet colas.

Once she served them, Carla returned to her pack of cigarettes.

"Gonna be a busy night," I offered.

"Looks like."

"Do you have any kids?"

Her eyes raced to my face and seemed to look at me full on for the first time. The moment was tense, and then she laughed. "None worth keeping."

"What does that mean?"

"It means I don't want to talk about it. Why are you asking so many questions?"

"Making small talk." I nodded toward the stage, where Iron Steel was preparing to start. "I have a friend coming on after these guys, so I've got time to kill."

She seemed to take this at face value. "You got any kids?"

"Nope." I swiveled on my stool to knock on bar wood. "Can I ask you something? Out of curiosity?"

She tapped a long ash off her cigarette. "You want to know where Clive got the money, right? I don't blame you. I would too. Anyhow, it's no secret. He got it from the Fergus attorney. The same one who was at the library event."

I mentally ran through the guest list. I didn't know over half the people who were at the gathering, or what they did for a living. "What's the attorney's name?"

"You'd have to ask Clive." Another large group pushed through the door, this one co-ed, and Carla smashed out her second but certainly not her last half-smoked cigarette of the night.

I stayed long enough to hear Iron Steel's entire set, and I had to reluctantly admit that they weren't half bad. They were closer to 40 percent crap, which was an evolution for Brad. I wasn't staying to hear him, though. I was here for Johnny. He'd suffered through my gastrointestinal distress and still requested that I come and see him play tonight. I'd been running all day, starting with taking Peggy to church this morning—shoot, I'd only had enough time over lunch to run home and let the animals out and grab a sandwich. I knew I looked faded and stressed, but he'd seen me worse.

That's what I told myself until I saw him stride through the rear door of the bar, equipment in hand, oblivious to the appreciative stares he drew from the female crowd. Most of them were here to see Johnny, and I couldn't blame them. His thick hair curled around his ears, and the rosy cold on his cheeks turned his eyes so blue they glowed. It was his hands that made me weak in the knees, though, those strong-fingered, lean, lovemaking hands. I quickly swiveled in my seat and dug frantically in my purse for lipgloss. I had the wand to my lips and was pinching my cheeks to add color when I felt his hand on my shoulder. He slid his other hand on my cheek, chilled from the outdoors, and leaned in to whisper over the clamor of Iron Steel.

"You made it." His warm breath seemed to travel over my entire body.

I nodded, but he was too close to my ear to see it. He kissed the spot directly below my earlobe, and I quivered. He pulled back with a smile, nodded toward his equipment, and went off to set up. I was aware that I was now being stared at, an impotent lipgloss wand in my hands. I shoved it back into the container and ordered a refill on my beverage.

By the time his band was on stage, Bonnie & Clyde's was packed. I held my seat at the bar and admired from a distance as Johnny sang everything from smoky love songs to pulsing rock. On break, he took me by the hand and led me to the basement, smiling at the people who wanted to talk to him but not stopping until he had me at the bottom of the stairs, where he closed the door, pushed me gently against it, and kissed me like he meant it. I was able to stand seven full minutes of passionate petting before my hand went to his zipper. He pulled it away and moved it to his hard chest.

"Remember the rules," he whispered huskily.

"I can't even remember my own name."

He chuckled, a throaty sound that never failed to make me smile. He played his finger across my lips. "I have to go back upstairs. You're probably not going to stay through the whole second set, are you?"

I heard the hope in his voice, but he was a realist. He knew once I cooled off, I'd sense the danger of going home with him and flee. Still, I found myself wanting to share with him all that I was discovering, but it felt too intimate, and I didn't want him worrying about me. I walked him back upstairs, emotions and questions swimming between us, and slipped out the front door a few songs into the set.

TWENTY-SIX

SATURDAY MORNING, MY FIRST order of business was to call Lyle. I was going to find out who those other three Musketeers were. I had a hunch that one of them was Clive's generous donor. If my fledgling theory that Clive was dating the victim was correct, it would make sense that one of the Musketeers would bribe him to keep him silent about the facts of their horrible crime. Unfortunately, no one answered the phone at Lyle's. I got ready for work and drove to town to open up the library. The day was gray and heavy, a pillow of cold and dirt pressing down from the sky and making the air feel scarce. The temperature was hovering below zero, cold enough to sting, and I reconsidered the threat of the storm. It wouldn't be the snow that would bury us. It'd be the heavy, frozen air, too thick with ice to breathe in.

At work, I felt edgy, like I'd drank too much coffee and everyone was looking at me wrong. I tried Lyle again. No answer. I pulled out the Love-Your-Library guest list and crosschecked it for all the guests with a Fergus Falls prefix in their number. I came up with 23 names. After searching for those names online, I found that three were attorneys: Frederick Milton, Jason Paul, and Margery Flax.

I scratched out the work phone numbers of all three and gave each a call. None of them were in their office on a weekend, but their answering services were on duty. I was able to schedule an appointment with both Margery and Jason for Monday. Frederick's first free spot was next Wednesday. I made an appointment for that day, though I intended to drop by earlier. My plan was to get someone to cover my Monday shift at the library and run to Fergus to see if Julius would be willing to tell me who the Musketeers were, and then to meet with the available attorneys to discover which one had given Clive money, and why.

Lacking the focus to do anything productive, I researched the Internet for information on purity pledges. After last night's passion and very specifically discovering that my traitorous hands were set on hunting Mr. Happy, I was in the market for a mental chastity belt, or at least one that didn't leave a panty line.

My first hit, a site called "Pledge Power," creeped me right out. The website offered a two-part pledge, one for fathers to swear to fight the war for their daughter's virginity, and one for daughters who promised their fathers they'd keep their virginity intact for their husbands. The bottom of the page had a link for "secondary" virgins, the used-cars-with-a-heart of the virgin world, those of us who might have slipped and fallen onto a penis or two but who were trying to right our ways. I clicked on that link and was told that there was hope for me to revirginate, which seemed to belie the website's slogan that "once you slide, you can't hide."

I exited that page and returned to my search. After twenty minutes, I decided the purity pledge movement was predicated on a mixture of peer pressure and wishful thinking. I liked the emphasis on creating a relationship built on friendship, love, and romance instead of hormones, but none of the hits explained what to do once you had all that and still longed to get biblical with your boyfriend. Several pages offered a purity ring, but unless it slipped around both thighs at once, I didn't see how it would do me any good. Sigh. The day was getting worse. I closed the purity pledge sites and cleared my computer's history before ringing Lyle again. Still no answer. He must not be working today, and I wasn't willing to drive the 45 minutes to be sure. I'd try him again tomorrow.

Not knowing made me antsy, though, and I kept pacing the library in between helping patrons. It was during one of these stalk-fests to the front door that I noticed Clive's silver Mercury Cougar, a boat of a car, parked in the lot. Clive was behind the wheel, staring intently at me through the glass doors of the library. I pulled back, my heart racing. I'd never seen him in the library before, outside of the party he'd crashed last week. I made like someone was talking to me and turned away in imaginary conversation, scrambling to the computer as soon as I was out of sight of the door. A quick search proved that Clive Majors did not possess a Battle Lake Public Library account.

I glanced back toward the door, my mouth dry. Only one patron remained in the library, an older woman who was looking through the Westerns for her husband. Once she was gone, I'd be alone.

She set five paperbacks in front of me. "Is this all the Louis L'Amour you carry?"

"Let me see." I searched, saw that it was, and then pretended to scour the database for another five minutes.

"Are you finding it?"

"Computer's slow." I didn't want her to leave.

She pushed her library card toward me. "That's okay. This will be good for now."

"We have a lot of Western authors. Would you like to look at those, too?"

She shook her head. "He probably won't even open these. I keep hoping, but he's not much of a reader."

"Maybe I could help you find something. What do you like to read?"

Her smile drew tight. "Just these."

"You sure?"

"I have to get going."

I couldn't push it anymore without making her uncomfortable. I reluctantly checked out her books and then watched the cold-frosted front door. Five minutes passed, then ten. It was later in the afternoon, I began to think. Even if Clive did storm through that door, we wouldn't be alone for long. Not on a Saturday. It was our busiest day, even in this weather. Heck, maybe Clive had already gone home. Might as well check. I forced myself to the door in time to see him striding toward the library, his eyes burning, arms hidden behind his back.

TWENTY-SEVEN

I WAS TRAPPED. I rushed behind the counter to put furniture between me and him but that's all I had time to do before he ripped the door open so far the hinges made a scraping noise. He entered with such force that he pushed the icy blue smell of winter ahead of him.

He marched to the waist-high desk and leaned forward into it, his lips trembling and flecked with spit. "What are you sticking your goddamned nose into?" A greasy hank of hair fell into his face. He looked like a man unraveling.

I kept my voice steady. "I don't know what you're talking about."

"You were at my place." He slammed his hands on the counter.

The relief at finding out he was unarmed left my knees weak. "I told you that at the Love-Your-Library event that I was there. I was walking Luna and got lost. I stopped by again the other night to drop off cookies, but you weren't there that time, either."

He reached across to grab at my shirt and then drew back inches shy of my collar. His hand was shaking with whatever internal battle he was waging, and the smell of cheap whiskey and sweat poured off of him. "Goddamn it, that's not true! You looked in every window I own."

He must have more than one camera. "I'm nosy."

"You're stupid."

I couldn't disagree at the moment. And the situation was too dangerous to risk a lie. "I saw your pot operation, if that's what you're worried about. I didn't rat you out, and I'm not going to."

His eyes looked like sunken tar pits. I guessed it'd been a very long time since he'd slept. His voice slunk low into a snarl. "Because dead girls tell no tales?"

My fight kicked in and I leaned toward him across the desk, forcing him back a few inches. "Fuck you, Clive."

He nodded as if I'd commented on the price of potatoes. Then he looked away. His eyes couldn't settle on any one object, so they returned to my face. "You ever kill anyone?"

Under the counter, my hand had located a stapler, its cool metal riding in the curve of my palm. It wasn't much, but if I could shove it into his throat, it might be enough to get me free of the library.

"I have. I killed my goddamned best friend." His rabid eyes grew wet, and tears streamed down his face. "You fall asleep with that every night." He strode back out the door, across the parking lot, into his car, and drove away.

I watched him from the door, hot juice pumping through my adrenal glands. I forced myself to breathe deeply, but I couldn't stop the shaking. Clive was on a razor's edge, and he had targeted me as an enemy. I glanced at the clock. I had two hours left in my shift, and I didn't want to be alone. I ran back to the phone. I couldn't reach Jed or Kennie, and I wasn't going to call Gary or Johnny, so that was how Peggy ended up learning the ropes of the library system.

She came right away, for which I was grateful. I brushed off her question about whether I was feeling well and welcomed her self-involved chatter about her mojo, her medical conditions, her life. It kept me from needing to think my own thoughts. After I locked up the library, I agreed to walk with her to the Art of the Lakes, Battle Lake's eclectic and dynamic art gallery, because I wasn't ready to go home yet. Both she and I enjoyed the watercolors and fiber art, and I was happy to see one of Monty's glass swans on display, but Peggy still refused to be inspired. Since she agreed to watch the library for me on Monday so I could run to Fergus, though, I counted it a good use of the early evening. I was still too tense to eat, so I declined her offer of going out for supper, and we parted ways.

I considered cruising home for a night of mindless TV, but placing myself that close to Clive didn't sit well. I decided I could race over to Parkers Prairie and back in little more than an hour on the off chance that Lyle would be in. If he was, I could satisfy my curiosity about the identity of the Musketeers. If he wasn't, I'd hopefully have a better idea of where I was going to take Tiger Pop and Luna to spend the night.

When I arrived at the edge of Parkers Prairie it was nearly seven, and the handful of streetlights were shining a diffuse, silver glow. They each held either a Christmas wreath or a giant red and white candy cane strung with green garland, alternating one and then the other. The decorations gave the small town a cozy, welcoming feel. At Lyle's, the light was on in his office, but no customer cars were parked in the lot. I let myself in, noticing the usual disarray in the front room.

"Hello?" I didn't wait for an answer. I'd only said it out loud to be polite. I shoved my way through the door to the garage, the stress of today making me aggressive. "Lyle?"

I saw his legs pointing out near a brown van and stomped over. "It's Mira. And I'm not leaving this garage until you tell me who the Musketeers were. I can find it out myself, but it'd be easier if—"

The words caught in my throat and choked me. Lyle wasn't under the van. He was lying on his back next to it, two syrupy, brackish holes staining his jumpsuit. A pool of coagulating blood spilled out from underneath him like a lily pad. Both eyes stared up at the ceiling of the garage, filmy and unblinking.

TWENTY-EIGHT

I SCRAMBLED BACKWARD AND tripped over a dolly. I fell to the floor hard, twisting my left wrist. I whimpered. I was now on the same level as Lyle's corpse, and I was staring at the uneven tread of his work boots. One of his hands appeared relaxed, wading in a pool of his own cooling blood, but the other was clenched except for the pointer finger. It was aimed skyward. The coppery, salty smell of so much fresh blood gagged me. I turned away, retching, and vomited by the garage door. Shaking, I ran my mittened hand across my mouth.

I pushed myself off the floor. My eyes fought between pinning themselves to Lyle's dead body and scouring the cavernous garage for the killer. Every molecule in me hummed and bounced. My instinct to escape was strong, but I forced myself to grab a rag and wipe up my mess. Even though my hands were shaking so hard it made it difficult to grasp the cloth, I knew I couldn't leave my own bodily fluids at the scene. There was little more than foam to wipe up. I bunched the rag into the pocket of my coat and turned once more to look at Lyle. The rictus of his mouth suggested he'd died yelling, or maybe begging for his life. His skin was blue-tinged, and I knew it'd feel like marble if I touched it. My stomach turned again.

I backed toward the office, my eyes darting, trying to see everywhere at once. I had a horrible vision of Lyle's body rising, accusing me of leaving him last night to be murdered by the driver in the Jeep. His black-booted feet didn't so much as twitch, but that didn't calm me. The light in the office felt too bright, exposing me to a murderer who might be lurking just outside the door. I kept my back to the wall, feeling along the outdated candy machines, toward freedom.

RING.

The squeal of the phone made me jump and pee, one more than the other. The sound pinned me to the pop machine.

RING. RING. RING.

The silence that followed was terrifying. I was paralyzed. I felt shadows crawl toward me, inky oily fingers grabbing at my neck, slipping down my spine, pulling me into the grave. "Get out," I whispered to myself. "Get out of here." But the words wouldn't leave my throat. I felt a ridiculous safeness where I was, pinned in the light. Behind me was a dead body. Outside was maybe a killer. Here was safety.

But here I was an easy target. I pushed off the wall and toward the phone. I still had my gloves on. I picked up the handset and dialed 911 before the suffocating fist of fear gripped me entirely. "I'm at Lyle's in Parkers Prairie. Lyle's been shot. Dead. Send an ambulance and police."

I dropped the phone and ran for my car, but not before I saw the desk had been cleared to expose a single line of scribbling in today's box on the calendar: "5:00 FCM/$."

TWENTY-NINE

I MADE A BED in the corner of my closet and slept like a person who has made a bed in a corner of her closet. I knew I should have been a responsible citizen and stayed on the scene until the police arrived, but I couldn't. Once I had made it into my car and slammed the locks tight, my instincts drove me all the way home with only a stop at a gas station to deposit the smelly rag into the garbage.

The next morning, I was fuzzy-headed and blurry-eyed, but no longer cold-blood terrified. It helped that Luna and Tiger Pop were both attentive and reassuringly present. I ran a comb through my hair, splashed some water on my face, and drove to the Battle Lake Police station.

I'd spent more than my share of time in the squat brick building behind Lake Street. The windows were barred, ostensibly to retain the dangerous prisoners. The inside was sparse with one main room that visitors entered, a conference room to the right, a break room in back, and several holding cells off to the left. I was less than happy to find Police Chief Gary Wohnt bent over the keyboard at the main desk. Why couldn't one of his deputies have been working? He glanced up when I entered and immediately returned to what he was typing. Behind him, the Fleet Farm calendar was open to December, a photo of a horse-drawn sleigh featured above the dates. On the far side of the room, a Charlie Brown Christmas tree guarded three poorly-wrapped gifts, probably props. The soda machine hummed.

I figured I'd best start on neutral ground. "When do we get the grant checks?"

He continued to type. For some reason, his refusal to acknowledge my presence enraged me. It was the combined stress of my recent nearness to death and being stretched too thin. I strode to the filing cabinet off to the side of his desk. It was partially open. I yanked it out the rest of the way and began rifling through the files.

"What the hell are you doing?" Gary flew out of his chair and grabbed my hand as I was pulling out Anderson, Charles' file. His angry breath on my cheek smelled like peppermint and aftershave.

"Oh, you *can* see me. I wasn't sure." He was gripping my left wrist, the one I'd twisted last night. The pain was excruciating. I bit the inside of my cheek to keep from showing him how much it hurt.

"Put that back," he growled.

"I can't. You've got my hand."

Without letting go, he reached across with his free hand, plucked the file from mine, and reinserted it. "What do you want?"

I twisted so I could push a sharp elbow into his stomach. He neatly sidestepped my move but released my arm, returning to sit behind his desk.

I followed, sitting across from him. "I heard Lyle Christopherson was shot last night."

He flared his nostrils. His body was otherwise dangerously still. "Who's Lyle Christopherson?"

My heart thudded to a stop and the backlash of blood flooded my face. I forced myself to breathe. Either he was bluffing or this was all much larger and much more malignant than I had imagined. I chose the route of least screwed. "The guy who's dead body is in the county morgue in Fergus. The mechanic from Parkers Prairie. I heard it on the police scanner last night."

I really should get a police scanner. I bet I could pick up all sorts of interesting bits.

He selected a navy blue pen from the cup on his desk and click clicked the end. His eyes traveled like steel wool from my chest up to my face. "You don't look like you slept very well last night. Are you here to confess?" A taut muscle in his jaw jumped.

"I was at Lyle's recently. He put a new thermostat in my car and changed the oil." I watched for a reaction. I'd given the facts I thought Gary would uncover on his own without offering any information I hoped he wouldn't. Had I given him too much or not enough?

"That's a long drive for an oil change."

"The price was right."

Gary's eyes gleamed and the pen continued to click click. We'd been here before. He couldn't accuse me of withholding information without inadvertently uncovering some of his own.

The door opened behind me, letting in a cold sweep of air. I tensed, then shot a quick glance at Gary before turning to see who had entered. *I see how scared you are, make no mistake*, his eyes said. I wanted to tell him that this was actually progress because my pants were dry, but the agitated woman who blew through the door consumed my attention. She was older than me, close to Hallie's age by the dim of her hair and lines on her face, and her face looked puffy from crying. She acted like she'd been here before.

"My dad here?"

Gary stood. "You know he can't get out yet, Melissa. The judge hasn't set bail."

I looked from one to the other. I could tell by the set of his shoulders that Gary sorely wanted me to not be witnessing this.

"I'm not leaving without him."

I walked toward the holding cells. I knew going into that off-limits area would get me in a lot of trouble. Something about seeing a bloody corpse and peeing your pants resets the rules. The first cell was empty. So was the second. I didn't make it all the way to the third before Gary's arm clamped onto my shoulder like a metal vise, but I made it far enough to spot Clive Majors, both eyes blackened, slumped over on a bunk.

THIRTY

GARY LITERALLY KICKED ME out of the police station. I didn't fight it. I'd seen enough. I drove directly to Kennie's house, six blocks from the station. She was home, no longer orange or mustachioed, and looking like she'd just danced out of a beauty salon.

"Do you sleep in make-up?" I asked crossly, pushing past her. I'd never been in her house before and halted my forward charge in shock. The interior was done in shades of pink, the furniture was overstuffed, and the white shag carpet was thick enough to lose a hamster in. The air was redolent with a flowery perfume. The walls were covered with framed posters of kittens and butterflies. It was like being inside a Barbie dreamhouse.

"Do you brush your teeth?" she said acidly, directly behind my shoulder.

I considered. I actually hadn't that morning. That left me without a snappy comeback and even angrier for it. "How's your hair problem?"

"You wanna start over?" She indicated the door.

I collected myself. I technically was being an asshat, and that was supposed to be her responsibility. The role switch was uncomfortable. "Look, I'm sorry. It's been a bad 24 hours."

She fluffed her hair. "Just cuz someone stuck you in a toilet doesn't mean you should act like a turd."

"You ever take your own advice?"

"Rarely. Can I offer you some coffee, or did you just come to insult me before church?"

I took a deep breath. "Church isn't such a bad idea. I might be in the market for soul insurance, though it's a little late in life to take up another bad habit. In the meanwhile, any idea why Clive Majors is in jail?" Part of me didn't want to hear the response. If he'd been accused of Lyle's murder, that implicated me because I hadn't reported his crazy behavior earlier in the day.

She piffed. "The usual. DWI. It's his second since Tom died. His daughter should be down to bail him out any time now."

I played dumb. The role was feeling particularly well cast this weekend. "Clive has a daughter?"

"Her name is Missy. I graduated Battle Lake High with her."

"Where's she live now?"

"Alexandria. She's a home health nurse. Makes sense, since she grew up taking care of Clive. I heard talk that she's planning an intervention to get him into treatment. He hasn't been right since the accident."

I was trying to absorb the information Kennie was throwing at me. "Who's Missy's mom?"

Kennie cocked her head to glance backward along the time continuum. "I'm not sure anyone knows except Clive. Missy just showed up in kindergarten one day. He kept her clothed and fed, but I never saw a woman around, except those he'd date for awhile. Like Carla. Those two have been going strong for a few months now."

"You ever heard of the Four Musketeers?"

"The candy bar?"

"No, a Battle Lake gang back in the late fifties, early sixties."

She laughed, and then looked offended. "I'm not that old, and Battle Lake doesn't have gangs."

"I need a nap."

She watched me walk out the door. "A hairbrush wouldn't kill you either."

Needing to self-medicate, I stopped at the Apothecary to purchase a fistful of Nut Goodies and a Chia pet herb pig. *Sugar and gardening*, I thought. *I'll get through this with sugar and gardening.* I went home and got ugly.

THIRTY-ONE

MONDAY FOUND ME THREE pounds heavier and no wiser. I also realized that Hallie deserved to know what was going on. I was not unclear on that point. I just didn't possess the cojones to tell her all the bad news. I rationalized my cowardice by convincing myself that I only knew part of the story. She would naturally have questions, and she deserved answers. I needed the whole mess straight before I told her that her dear departed father had been murdered for a horrible crime he'd been a part of decades earlier, and that the murderer may not be through yet.

So I'd find her some answers. At least that was the plan. My first attempt was foiled when I visited the Fergus Falls nursing home to discover that Julius had been transported to the hospital to treat a recent case of pneumonia. He was currently in an oxygen chamber and not allowed visitors. I stopped by the hospital anyways to send up some flowers and a box of donuts. I was certain he wouldn't be able to eat them, but I hoped they'd give him a smile.

My next stop was the office of Jason Paul. I recognized him as the young African American who had attended the Love-Your-Library event. It turned out he was new to town and had never been to Battle Lake before or since the library celebration. I thanked him for his time and drove to Margery Flax's office. I had not forgotten the initials written on Lyle's calendar—FCM and a dollar sign. Clive had received a windfall from a Fergus Falls attorney. Lyle was possibly expecting money from someone with the initials "FCM." Two of the Fergus Falls attorneys on my list had the initials "F" and "M" in their names. I didn't need to be Nancy Drew to know that either my meeting with Margery or my meeting with Frederick was going to be very illuminating, and my money was on Frederick.

Margery turned out to be a busy woman who was in a constant state of motion, alternating between texting, searching on her computer, and writing on a notepad the whole time we were talking. She quickly established that I wasn't here as a potential client and got me straight to my point in an uncharacteristically—for Minnesota—straightforward manner.

"You were at the Love-Your-Library event, right?" She'd been on the guest list, but I didn't recognize her face.

She nodded while scribbling something on her desk pad and keeping one eye on her computer screen. "Briefly."

"Were you there at the end when a large donation was made to the library?"

"I came around 7:40 and left at 8:00. I had a dinner engagement with friends. Is that all?"

"You didn't write Clive Majors a check for $5,000?"

She snorted. "Not unless he's the guy who holds the mortgage on my house."

I felt embarrassed. I was obviously barking up the wrong tree. "Your middle name doesn't happen to start with a "C," does it?"

"My middle name is Jean. Now, if you'll excuse me." She glanced suggestively at the door.

I didn't see anybody waiting to break it down but I had no doubt her time was worth more than mine. I thanked her for it and drove to the office of Frederick Milton. According to the name on the sign, he was the senior partner in a law office of four. The thick carpeting and dark wood of the lobby suggested that they were doing just fine.

"I'm here to see Mr. Milton."

The pleasant-faced secretary smiled from behind the counter. "Do you have an appointment?"

"No, but he's expecting me."

Her nose wrinkled with puzzlement, but her smile stayed intact. "I'm afraid he's in court today."

"I'll wait." Before leaving Battle Lake, I'd called Hallie's attorney from the Litchfield Law Firm. I'd ostensibly called to turn in my billing for the week, but I'd also asked him about the three attorneys on my list. He'd heard of Margery and Frederick, but not Paul. He'd informed me that Margery specialized in family law and that Frederick was a business lawyer who rarely took a case these days. His focus was on running for county commissioner.

"Can I ask who's waiting?"

"Mira James. I'm a reporter with the *Battle Lake Recall*."

She nodded as if that made sense and typed on her computer. She looked up a few minutes later. "He'll be back within the hour. I might be able to squeeze you in, but he'd only have a minute or two."

"That's all I'll need." I spent the next two hours reading the Fergus Falls *Daily Journal*, then *American Lawyer*, and then *New American*. I was ready to slice my eyes out by the time I was finally ushered into a back office. I was unsurprised to find that I immediately recognized Frederick Milton as the lip-muff-sporting gentleman who had been chatting with Mitchell and retired Sheriff Mike at the library event, the one who couldn't take his eyes off of Clive. Pieces were falling into place.

"Ms. James. So nice to see you again. Were you waiting long?" He had stood to greet me, but the handshake he offered was little more than a mildly obscene brushing of his warm, flaccid palm.

"No," I lied. "I'm here to ask you some questions." We both sat. His suit wasn't cheap, but I couldn't shake the feeling that it hid scabs and scars underneath. It was a combination of his arrogant manner and greasy eyes.

"I assume for an article on my bid for county commissioner?"

"Okay. When did you throw your hat in the ring?"

He sat forward, stroking his mouth pelt like an old-school villain. "This past summer. You sure you don't want something to write with?"

"Memory like a steel trap." I tapped my noggin. "Do you know Clive Majors?"

Frederick's eyes narrowed. "I went to high school with a person with that name."

"Did you recently give him a chunk of cash?"

To my surprise, Frederick laughed. It was a rich, friendly sound. It almost made me want to smile, and I had a glimpse into the personal charisma that might get him elected to public office. "I've been donating money to a lot of charities lately. It's hard to keep track of them all. If you're looking for a scandal, though, I'm afraid you won't find one here. I did know Clive. Not well, but Battle Lake isn't so big that anyone's a stranger. He sold me a piece of land back in October. The deed just went through. The land is undeveloped, right on Bass Lake outside of town. I hope to build a summer cabin there, time willing."

I was sniffing around his corners, looking for the lie in his words, but they made sense on the surface. "What's your middle name?"

"My, you get around a conversation. It's Craig. What's yours?"

"Rayn." I stood and turned toward the door. "I'll show myself out." I was mad that I'd revealed my real middle name and even angrier that he'd had a smug answer, but I'd gotten my information. He was tied to this, no doubt, and a quick search of my bionic database would reveal the truth about his supposed land purchase. In the meantime, I couldn't shake the feeling that I'd just disturbed a rattlesnake.

THIRTY-TWO

When I returned to Battle Lake, I found Peggy had done a nice job with the library. In fact, she seemed entirely in her element helping people locate what they needed. Maybe she hadn't yet tapped into the type of inspiration she was looking for, but she seemed a lot happier than when I first met her. She asked to stay on until close. Together we shut down the library, but not before I went online to search land tract sales and confirm that Clive Majors had not sold and Frederick Craig Milton had not bought any land in the past ten years. Frederick was a slimy liar. That fact, combined with the check he'd written Tom's killer, on top of his initials placing him at the scene of Lyle's murder, strongly suggested that he was one of the original Musketeers. But why start killing off those tied to the rape after all these years? I had no answers.

When I got home after work, I discovered a phone bill and a postcard in my mailbox, the latter from Mrs. Berns:

Arizona is crap. Everyone around here says it's the grandest state in America, but calling your ass a turkey doesn't make it Thanksgiving. And there's old people everywhere you look. It's disturbing. Do you believe someone asked me to golf? Do I look like I'm dead? I'm coming home next Wednesday. Pick me up at the airport at 2:00, and you better have the case solved so you can tell me all about it.

　　—Your friend, Mrs. Berns

　　p.s. I got you a t-shirt.

I smiled. Inside, I gave Tiger Pop and Luna a strong dose of attention before tending to the blinking red dot on my answering machine.

Mira. It's Hallie. Call me. It's urgent.

Her voice sounded as if she had been exercising or crying or both. The record indicated she'd called a half an hour ago. I rang her up immediately.

"Mira."

Boy, caller ID was unnerving. "What's wrong?"

"Everybody at work is talking about a mechanic in Parkers Prairie who was shot last night. Was it the one my dad brought his car to? Lyle?"

I cursed my stupidity. Of course she would hear of Lyle's death. Small towns, small county. "Yeah. It was Lyle."

"I knew it!" She exhaled deeply on the other end, and her voice, when it came back on the line, contained a tremor. "It's connected to my dad's death. There's something else going on. What have you found out?"

"Nothing for sure," I said carefully. "I spoke with Julius, the man you were concerned had the original idea for Battle Sacks.

There's no axe to grind there. Your dad actually visited Julius regularly. They were friends. Your stepmom had nothing but good to say about Tom, as well."

"Did you find out why my dad brought his car all the way out to Lyle to get it fixed?"

"Lyle believed that your dad owed him, although he never said exactly what for. I'm still looking into that." I measured my options and decided to come at it from the side. "Would you know anything about the Four Musketeers of Battle Lake, a group of friends your dad would have hung out with in high school or right after?"

There was a pause at the other end of the line, then a laugh. The scoff in it was irritating. "Well, not just high school. They were lifelong friends. Mitch Courier, Fred Milton, and my dad were thick as thieves. He never called them the Musketeers, but I heard others refer to the group and put two and two together. My dad always tried to include Clive, too, but he never quite fit in. My dad didn't give up on him, though. He said they grew up together, went to school together, and would take care of each other until the end. Do you think Clive killing my dad had anything to do with the Musketeers? Jealousy over their connection, maybe?"

I slapped my forehead. All this running around to discover for her what she already knew. The best-laid plans of detectives and women ... "It's a possibility. Why didn't you tell me about the Musketeers?"

"You asked me for a list of people who might have it out for my dad. They were his friends."

Of course. "Can you think of anything else your dad was stressed about before he died, anything he said or something unusual he did?"

"He was stressed about my health. That's all we talked about the weeks leading up to his death."

"Ach. I'm an ass for not even asking. How are you feeling?"

"Pretty good, for someone with chronic kidney failure."

"Failure? I'm so sorry."

She made a dismissive sound. "It's not nearly as bad as it sounds. I'm in the early stages. The doctors say I could live for decades like this, with regular dialysis. I just need to manage my stress and diet. Of course, my dad didn't live long enough to hear that good news. He just knew my kidneys were failing. It was driving him crazy. I suppose that's another reason I feel like I need to uncover what happened. I was responsible for so much stress in his life. If it wasn't for Fred, Clive, and Mitch hunting and fishing with him and making sure he relaxed, he probably would have died of a heart attack any day now. The irony, right?"

The click in my brain was as loud as a femur snapping. The three letters that Lyle had written on his calendar right before he'd been shot in the chest were not the initials of a single person. They were the initials of the remaining Musketeers. FCM: Frederick, Clive, and Mitchell.

THIRTY-THREE

ANY DAY THAT STARTS with me driving to Alexandria, Minnesota, to buy sheer black nylons and a $14.99 pair of black pleather heels isn't going to end well. Or can only get better, if you prefer that your empty-headed clichés have rosy cheeks. On the drive to Alex, I'd contemplated what solving the FCM initials did for my case. If I was right, the three men had been on their way to pay off Lyle, but why now, so many decades after the crime? And why had they killed him instead? He'd already done the time. There was nothing new he could tell anyone. And how was Carla and Clive's relationship tied up with all of it?

I considered going to the police with what I knew, but they wouldn't believe my far-out accusations that an upstanding attorney who was now running for county commissioner, a wealthy hunt club owner with sterling connections to the law, and the owner of the most successful business in the county had raped a woman four decades earlier, framed another man for the crime, and intended to bribe him but then killed him instead. Oh, and that the fourth sometimes-member of the gang was now coincidentally dating the victim? Even if they believed all that, the circumstances still wouldn't connect to Tom's death, a connection which I couldn't even see clearly myself.

The problem was, the killers might not realize that I was still without answers, which placed me in the direct line of danger until I solved this crime. The men clearly weren't picky about offing anyone who stood in the way of their goal, whatever it was. Those pleasant thoughts carried me all the way through the shoe store, to the front counter to purchase my little iron maidens, and back to the hunt club, which was so busy that I had instructions to park in a plowed field across the road, from which point I would be shuttled to the main lodge.

When I'd first poked into the main lobby, I was worried that I was going to run into Mitchell and be kicked out on my bumper, but the place was humming like a hive and it was easy to blend in. That left me time for a new worry: the skanky "uniform" that I'd been handed as I entered the changing room, a large closet designated as our private area, my new shoes and nylons in a plastic bag dangling from my hand. When I unfolded the uniform, I realized that the skirt that was supposed to reach my knees would have, if I were five. The tight red sweater was a fake-fur-trimmed and low cut v-neck designed to display cleavage, but here the joke was on them: I didn't have any. Ha.

The Fates intervened before I got too cocky, though, revealing that I'd accidentally bought control top nylons. I'm not saying that I didn't have a top to control. I'm saying that the top of these nylons was better suited to choking a snake than supporting my lady parts. Once I'd slid the nylon vise grip over my belly, did the knees-out wedgie bend to align the pantyhose so they weren't cutting off all the blood to any one area, and yanked on the sweater and the skirt, I had only to slide into the two-inch heels and walk out to get my serving directions. Easy peasy.

"Whoa, have you been drinking?"

I stabbed a look at the woman who'd spoken. She was short, maybe 5'2", but she had enough boobage for the both of us. "No. Why?"

"Weak ankles, then?" She pointed at my feet, her expression sympathetic.

"I don't understand."

"Honey, you're walking like a dog with shit on its feet."

I took in the ridiculousness of my body from the neck down. If 13-year-old boys ruled the universe, this is what we'd all be required to wear. The women, anyhow. The guys would be in t-shirts, blue jeans, and laser-gun belts. "It's been a while since I wore heels."

"When you say 'a while,' what do you mean?"

I thought. "Maybe since the fifth of Never."

"That's what I figured. Here. Let me show you how."

I spent the next ten minutes receiving a crash course in stilt walking. The woman, Connie was her name, started out with big, "heel-toe, heel-toe" aspirations for me, but it turned out she was a realist, too. She ended up showing me how to keep everything stiff from the knee down and shuffling forward. It wasn't pretty, but it was an improvement from my Frankenstein stomp.

"That looks fine, honey. No one is going to look at your feet anyhow, not with those legs and that face. And I have one more thing."

Before I could object, she pressed a shot glass against my lips. I smelled peppermint and felt the hot liquid brushing my mouth like a lover, and damn if I didn't take it in one swallow. It burned on the way down and brought its heat all the way to the edge of my toes. I smiled.

"That's right. That's our health plan in the waitressing world. Every break you get, take a swig of that. It's ours to enjoy back here in the changing room." She patted me reassuringly on the back. "It'll make all your customers smarter."

She shoved me out the door, where I was assigned my role. Some of us Santa babies were put on hors d'oeuvre duty, some were "conversationalists," and others were cocktail waitresses. The woman I took to be Mitchell's wife, Maggie, assigned us our positions. She was thin-lipped, short-haired, and down to business. Based on my past waitressing experience and the scowl on my face, she assigned me cocktail duty, shoving an empty tray, a pen, a pad, and a swirl of cocktail napkins into my hands.

The main dining hall had been converted into a winter wonderland, all fake puffs of snow, twinkle lights, and glass ornaments. There were easily a hundred and fifty guests, and I had counted 15 Santa babies. The majority of guests were male, though many of them had brought their wives or girlfriends, and a sprinkling of women seemed to be there on their own, or at least comfortable with their own company. I recognized faces from the Love-Your-Library event, but had yet to spot Mitchell, Clive, or Frederick. Three doors down from the main dining room was the Men's Smoke Room, the one with the secret chamber. Whenever I started to waver in my heels, I remembered that room, and the fact that I was only waiting for an opportunity to scope it out. Tying Mitchell to Lyle had only upped the ante.

Someone grabbed my arm. "Vodka tonic, two limes."

"Sure." I nodded over the strains of Dean Martin crooning "The Little Drummer Boy." "Be right back." *And if I'm not, feel free to complain about the woman dressed like Playboy Santa*, I thought, as I wove my way into the crowd. I thought I caught a glimpse of Mitchell in a blue dress shirt and tie, but the crowd closed in before I could make my way to him.

"Can we get two whiskey sours, and a glass of red wine?"

"Sure." I kept moving. I'd be forced to fetch drinks for some people, or my night would be over too soon. At the bar, I put in my orders. The bartender, a lantern-jawed, buzz-sawed blonde at least five years younger than me, slipped me a clear shot of liquid as he whipped up the drinks. I swallowed it, and I'm pretty sure it made my boobs a little bigger. I chose not to consider the implications of falling off the wagon. It was just a single night, not a habit.

"Thanks." I brought the drinks to their respective owners and was surprised when I was handed a $10 tip. Out of habit, I folded the bill in half the long way and then folded it in half again over the pointer finger of the hand bracing the tray. I'd forgotten how nice it was to have people hand you money. After that, I began to take drink orders with a vengeance. I caught snatches of conversation as I threaded through the crowd, most of it authoritative rants about what was wrong with the tax system, the health system, the education system. The only areas off limits seemed to be the military, Wall Street, and religion, as long as we were talking Christian. I swear I felt the invisible hand of capitalism pinch me on the butt at one point. I was in the belly of the beast, surrounded by a cadre of gun-loving, money-making white guys who could turn on me at the drop of an olive. But man, they tipped great when I brought them the right drinks.

One hour and three hundred and seventy dollars in tips later, Mitchell was the only one of my three targets that I'd spotted. He was bellicose, flushed with good cheer, and greeting people like a Mafia don. I did spot Mike, the retired sheriff, and stopped to say hi. Other than him, and the rich folks I recognized from Love-Your-Library, tonight's attendees seemed almost entirely to be out-of-towners. Clive hadn't shown, and my feet felt like bloody stumps. I hunted down Connie, told her I needed a break, and asked her to cover for me. I stopped at the changing room to down a shot, stuff my wad of tips into the tourniquet of my nylons, and then slip into the hallway.

Directly across from me were the restrooms. I used the ladies' room, slipped my heels off on the way out, and made my way to the Men's Smoke Room. I walked like I had a purpose, and damn, it felt good to get those shoes off. If someone stopped me, I'd say I was lost. The only people currently in the hall were here to use the restroom, though, and they had no reason to question an employee. I vanished into the unlit smoke room.

The smell of rich cigars overlaid the mildewed scent of old books. My eyes quickly adjusted to the dimness, the only illumination spears of moonlight filtering in through the half-closed curtains. I grabbed a lighter off the nearest table and strode to the bookcase that hid the secret room. I knew Scooby Doo would lean against the bookshelf in frustration and accidentally trip the switch to open the door, so I tried that. No luck. Maybe I shouldn't have downed that last shot. Next I tried pulling out combinations of

231

books, but it wasn't until I slid my hand under the bottom of each shelf in desperation that I happened upon the recessed button.

I shoved my finger into it, and the catch on the secret door released. Instead of swinging open, the door sighed and fell slightly ajar. I slipped into the room and pulled the door almost shut but not so tight that it would latch. The utter darkness was disorienting and made me hyper-aware of the smells of cheap perfume and tobacco. I flicked the lighter. My first glimpse showed a smaller version of the library I'd just left, maybe fifteen by fifteen with shelves lining the wall and a couch and chairs in the center, and in the circle of the furniture, a coffee table strewn with what looked like reports of some kind. On the other side of the room I spotted a mounted, flat-screen TV large enough to make a football fan weep, and then the flame died. I flicked it again and this time held it.

"Phoo-ey," I whistled, making the sound because I couldn't whistle. Glancing around, I realized I'd stumbled on the Library of Physical Congress. Surrounding me were the spines of possibly the grossest films ever conceived. I peered at the shelf nearest me: *Days of our Vibes, The Young and the Breastless,* and *Thighnasty.* Out of curiosity, I tugged one out to look at the cover. Out of disgust, I pushed it back in.

My thumb was growing hot from the lighter, so I released the tab and navigated by memory to the table I'd spotted in the center of the room. Was this secret room a complete waste, just a porno fort? I bumped into the main couch and fell into it. The furniture felt like leather, which I believed was a questionable choice given the viewing material in here. Around me, the darkness closed in like fingers.

I felt along the sofa until I stumbled on the table, and I knelt down beside it. I tapped the wheel of the lighter with my thumb. Still hot. I'd decided to sit there until it cooled when I heard the soft thump of laughter being absorbed by thick walls. My stomach clenched. That was the first sound I'd heard since I'd been in here. Could it be coming from the main dining hall? Then it came again, only this time I could make out words.

"Party … ever … scrooged …

There were people in the smoking room! I was trapped like a raccoon in a garbage pail. If they decided to come in here, there was nowhere to hide, at least for any length of time. My best bet would be to sneak closer to the wall by the door, which would poise me to dart out should they make their way into here. If I kept my head down and ran fast, they might be so surprised that they wouldn't remember any details other than the Santa Baby costume. I crawled toward the door, then, on a whim, returned to the center table to grab a couple sheets of the reports I'd seen there. I folded them into my nylons, barely, and made my way back to the door. I slowly eased into a standing position and tuned my ear into the conversation in the Men's room, which was trickling in clearly through the crack I'd left in the door.

"… ever change, do you?" asked a whiny voice.

"Why would I?" I recognized Mitchell's deep baritone immediately. "Life's worked out pretty well for me so far!"

"We all knew it would," said a third voice. "So you gonna let us in that hidden room of yours for some adult viewing, or is that only for the rich guys from the Cities rather than your ol' classmates from Brandon High?"

"Help yourself. I'll join you after the party dies down."

My heart placed a call to my stomach, and they agreed it was a good time to drop. I pressed my back hard enough into the wall to leave marks.

"The button is here." The closeness of Mitchell's voice smacked me like ice water. He couldn't have been more than three feet away, on the other side of the wall. "Dammit, it's already open. Maggie said she'd get that fixed."

Dim light poured into the room. I could make out the lighter I'd left on the table when I'd grabbed the papers. My own mortality brushed against me like a puff of wind.

"You know how to work a DVD player?"

The man with the whiny voice backed in. "Sure, if I can find the lights."

"They're out here." I heard a click, and then I was lit up like a firefly.

"Mitchell." Maggie's voice. "Someone wants to talk with you. Big bucks."

"Coming."

I heard his heavy footsteps, or it may have been the drumming of the blood in my ears. And then the whiner turned and caught sight of me. His expression was astonishment followed by pleasure spreading across his mousy features. He was about my height and soft-looking, the perfect vehicle for his petulant voice. "Hello, Santa," he said, smiling.

I prayed three long strides had already taken Mitchell out of the smoke room. I held up my hands like I was jumping out of a cake, my slingback heels still laced through the fingers of one hand. "Surprise!"

"I'll say. Jerry, come here. This room has a secret center!"

The other guy poked his head in. They were both variations on a theme—the sandy-haired, beer-bellied, small-town guy with bland features and a big heart, if you asked his wife and kids and if they didn't know he was visiting a porno room.

"What can I get you two to drink?"

Whiner smiled. "Coors light. One for Jerry, too. You'll come right back?"

"You betcha," I said. I felt a little sorry for them, despite the proclivities that had brought them to this room. I bet they felt as out of their element at the party as I had. From what I'd caught of their conversation, they were hometown guys calling in a favor, not hunt club regulars.

I couldn't hide the surge of relief I felt when I exited the secret room. I wasn't safe yet, but I let my breath trickle more naturally. The Men's Smoke Room reeked of freshly lit cigarettes, and a partially extinguished ember glowed orange in the darkness. I tried to walk naturally, heels in my hand, but all the paper crowding my nylons was chafing against my skin. I didn't dare to move fast until I was at the door, when I dashed out. Free at last.

"What the hell were you doing in there?"

My eyes shot to the right. Maggie was barreling down the hall toward me, looking mightily displeased.

"Ah, getting drinks for a couple guests."

Her eyebrow raised. "They're in there now?"

"Yes."

She wasn't entirely buying it, but her options were limited. If I was telling the truth and she went in there to check, she ran the risk of embarrassing a client. If I was lying and I'd been in there snooping or stealing, I was out now, and there weren't many places for me to hide stuff. "Get back to work. I'll wait for them to come out."

"Thanks," I said. And I walked directly to the changing room, swapped out heels for Sorels, grabbed my clothes, and jogged to my car.

THIRTY-FOUR

"THOSE ARE BOOKIE SHEETS."

Curtis sat across from me, the steel-gray sky of the storm finally on us. His window blinds were open, but there was little light to allow in, even though it was only 4:00 in the afternoon. I'd had Peggy watch the library for me so I could run to the Battle Lake Senior Sunset during visiting hours. If anyone would know what the number-scribbled sheets I'd pinched from the hunt club meant, Curtis would. He was the town's memory. Many people wrote him off because he was pushing 100 and fished off the roof of the nursing home whenever he could sneak out, but one look into his ice-blue eyes and you knew he was fully in possession of his faculties.

"Gambling? What kind?"

"Can't be sure. Looks like football based on the numbers, but it's all in code. It'd be impossible to say."

"Is it legal?"

"How many of these sheets did you see?"

"At least fifty, I'd say."

"Gambling on that level would get a person in a lot of trouble in Minnesota. If any money is changing hands, that is. You see the initials in this first column?"

I nodded.

"Those are likely the gamblers. These here numbers are the teams—VKS could be the Vikings and SKS might be the Sea-hawks—and these are the points. This last column covers the amounts. This appears to be a profitable business. These sheets alone are worth tens of thousands of dollars."

I ran my finger down the first column of the three pages I'd stolen. It wasn't until the third that I saw it: FCM, Frederick Craig Milton. "What would you do with these sheets if you were me?"

"You friends with the people they belong to?"

"Nope. I'm actually feeling a little poorly toward them."

"Then I'd bring them to the police. That is, if I wanted to an-swer a lot of questions about how I acquired them." Curtis winked at me and then cocked his head toward the window. "You best run home and pick up some candles and nonperishable food on your way. I've seen a lot of storms, but none with teeth like this one. Once she bites down, she's not going to let up for days."

The slate of the sky reflected off his eyes, turning them as gray as mercury. I shivered. "That's good advice. Thanks." I stood and kissed him on his forehead.

I was almost out the door when he stopped me with a ques-tion. "When is Mrs. Berns coming back?"

"Soon. Next Wednesday."

"Good. It gets too quiet around here without her."

I smiled and left him by the window, shaving wood off a stick with his pen knife. I knew he'd hide both if a caregiver poked her head in.

Outside, the weather was a sterling haze, thick with unshed snow. I sniffed the air. The clean pre-scent of a blizzard was strong. Curtis was right. All smart people would go home and wait this one out. I couldn't do it, though. I sensed I was close to something big, but I didn't know how to string all the clues together. Was the gambling operation tied to the two murders? If so, how? It didn't help matters that I was hungover from three shots of schnapps. Like a bad one-night stand, I was trying to put it behind me, but I was ashamed. I needed someone to make me feel better about my bad choices. I cruised to Sid and Nancy's, but they'd closed up early. The sign on their door said, "Snow Coming. Stay Safe."

I could go around the back and ring the bell wired to their living quarters on the second floor, but I didn't want to bother them. They got so little time off together. With Mrs. Berns gone, that left only one option. The Glass Menagerie. A light was on in the front window across the street. The first snowflake fell as I crossed. It was huge, as puffy as a pillow and trembling with the news: a storm was coming.

Mrs. Berns had once said of Jed that he'd have a hard time stacking boxes to reach a banana. He wasn't the most linear thinker, that was true, but maybe that was exactly what I needed right now, someone to help me tackle this puzzle from an unconventional angle. The sign in the storefront window said "Closed," but the front door was unlocked. I let myself in, accompanied by the fairy song of door chimes. I made a beeline toward the shelf of glass sea creatures.

"Can I help you?"

I turned, startled. "Hi, Monty. I stopped by to see Jed. Is he here?"

"Naw." He wiped his hands on a towel streaked with bright colors and dingy black ash. "He's working. Battle Sacks." The acrid smell of the furnace dominated the air.

"Shoot! That's right."

"Something I can help you with?"

I took in his ever-present rainbow pompom hat, worn flannel shirt, and frayed jeans. His hands were scarred and dirty with hard work. "How good are you with puzzles?"

He smiled. "Not very. I'm better with sandwiches. You eat yet?"

I considered lying, but my stomach mutinied and let out a growl. "Not yet. I don't eat red meat, though."

"You're in luck. Neither do I. How does a hummus on pita bread with lettuce, tomato, and black olives sound?"

"Like the best proposal I'll get in this lifetime."

He chuckled. "Good enough. I just have to shut down my work in back."

I followed him to the rear door, fascinated and yet repelled by the hellish glow of the furnace. When Monty leaned in to adjust the knobs, it cast his face in red. "Storm coming," I commented, to get my mind off the vision.

"This'll just take a minute." He turned, closed the nearest canisters, and returned tools to drawers before leading me upstairs.

"Do you live here, too?"

"Yup. One half is a one-bedroom apartment. The other half is an efficiency. I get the efficiency." He led me into his one-room living space, a neat arrangement with a bed, a bookshelf, a tiny kitchen with a table and four chairs, and a door to what I presumed was a bathroom. "Have a seat."

I obliged and watched him whip up the best sandwich I'd ever eaten in my life. It was the perfect mixture of creamy and crunchy, sweet and salty, with a solid umami flavor in the hummus. "Did you make this yourself?"

"From scratch. I even boil the beans. Care for a beer?"

Outside, huge snowflakes were scratching softly at the window, pausing to take in every view they could before they fell to the ground forever. Although it had left me feeling guilty, the schnapps last night had tasted good. A beer with this sandwich would be even better. I could schedule time next week to think about the implications of both. "Do you have potato chips?"

"Only plain rippled, lotsa salt."

Shame is for sissies. "I'm in."

He leaned back in his chair, grabbed a silver bag from the nearest cupboard, and tossed it to me. Then he stood to pull two Heinekens out of the fridge, popped their caps with the edge of a lighter, and passed me one. I took a deep swallow, letting the rich, bitter liquid coat my tongue before swallowing.

"I see you're a fan of beer."

I opened my eyes. "Haven't had one in a while."

He nodded as if he understood, and went back to his sandwich. He'd done a lot for me. He'd saved me from an ice cubing when we'd first met and nurtured Jed's creativity and responsibility. I popped a potato chip in my mouth. "When you were in high school, do you remember hearing about a group of guys who called themselves the Four Musketeers?"

"Sure." He drank an inch of beer. "Everyone knew about the Musketeers. Tom Kicker was one of them. That why you're asking?"

"Yeah. What were they like?"

He considered my question, playing with his beer cap. "Young. Entitled. All of them except for Clive was the son of a rich man. Nothing special in any of them, that I saw. I suppose none of them moved very far away from here. This area's been good to them."

"You know where Clive and Tom ended up. Mitchell inherited his dad's hunt club over by Millerville. Frederick ended up a lawyer in Fergus."

Something flashed in Monty's eyes. "Frederick? You mean Freddy 'Fingers' Milton?"

"I suppose."

"He added some respectable syllables to his name to distance himself from his shoplifting days, then."

"He's running for county commissioner."

Monty sighed. "That's the way that works. Let's hope he's a changed man."

"I'm not sure," I said, the beer warming my belly pleasantly. "Were you around in 1962 when the girl was raped?" I recounted the story and filled him in on my belief that three of the Four Musketeers had been responsible for the attack, and that Clive was now dating the woman they'd assaulted. The more I talked, the quieter Monty grew. When I finished, he was gripping his green bottle so tightly I was afraid it'd shatter.

"You need to warn Carla. Now."

The urgency in his voice tripped my panic wire. "You think she's in danger?"

"Your theory has a hole. A hole big enough to drive a truck through. Clive was no innocent to that attack. They didn't call them the Four Musketeers for nothing."

"But that makes no sense. Why would he date a woman he'd attacked?"

"You've met Mitchell, Clive, and Freddy. Right? And you know of Tom and Lyle. How would you describe the first three?"

"Mitchell and Frederick make my skin crawl. Clive may be a good guy, but he's made a lot of bad choices."

"Would you call him easily influenced?"

I thought back to what I knew of him. "I'm not sure. You probably know him better than me."

"Then neither of us knows him well. What's your take on Tom and Lyle?"

"Tom was a saint, by all accounts. Lyle was rough around the edges, but he didn't send up any red flags."

"Exactly. From what you've told me tonight, Clive, Tom, and Lyle were the weak links. If someone wanted to make sure the story of the rape was buried forever, say someone running for county commissioner who had to make sure his ugly past didn't find him, he'd need to deal with those three. He bribes Clive to shoot Tom and then Lyle. Once Clive's in that deep, he'll never talk. That leaves only one person who could ever damage Frederick or Mitchell."

My stomach tightened into a fist. "Carla."

"Do you know where she lives?"

"No, but she's probably at work." I glanced toward the window. The snow was swirling as thick as fog. "Can I use your phone?" I dialed Bonnie & Clyde's. It rang, and rang, and rang. There was no

243

answering machine. I wasn't surprised that Ruby didn't own one. If she was too busy to answer, she'd figure the person could call back. I hung up after the twelfth ring.

"No answer?" he asked.

I shook my head and looked toward the window again. I could no longer make out the street lights.

He grimaced. "You want me to drive?"

"It'd save you from pulling me out of the ditch later."

We both bundled up and headed to his old Ford pickup, the safest tank in the Minnesota arsenal. The drive to Bonnie & Clyde's was tense. When we arrived, the parking lot was jammed with snowmobiles fast becoming drifted over with hungry snow. Inside, the place was crawling with sled riders, bulky in their snowsuits open to their waists, drinking with the fervor of someone who doesn't think they'll need to drive home. I elbowed my way through, ignoring the greetings from those who recognized me from the library. The smell of melting snow and two-stroke fuel was strong. When I finally caught Ruby's attention, she said Carla had the night off and gave me directions to her house.

Monty barreled along the dirt roads. I held on to his dashboard to keep from flying against the passenger door. I loved my Toyota, but she wouldn't have stood a fighting chance in this white-out. We already had over two inches of snow accumulation, and the storm hadn't even tuned its piano. The swirling white was disorienting, blanketing everything equally so the unplowed road blended with the ditch.

Carla's was the last house on a dead end road, an ugly single-wide trailer in a copse of scraggly elms. Her rusted Buick was a car-shaped snow sculpture leading to the front door. I felt a respite from the panic that had been riding me here. There were no foot-prints in the snow, no tracks in the driveway. Carla could be home safe, riding out the storm.

I hopped out of the pickup and waded through the snow to the front entrance. I had to kick aside a drift to yank open the screen door. No one answered my insistent knocking. I tried yelling, but no response.

"No." Monty peering through the front window, hands cupped around his eyes.

I jumped off the steps and waded over next to him, disregarding the scratching skeleton of a rose bush. I had to perch on tiptoes to spot what he saw. All around the main room was the evidence of a struggle—a plant fallen to the floor, its black dirt spread out like a fan, a broken glass, a shelf tipped over. In the middle of the mess sprawled Carla, motionless, her arm twisted underneath her.

THIRTY-FIVE

I SCRAMBLED BACK ONTO the steps and tried the door. Locked. I felt the top of the frame for a spare key and only succeeded in bringing snow down on my head. Monty pushed me aside and put his shoulder to the door. It didn't budge. He ran back to his truck and returned with a crowbar, which he slid between the lock and the door jamb. He grunted and gave it a heave. The entrance gave way. He rushed in with me on his heels. We flipped Carla over, gently. Her dishwater-blonde hair was matted to her face, and her mouth was slack. Unconscious and without her make-up, she looked much younger, vulnerable.

"She's breathing," he said.

"Are there any wounds?"

"Not that I can see." He patted her face lightly. "Carla."

She moaned and shifted her head away from his hand.

"Her neck seems to be okay. Let's get her on the couch."

I bent forward to help. "Cripes. Her breath smells like 100-proof rubbing alcohol."

Monty nodded grimly, checking her face and arms for bruises and finding none. "You better put some coffee on. I'd say she wasn't attacked. She's on a fall-down drunk bender."

Disgusted and relieved, I did as he suggested. I found the kitchen in the same state as the living room. I picked up as best I could while the coffee brewed, closing cereal boxes and stashing them in the cupboard, loading the dishwasher, wiping off counters. I knew how demoralizing it is to wake up painfully hung over with a messy kitchen to boot. When I returned with a steaming cup of brew, Monty had the front door closed and Carla awake, more or less.

"Here you go." I handed her the mug. She took it, bleary-eyed, just another small town gal who drank too much. "Sorry about your lock. We thought you were dead."

"Then what was your hurry?" She took a sip of the coffee. It was hot enough to burn her lips, but she didn't flinch.

I didn't see a reason to mince words. "I know your story. About what happened in '62. I think you're in danger now because of it."

She shot me a face so comically puzzled that I'd have laughed if it wasn't for the seriousness of the situation. "Hunh?"

"In 1962, a Battle Lake woman was raped. The Four Musketeers were there that night, but a guy named Lyle Christopherson ended up going to jail for the crime. The woman was never identified in the papers."

"And you think I'm her?"

"You're not?" Monty asked.

She laughed, and it turned into a smoker's hack. She took the reminder to heart and grabbed for a crumpled pack of Merit cigarettes. "No. I know the story too, but it's not mine. Clive told me all about it during one of his more talkative drinking sprees. He was one of them Musketeers. All four of them did wrong by that girl. Every one of them, including Tom Kicker. Clive made a point of saying Tom wasn't in on the worst of it, but he wasn't no prince either, not like he wanted people to believe. Clive said Tom tried to buy his way into heaven every day after that, whatever the hell that means."

I slanted my eyes at Monty. He'd been right about all four of the Musketeers being involved, including Clive. He was standing, tense, his fists clenched at his side.

"So Clive admitted to the rape? Did he tell you the four of them let another man go to jail for it?"

"He never mentioned that."

"Who was the girl?" The question rose like thunder from Monty's chest.

"It wasn't me, and that's all I know for sure. Is there any more coffee?"

I took her mug and brought her back a refill. When I returned, Monty was at the front window, watching the snow channel. I sat next to Carla. "Did Clive ever talk about shooting Tom?"

"God, no. That's a subject we did not touch."

"Do you think it was an accident?"

She checked out my face. "Of course it was. Tom was Clive's only steady friend. It was a terrible accident. It was a tragedy for Clive and a sad day for the whole damn county. Tom did good by people around here. I suppose it's the worst for his girl though, Hallie. I feel terrible for her, losing her dad like that and with no mom. Without her real mom, I mean. Clara."

My heart felt as if a cold wet thread was being drawn slowly out of it. "What did you say?"

"Clara. Hallie's birth mom."

THIRTY-SIX

"CLIVE MENTIONED HER ONCE or twice. Her name's real close to mine, is I guess why it stuck. I just think it's a shame that a woman can lose her father and be in and out of the hospital like that poor Hallie, and with her mother no longer around to comfort her. She died giving birth to Hallie. I'm sure her stepmom did just fine, but there's nothing like your real mom when life gets hard."

I'd tuned her out after I heard the name. Catherine, Tom's ex, hadn't been certain of the name of the girl who had been raped. Carla, she'd thought. She'd been real close. *Clara.* Tom had married his victim and raised her child as if she were his own. *Clive said Tom tried to buy his way into heaven every day after that, whatever the hell that means.*

Monty was at my side. "What is it?"

"We have to go." Numb, I wandered outside. The air smelled a bit like steel, and the icy edges of plummeting flakes scratched at my cheeks. There was a total hush in the jaws of the snowstorm, an absence of sound that raised my hackles. Tom had told Catherine part of the truth, which is the main ingredient of all good lies. Clara had been pregnant by the rape, and a man had married her and raised the daughter. What he hadn't told her, of course, was that he was the man.

Monty followed me, making sure that Carla's front door closed tightly before jogging ahead to start the truck.

When I climbed into the vehicle, he told me he felt bad about her door. I didn't care. "Monty, I had it all wrong."

"It was an honest mistake. I'll come back out tomorrow and fix it, when the snow lets up." He started the truck and steered us onto the back road.

"No, I know the identity of the woman who was attacked. Her name was Clara, not Carla. Tom Kicker's first wife and Hallie's mom."

An icy shoulder caught the truck and began pulling it into the ditch, but Monty fought back with a sharp turn of the wheel. "Tom Kicker married the woman he raped?"

"We don't know whether or not he raped her. You heard Carla. Clive said Tom wasn't in on the worst of it, although it appears he didn't do anything to stop it, either."

"Holy terror," he said. "What men will do."

I rubbed my mittened hands together. It had grown cold in the cab. "The others must know that Tom married Clara, and that one of the three of them has a daughter."

"That'd be a difficult fact to hide. So why kill Tom and Lyle now?"

Why is it that the truth is so obvious once you know it? "I told you Hallie's in and out of the hospital."

"Right. Kidney problems."

"Yeah. She said she's in the early stages of kidney failure."

Monty closed his eyes in understanding. "She needs a kidney."

"I'm guessing. And if I'm not mistaken, family is the first place you'd look for a donation." I wanted to smack my own head. "She'll find out soon if she doesn't know already that Tom isn't her birth father."

"Not her birth father, but the man who raised her. If he loved her, he'd need to tell her who her other potential matches would be."

"Which explains the fight Hallie overheard between Tom and Clive, right before Clive shot Tom."

Monty picked up the thread of my story. "Clive must have gone to Frederick and Mitchell to let them know what was in the pipeline. They pool their money and convince Clive to shoot Tom and then Lyle, leaving only the victim as their weak link. Clara. But she's already dead."

"You think they'll stop there?"

"I wouldn't. Not if I'd come this far. Hallie may know about the incident, or find out one day. As long as she's alive, she's walking DNA proof of something three men have already killed to keep silent."

"How fast can we get to Hallie's place?"

"I'm on it."

THIRTY-SEVEN

FROM A DRIVING PERSPECTIVE, the only positive of a screaming blizzard is that it keeps everyone else off the highway. Even so, Monty crawled along at 30 mph, using the occasional road sign as visual evidence that we were still on the road and not four-wheeling through some field. Both of us leaned forward tensely, our heads unconsciously trying to arrive at our destination as soon as possible.

Monty stabbed on the radio.

"... worst blizzard of the decade. Mn/DOT has shut down Interstate 94 from Fargo to St. Cloud. If you don't need to be on the roads..."

He punched the button again to drown out the sound. "I'd pay money to be able to tune in a jazz station around these parts."

"You could get a portable CD player, maybe." He didn't respond. I found I needed to cover the animal howl of the storm, so I filled the air with inane chatter. "So you lived in Turkey. Is that where you learned to make hummus?"

"I lived all over."

"But you or Jed, I forget which, mentioned that you learned to blow glass in Turkey."

"That's true. I learned it in prison."

I glared sharply at him. "What were you in prison for?"

"In Turkey, it doesn't take much. Being in the wrong place at the wrong time."

"That's all?"

"The pocket full of opium didn't do me any favors."

"I see. Turkish prison as bad as they say?"

"A thousand times worse. Can we talk about something else?"

"Sure. How old were you when you left Battle Lake?"

"Nineteen."

"What'd your parents do?"

"Farmers. They owned nearly eight hundred acres in the county and did very well by it."

"Are they still around?"

"Dead. Came back for my mother's funeral and didn't leave, remember? I have one sister. She lives in Des Moines. I haven't seen her in years."

I peeked at the road. Snowflakes attacked the windshield and headlights like tiny tentacles, sticking, confusing. "I'm sorry."

His shoulders tightened. It might have been a shrug.

"Who'd you hang out with back when you lived here?"

"Always been a loner."

"But you knew about the Four Musketeers."

"Sure enough."

"You never said if you were around in 1962 when Clara was attacked."

"I was. I'd be mighty happy to see some justice done. I've always felt bad for that girl in the yellow dress."

Watching him, I felt hot worms begin to crawl over my skin. How was it that I could have been so close to solving this mystery, but so horribly wrong? The newspaper hadn't mentioned the yellow dress. I hadn't told Monty about the yellow dress. I only knew what the girl had been wearing the night she'd been raped because Lyle had confessed it to me. Someone would have had to have been there that night to know.

Monty kept his eyes pinned to the road, his face tight under the ridiculous pompom hat. When I was in the secret room at the hunt club, I'd overheard that Mitchell hailed from Brandon and not Battle Lake, but I hadn't registered the importance of that fact. The Four Musketeers had all gone to high school in Battle Lake. Monty, not Mitchell, was the fourth Musketeer.

THIRTY-EIGHT

It was Monty who had fled Battle Lake shortly after the incident, who knew too much about it, who had made sure to drive me tonight once he knew I was getting too close to the truth. It was likely even he who had placed the threatening phone call. He was the fourth Musketeer, the missing link, the man who had a record and a lot of incentive to not return to prison.

"What's the most difficult item you've ever blown?" My voice came out squeaky.

He shot me a glance. "Trees are hard. People request them a lot around Christmas."

"What sizes do they come in?" I was inching toward the passenger door. I slid my mittened hand around the solid metal of the handle. As soon as we reached Battle Lake, I was jumping out, running to the nearest car or house and begging the owner to bring me to the police station.

Monty looked at me again. Ahead, a twinkle of light broke through, marking the Standard Oil gas station on the south edge of town. "It was the dress, wasn't it?"

"I don't know what you mean." My pulse was knocking at the back of my throat with gagging force.

"I mentioned the color of her dress. It gave me away." He reached inside his jacket and pulled out a handgun. It was long-nosed, a poison shade of silver, glittering in the dashboard lights. "My apologies."

A wave of nausea-crested inertia threatened to overwhelm me. I forced myself to stay focused. "Did you talk Clive into shooting Tom?"

"I was there the night the suggestion was made and the check written." He flicked his right turn signal and steered with the same hand, easing onto a back road to Hallie's. The black eye of the gun stayed trained on my face. "I'd ask you to move away from that door. There's no place to run. This town is asleep."

He was right. The unplowed streets were virgin white, unmarred by prints, animal or vehicle. The heavy snow made it difficult to see farther than twenty feet. A person would be crazy to be out in a night like this. "How could he have done it? They were best friends."

"Jealousy is an ugly incubator."

"How about Lyle? Did Clive do that?"

"I'm afraid that was me. Clive got cold feet."

I pictured the vehicles raised on car lifts in Lyle's garage the night he was murdered. How had I not recognized the old Ford pickup I was currently sitting in? The Jeep must have been a rental. "And you think Hallie is the only loose end."

"Besides you. I'm sorry. That's the way it has to be. I'm not going back to the stony lonesome for anyone."

I grabbed for purchase. "What about the statute of limitations?"

He was gripping the steering wheel so tightly that the knuckles of his left hand were white. "Doesn't apply when there's DNA evidence."

"You'll get caught."

He curled his lips. "I imagine someone will. My guess is Clive. He's already looking suspicious after Tom's death. This is one of his guns." He tipped the pistol before retraining it on my face. "I used it to shoot Lyle, and left some of Clive's belongings at Lyle's. Freddie's got almost as much as I to lose. He'll never talk."

"Hallie doesn't know. I'm sure of it."

"Too many chances of her finding out with all those medical tests they run. We already covered that." He pulled up in front of her grand old Victorian. The bay windows facing the street flickered with the glow of a fireplace. "Let's go. Quick will be better."

I stepped out of the car, acutely aware of the gun pointed at me. I landed in snow halfway up my calf. The street was deserted. I could make out one street light on either side of me through the blizzard. The only sound was the mouse-soft footsteps of snowfall.

Monty came around the truck and stood behind me. "Come on."

I started trudging with him at my back. I couldn't bring the devil through Hallie's door. If I yelled for help, though, I'd be shot. My survival instinct warred with reality. Better one dead than two, I decided. Before I had a chance to talk myself out of it, I pretended to fall, twisting to the side and away from the barrel of the gun. On my way to the ground, I shot out my foot, kicking toward

Monty's knee. I heard the sickening wet sound of knee cap popping, and Monty toppled into the snow with a scream.

Frantic, I searched for his gun, but it must have landed underneath him. I tried to run, but the deep drifts handicapped me. I didn't know where I was going, but I knew it had to be away from Hallie's. All her neighbors' lights were off. If I risked one of their doors to find out it was locked, I was dead. I plowed through the snow toward the alleyway on the opposite side of the street. My navigation wasn't always true, but I was pretty sure if I followed it three blocks, I'd come out at the Rusty Nail parking lot. The bar would be open. I risked a glance behind me. Monty was dragging his leg 20 yards away and moving toward me with superhuman speed, a black demon in the howling snow.

A sob pushed out my lips and I forced my legs to pump faster. I felt the rush of the bullet past my ear before I heard the crack of it firing. I screamed in fear and zagged left, into the alley. I was out of his line of vision and prepared to bolt toward civilization when I came face to face with the wall of ice. The city had been storing the snow plowed from the street here. I was trapped.

"I'm sorry, Mira. I really am," he yelled over the shrieking wind.

I whipped around and backed against the two-story snow bank. Monty stood at the mouth of the alley, his face screwed up in pain. He held the gun with two bare, shaking hands.

The shot exploded.

I screamed.

THIRTY-NINE

MONTY'S HANDS SHATTERED IN a spray of red. The gun fell to the ground, and he quickly followed. First I was paralyzed, but then some B-team gland jolted my brain. *You're a sitting duck here*, it urged me. I pushed through the snow to seize the handgun from the obscenely red puddle of Monty's blood and bone. The weapon felt warm and sick through my mittens. I didn't know whether to point it at Monty, who was writhing in pain and cursing in an unrecognizable language, or in the direction from which he'd been shot. The snow was blinding, disorienting, and I wanted to cry out, but I didn't know who was friend or foe.

A black form emerged from the snowfall in the direction of Hallie's house. It was tall and moving slowly.

"I have a gun." I held up the weapon, my mittened finger just curving the trigger. I was surprised to see my hands were steady even if my voice wasn't. I'd have an adrenaline debt to pay later.

"So do I."

"Clive?"

He stepped underneath a street light, ten yards away. He was dressed for a snowstorm, the only identifiable features his face and the one hand holding a rifle directed at the ground. I pointed at it with the handgun. "You shot Monty."

"You best go home. I have business to finish."

I closed the distance between us, fighting the urge to faint so I could just wake up when the worst of this was over. "What are you doing here?"

"Carla called to tell me about your visit. I figured where he'd take you next."

"You came to shoot Monty?"

"I came to end all this."

I was within five feet of him. He was a scarecrow of a man, his face haunted. The imbalance that had rimmed his eyes the day he'd threatened me in the library was gone, replaced by resignation. I stared him straight on. "He confessed to shooting Lyle. If you let him live, you won't have to go to jail."

"I was sober when I shot Tom." He kept his eyes on mine, but the pain that crossed his face was crippling. He was stripped raw, his mask gone and his vulnerabilities laid bare. I saw it all in that moment. He'd never be free. He'd been offered money to shoot his friend, and he'd taken it. Maybe he'd shot Tom because of years of jealousy coming to a head. Possibly it was greed. Or, it could have been the worst option of all—a moment of *what if* triggering a flash-second of immutable action. We'd all stood on the edge of that cliff. Maybe it was that Clive had jumped. His eyes told me that no one would ever know for sure the final reason, possibly not even him.

"Come on, Clive. It's over." I pointed him toward Hallie's house. He resisted at first, glaring at the spot where Monty finally lay still, his body saturating the snow with a pulsating red. But then Clive gave in, all the fight leaking out of him. As we walked, I wondered what the largest size plastic underpants came in. At this rate, it'd be worth it for me to invest in some.

FORTY

Despite the blizzard, the Battle Lake police were on the scene
in under ten minutes. The ambulance, on the other hand, had to
come all the way from Fergus and took over an hour in the storm.
By the time they arrived, Monty had regained consciousness. Chief
Gary Wohnt, the first officer on the scene, had staunched the
bleeding in the area where Monty's hands used to be, but it was
clear that he would be forever maimed. *It was a helluva shot*, I
overheard one of his deputies saying, *and in a snowstorm*.

Once Gary had Monty stabilized, he led me out of the snowstorm and into Hallie's house. Clive was taken to the station. While
Hallie fed me warm apple cider, I repeated what Monty had told
me. The deeper I got into the story, the more my teeth started
chattering, despite the warmth of the fireplace. Gary leaned over
and grabbed my hand.

"You're safe," he said gruffly.

I couldn't stop the shaking that threatened to control me. He
reached to hold me, but Hallie was quicker. Despite her illness, and

the pain of hearing the whole story of her father, she was born with a made-for-hugging body. And maybe she was as scared as I was. She held me tight and smoothed my hair with her hands, apologizing over and over again.

"I'm the one who feels terrible," I said, my tremors reduced to a low staccato. "I uncovered that terrible story about your dad. You didn't need to know about it."

"He's responsible for his own actions, and it sounds like he paid his whole life for them." She pulled in a ragged sigh. "I had an inkling, you know. Not about the attack on that poor woman, of course, but children always know more than their parents tell them. I sensed there was more to my mother's story."

My nerves settled enough for me to take a quivery sip of the cider. I didn't know what to say. "I want to go home."

After waking one of her neighbors to stay with Hallie, Gary drove me, each of us deep in our own thoughts. He slipped his Jeep into four-wheel drive before tackling the driveway. I'd never been happier to see the doublewide.

"Thank you for the ride."

"I told you to drop the case." His voice had a raw edge. It wasn't anger. It was almost remorse.

I didn't have the energy to argue. "It's over." I started to get out.

"Mira—"

He grabbed my left wrist, the one still sore from my fall in Lyle's garage. I winced, and he dropped my hand like it was hot. "What?"

He looked away. "Take care of yourself."

I nodded, even though he couldn't see me, shut the door tight, and made my way to bed.

FORTY-ONE

WE GATHERED AT THE Fergus Falls nursing home, decorating the party room. Mrs. Berns had been in my company all of thirty minutes, and she'd pried most of the story from me as well as gotten the phone number of an attractive 50-something male nurse. She looked tan and fit, the warm caramel tone of her lined skin accenting her white hair beautifully. She wore a pretty blue sweater, jeggings, and a pair of white tennis shoes. "I tell you what, this is a whole damn lot better than Arizona. Everyone lays around there like vulture bait, swallowing their pills and rubbing on their jellies. Minnesota is where the action is!"

"Arizona doesn't sound so bad," I said. "No snow, right?"

"No young people, either. The whole state is a raisin ranch. But quit changing the subject. Do we know the full extent of Tom's crimes?"

"According to Kennie, when Gary questioned Clive later that night, he confirmed that Tom never laid a hand on Clara back in

'62. He'd served as the watchman for his friends and had carried the burden of that horrible choice every day for the rest of his life."

"The hell, you say." Mrs. Berns was standing next to the piñata, a stick in her hand.

If I had picked her up at the airport, she'd already know everything, but I'd sent Peggy so I could decorate for Julius' birthday party. It'd been almost a week since he'd first been admitted to the hospital for pneumonia and only two days since he'd been released. I'd reserved the nursing home activities room and decorated it as un-Christmas-y as possible, so the focus could be on Julius, a man who'd always had to share his special day with Jesus. Hence, the Cinco de Mayo birthday theme. Mrs. Berns had insisted on being driven straight to the festivities, and Peggy had been happy to oblige.

"No lie."

Mrs. Berns shook her head in disbelief. "I leave town for two weeks and you uncover the biggest scandal in its history. That blows."

"I could have used your help." I indicated her empty glass. "Can I get you another?"

"Margaritas are like boobs. You should only have two."

"But that's your first."

"Exactly." She passed me the glass.

I walked over to the contraband bag I'd smuggled in and topped off Mrs. Berns' plastic cup. Across the room, Peggy was engaged in a Go Fish rematch with the original group she'd met when we'd first visited. Their laughter was drowning out the salsa music I'd brought. Julius was in his wheelchair, a warm brown quilt across his lap. Johnny was swapping fishing stories with the old man, who looked as animated as a teenager. I caught Johnny's eye and gave him a big smile as I walked back to Mrs. Berns.

"Here you go."

She took a chug. "Sweet, but good. So what's going to happen to Frederick? And Mitchell?"

"Mitchell is under investigation for running illegal gambling at the hunt club. Seems someone anonymously turned in betting sheets and instructions to a secret room. A lot of money was at stake, and if the charges stick, the jail time could be significant."

Peggy broke away from her card game to interrupt our conversation. "Can either of you lend me $5? I just got cleaned out."

I dug in my back pocket and yanked out a ten. "I get interest if you win."

"That's fair. What're you two talking about so seriously over here?"

Despite describing her driver as "sharp as a marble" in a stage whisper when the two of them had first walked into the party room, Mrs. Berns and Peggy seemed to get along just fine. "Mira was just about to tell me what sort of awful consequences Frederick will have to face for his crimes."

I pursed my lips. "Don't know. Clive will only confess to his and Tom's part in the rape, and Frederick won't confess to anything."

A look of disgust crossed Mrs. Berns face. "But what if Frederick is Hallie's dad? Wouldn't that prove it all?"

"It might have, but he's not. Clive underwent the tests. He's definitely Hallie's father."

"Shit on a shingle," she said, whistling under her breath. "That poor thing has had a tough month."

"No doubt. But Clive is a perfect match and has agreed to donate one of his kidneys. She's not willing to talk to him yet, but I'm hoping she can find a way to make peace with it, for herself."

"Good thing that gal didn't need a liver," Mrs. Berns said. "And Clive's wacky tabaccky farm?"

"Gone. I went to grab Chuck the next morning until his daughter can pick him up. When I peeked in the windows of the barn, there was no green to be seen. Clive must have known the law was coming."

Mrs. Berns tsked. "It's funny how things work out, isn't it?"

"Yeah. Justice can be messy, I guess. Like life. You've got to learn to be happy with what you end up with."

Peggy sucked in her breath so loudly it sounded like a balloon popping.

"What is it?"

She stared at me, wide-eyed. "I've got it."

"What?"

"My mojo." She held out her hands expressively, serenely. Mrs. Berns and I watched. A hush seemed to fall over even the salsa music. Peggy cleared her throat. "For the best jewels, shop at Epiphanies."

Mrs. Berns crowed with laughter. "That's a doozy! I like that one."

I smiled. "You have your mojo back."

Mrs. Berns put up a hand. "Ach, don't talk to me about mojo. Have I mentioned how many woo-woo loonies live in Sedona? I felt like I was on some sort of commune but without the sex and drugs. And then what's the point, I ask you? Boy, I missed you all." She pulled me in for a spontaneous hug, then abruptly pushed me away. "I don't know what you're doing, hugging an old lady when you have that hot slab of beef over there. Not many boyfriends would go with their girlfriend to a nursing home on their only day off of work."

"He helped me decorate, too," I added on. "And I'm not his girlfriend."

She flicked me on the forehead. "Stop it with the control freak act. You still not sleeping with him?"

"Not for six months. I told you."

"How about that other move I told you about? You know, the cough-a-doodle."

I blushed.

"Ack. Knowing you, you probably ordered some books so you could figure out how to do it just right." She rolled her eyes. "Now you go over and grab that boy and pull him into a dark closet. Right now. I mean it." She turned me around and swatted me on the butt.

I recognized good advice when I heard it. I walked shyly over to Johnny. He immediately took my hand and smiled into my eyes. The touch of his palm on mine sent electric sparks from my hand all the way to the soles of my feet.

"Julius was sharing fishing secrets with me," he said, his deep voice caressing my ears.

"Not all of 'em, you hear." Julius wagged a finger. "You have to get me in the boat with you to find the real honey spots."

Johnny chuckled. "You have my word. Next summer we'll go muskie fishing. You think they'll let me take you out of here?"

"I'll break out if I have to."

I leaned into Johnny. I couldn't help it. He was hot goodness. "Can I come?"

"You like to fish?" Julius asked.

I shook my head. "Nope. But I could bring a book. Hey, you mind if I steal Johnny for a couple minutes?"

Julius shrugged and wheeled himself over to Mrs. Berns, whom he'd taken an immediate shine to.

"Thanks for helping me set up for the party."

"Thanks for asking me." Johnny leaned in to brush a kiss against my cheek. He let his hand linger on my neck. "Do you have plans later tonight?"

"I was hoping we could go back to my place and I could cook for you. Since last time, you know, didn't turn out exactly like planned." The thing was, Mrs. Berns was right. I had ordered a few books. Where high school and religious movements had failed me, hard facts had come through. Turns out there were all sorts of things we could do to pass the time for six months.

His eyes sparkled. "Outstanding."

I nodded. He had no idea.

THE END

NOVEMBER HUNT DISCUSSION QUESTIONS

1. This book didn't delve into Mira's past as much as previous books in the series. Do you feel that this improved pacing, or do you wish you had found out more about her?

2. Although all mysteries deal with murder, few comedic mysteries delve into the dark topic of rape. Do you prefer mysteries that deal with darker issues, or do you prefer your mysteries to be overall light? Why?

3. Police Chief Gary Wohnt first appeared in the series as an overbearing buffoon, but he's developed into a potential love interest for Mira. Do you see the two of them ending up together? Why or why not?

4. Along the same lines, do you believe Mira and Johnny will have their happily-ever-after before the series is over? Why or why not?

5. Which of the series' characters would you have liked to see more of in this book and why? Which would you have liked to see less of, and why?

6. What was your favorite scene in this book, and why?

7. Do you think a murder mystery series can be reasonably set in a small town, or does it defy reason to the point of annoyance to have so many deaths in a rural Minnesota location?

8. What would you title the December book in the series?

If you enjoyed reading November Hunt
read on for an excerpt from the next
Murder-by-Month Mystery.

ONE

IT'S TOASTY INSIDE THE car. The core-heated air smells of pungent pine freshener and coffee. Outside, a winter sky the color of lead blends with the gray snow-slush roads, morphing the landscape into a blurry daguerreotype day. The radio is set to AM. An announcer squawks about a history-making 57-yard Hail Mary. The game took place last Sunday. The show is a replay, its urgency offensively fake, a mystery already solved, shelved, and forgotten.

The killer stabs the radio button and cruises past the woman's house for the second time in an hour. It isn't difficult to blend in, even in a rural area. Silver sedans are a dime a dozen, especially "borrowed" older models with a hint of rust rimming the wheel housing.

The woman is shoveling snow from her sidewalk. A quick pass reveals her wide-mouthed shovel digging deep into the drifts and coming up loaded. Her shoulders are strong, her concentration absolute. She tosses the snow to the side, and her mutt tries to catch it before it lands. They've been at it for at least ten minutes, and the dog was now more snow than animal. Shovel. Toss. Catch. Shovel. Toss. Catch.

The killer isn't worried about the dog. Animals are easy to subdue, if one is quick. The woman wouldn't put up much of a fight, either, despite a toned upper body. Fear is the great paralyzer.

Although her ski cap is tucked low, the killer knows she's a brunette, just like the rest. She likes travelling and has been to Italy once. She loves a good debate, fried chicken, and tends toward the sarcastic side, though she doesn't mean anything by it. And she lives alone. The last point, the killer had uncovered by driving past her house, and twice taking her mail while she was at work. The rest had been in her online dating profile.

"Quiet," the killer snaps. "I know she shouldn't have put all that out there. A woman who advertises shouldn't be surprised when a buyer shows up, right?"

The only response is the hum of the heater. The 12-inch plastic doll strapped in the passenger seat has nothing to add. She sits in her perfect Jackie O dress suit, her immaculate brown hair pulled back into a bun. Her face poses a frustrating half-smile, always. The killer turns the radio back on.

TWO

THE ELF GRINNED AT me from my dinosaur of a Zenith TV, a row of bow-legged appliances dancing behind him. A seizure-inducing stream of flashing lights crawled across the bottom of the screen. The soundtrack offered a helium-voiced singer suggesting I deck my halls with boughs of holly. "Did you know there are only ten shopping days until Christmas?" the elf asked. His eyes begged me to say no.

"Yes," I told the TV, "and did you know that every time a television set is turned off, an elf dies?" I clicked the power button on my remote and showed my back to the tube. I didn't hate Christmas. In fact, you'll find no bigger fan of twinkle lights, old-fashioned peppermint candy, and picture cards featuring families in matching sweaters and forced smiles. It was the Christmas advertising that rubbed me raw every year, starting before Halloween and ending only when every American was corpulent with credit card debt and buyer's remorse. That's why I only turned on the TV this time of year to quick check the weather. If that made me a Grinch, so be it.

I sipped my tea and regarded Luna, the German shepherd mix that came with the double-wide I'd been trailer-sitting since last spring. "I forgot to pick up eggs and bread again last night."

She cocked her head at me and whined. She knew exactly where I was going with this.

"You're wrong," I protested. "I really forgot this time."

She looked away, sadly. She would not be party to my addiction.

I turned to my calico kitty, Tiger Pop. "You understand, don't you?"

He lay in a patch of winter sunlight, not even bothering to flick his tail. I studied him for a good two minutes and finally decided he was ignoring me with approval. That was all the encouragement I needed. I yanked a winter coat on over my pajama t-shirt and slipped my bare feet into lined winter boots before pulling open my front door.

It was one of those beautiful December days where the air feels so clean it scrubs your lungs. It was bracing but felt temperate after Minnesota's bitter-coldest November in decades. I sucked in a deep, cauterizing breath. The wind licked at but did not slice my bare knees. Glittering diamonds of light sparkled off the rolling sea of snow drifts that was my massive front yard. I crunched down the steps and over the shoveled path to my beloved Toyota Corolla. The two of us had been together for nearly a decade and except for a bunk thermostat that I'd had replaced last month, she'd never let me down.

The double-wide I'd just stepped out of was set within throwing distance of Whiskey Lake and on 100 acres of oak forests and undulating hills. It was located four miles outside of Battle Lake in upper west central Minnesota. In this part of the country, people rarely locked their houses and certainly did not lock their cars. I was a house locker—lived too long in the Cities for anything else—but there was nothing in my car worth stealing. Well, almost nothing. I flipped open the trunk and reached for the Folgers can tucked in the far corner. I peeled off the lid: two fat candles, a box of matches, a flashlight, a Leatherman, a camping knife, a survival blanket the size and consistency of a sheet of tin foil that I didn't think would keep a plucked chicken warm, and a single Nut Goodie greeted me. This was all that stood between me and hypothermic, starving death in the event that my car went into the ditch and disappeared into a towering snowdrift on some lonely country road.

Wait, just one Nut Goodie? I scrabbled around the bottom of the can I'd had a half dozen of the candy bars in there when I'd initially created the winter survival kit. I dumped the contents into the trunk sifted through them, but there was no changing the facts: only one Nut Goodie remained. I glanced guiltily at the house. Maybe Luna was right. Maybe I wasn't doing myself any favors with the Nut Goodie breakfasts. The thing is, the candy is heavenly. As big as the palm of your hand, it's a delight of chocolate and nuts wrapped around a maple candy center and encased year-round in a manic Christmas package of red, white, and green. I refused to keep them in the house because I can't stop eating them once I start. I'd hoped the inner reaches of my car would serve as a demilitarized zone. I'd been fooling only myself.

I sighed, dumping all but the candy bar back into the Folgers can. I held it in my hand, confronted with a Sophie's choice moment: immediate gratification or long-term survival? My knees and fingers were getting stiff with the cold, but I couldn't decide. I was already heavy on saliva imagining the frozen Nut Goodie melting in my mouth, but I knew I shouldn't recreationally eat all of the food in the emergency car kit. Then I remembered: I had granola bars in the house! They could be my emergency survival food. I pocketed the candy, popped the lid back on the coffee can, and charged to the house before my knees froze and fell off.

Luna forgave me my weakness, greeting me at the front door with an energetic wag like I'd been gone for a week. I patted her head, doffed my boots and coat, and planted myself at the kitchen counter to enjoy my chocolate breakfast and read yesterday's mail. I'd come in too late last night to sort it, after putting in extra hours at the library as well as finishing up a front page article for the *Battle Lake Recall*, the local newspaper where I freelanced. Both jobs had fallen into my lap after I moved here from the Twin Cities last March to housesit for a friend. I'd only intended to stay through the summer, but Battle Lake gets under your skin that way.

The top letter was a plea that I become a contributing member of Minnesota Public Radio. For the millionth time, I promised myself I'd do that. Soon. I hated feeling like a public radio parasite, but money was tight for those of us in the bottom of the food chain, even when working two jobs. I pried off a chunk of hard-frozen Nut Goodie and continued. Next on the pile was a holiday card, this one from Peyton McCormick and her mom, Leylanda. Peyton, a precocious eight-year-old, was one of my favorite attendees at the library's children's reading hour every Monday. She'd gone through a horrible ordeal last June. The entire town had pulled together to save her, and when she was finally rescued, she became a local hero. Her gap-toothed smile dominated the photograph, and a tongue-lolling golden lab wearing a Santa hat reclined between her and her mom. I showed the photo to Luna.

"Think we should do something like this next year?"

She licked my still-cold knee.

I made room on the fridge for the card and sifted through the rest of the mail: phone bill, Victoria's Secret catalog, and a card rimmed with red and white-striped candy canes, promising me a free box of the candy if I signed up for a one-year subscription to *Healthy Holidays*. I tossed it. Seemed like a mixed message, and besides, I could already feel the Nut Goodie knocking out a wall in my stomach to add on. I also trashed the catalog, wrote a check for and stamped the telephone bill, and got ready for work.

Freshly-showered and brushed, I gave Luna one last chance to paint the snow, made sure both animals had clean water, fisted some granola bars to restock my car kit, and headed to town, a smile on my face. Battle Lake and I had gotten off to a rocky start, but we'd recently come to an agreement: I'd appreciate her if she didn't squash me.

Otter Tail County hadn't had fresh snow since Monday, so the roads were clear. I'd arrive an hour early to work today, but that would give me time to finish the book ordering that I'd begun last night. I would have been early, that is, if not for the mob outside the police station on my way to the library.

I slowed the Toyota to a crawl and hand-cranked the window. The odors of car exhaust and winter air washed in. The crowd of twenty or so was dressed for the weather, mostly female, and appeared more scared than angry. I recognized a friend I hadn't seen in a while. "Gina!"

She caught sight of me and made her way to my car, no mean feat given the size of the crowd against the heft of her curves. She was a nurse, and like most healthcare professionals in this county, she was built like a Sherman tank. It's what the city folk called irony. "Mira! Did you get one too?" Her cheeks and the tip of her nose were rosy, and white puffs of air accented her words.

"One what?"

"This." She held up her mittened hand. It clutched a candy cane-rimmed card promising her twelve free candy canes if she signed up for a year of *Healthy Holidays*.

"Yeah. I tossed it into the trash this morning. What of it?"

She raised her eyebrows so high they disappeared under the edge of her knit cap. "Jesus. I know you live in a trailer, but is it also under a rock? Haven't you heard about the Candy Cane Killer?"

"Sure," I lied. "Candy. It's a killer."

"Gack." She reached in to slap my forehead. The woolen mitten cushioned the blow. "I'm not talking about candy. I'm talking about the Candy Cane Killer, the serial killer who only murders in December and only kills brown-haired ladies about your height and weight? He started two years ago in Chicago. Last year he targeted central Wisconsin. They think he's in Minnesota this year. A couple days ago seven women in White Plains got his calling card—a single candy cane—and yesterday, one of them showed up dead."

I wanted to ask how a person could show up dead, but I knew my fixation on clear English wouldn't be appreciated in the moment. That annoying habit was about all I had to show for my English bachelor's and a handful of grad credits in same. It could be argued that I used a preoccupation with detail to distance myself from emotions, by the way, but we'll leave that train of thought to the therapists. "But that's not an actual candy cane." I pointed at her card. "It's an advertisement for a magazine."

"You think you know more than the police? They want to speak with everyone who got one of these." She shook the card for emphasis, and it made a rippling noise in the wind. "If you have one, you better go get it. Now. You have time before the library has to be opened."

She forced her way back into the crowd, and I rolled up my window and motored away. I had three things on my mind: 1) Yes, I often did think I knew more than the police, at least the local chief of police, Gary Wohnt. 2) I'd scented hysteria brewing in that crowd, a faint sulfur smell that takes only a single match to ignite, and 3) I didn't want to be the dumb lady in the horror movie who ignored everyone's warnings. Unsure what to do about one and two but confident that I didn't want to be caught stupid, I pointed the car toward home. I'd snag the card, show it to one of the officers at the police station, and still have time to open up the library before ten.

I thought about the serial killer as my Toyota ate up the four short miles between town and home and remembered that I had heard of him. Coverage of his killings in Wisconsin and Illinois had also been on the news last year, but they'd seemed distant from my life and had been quickly overshadowed by news of wars and economies. I shivered involuntarily. White Plains was not far from Paynesville, the small town I'd grown up in. I didn't want to imagine a serial killer by my hometown, near my mom.

I pulled into my driveway on automatic, parked the car, and hurried to the house. I was so deep in thought that I'd yanked open the house's outer glass door and walked halfway through the inner before I realized it had been unlocked. I looked at the knob in my hand. Had I been in such a hurry this morning that I hadn't closed it tightly? That would be a first. I glanced around the living room. Everything seemed in place, except for one thing. No dog had greeted me.

"Luna!" She always met everyone at the door, tail wagging, no exceptions. My eyes swept the living room, the kitchen behind it, the open door to my left leading to the master bedroom and the hallway to the right leading to a bathroom, office, and spare bedroom. No movement. I glanced behind me again. The outer door was weighted and had self-closed behind me. It had definitely been latched this morning. Luna wasn't outside unless someone had opened the door for her, and she wasn't inside unless she was too hurt to move. I suddenly felt hollow.

"Luna?" This time it was a whisper.